Dear Reader,

This month, there's plenty to be thankful for—but romance should always be at the top of the list! And we have four dazzling new romances from Bouquet to offer!

What could be more romantic than a chance meeting? In Lori Handeland's **When You Wish,** a massage therapist couldn't be more surprised when the sexy man who walks into her office turns out to be an infuriatingly logical doctor—with a smile that melts her heart. And in **Her Best Man,** beloved author Lisa Plumley offers us the story of an impetuous heiress trying to do a simple favor for her best friend—and hijacking the wrong man! Unless he's right for her, of course . . .

When love takes you by surprise, there's only one thing to do—fall for it! In Cheryl Holt's **Mountain Dreams,** a sensible businesswoman does just that—when she meets a legendary ladies' man who just might be ready to fall in love, too. Finally, Adrienne Basso proves that when a financial analyst agrees to masquerade as her boss's date for the weekend, neither one of them anticipates **A Night To Remember.**

Enjoy!

Kate Duffy
Editorial Director

PRETTY WOMAN

Joshua's gaze flicked to Eleanor's bare shoulders, and he wondered if they were as satiny soft as they looked. He forced himself to look away, sternly reminding himself they were completely wrong for each other.

"You look great."

Eleanor managed a crooked smile. "Sure. I was born to wear designer clothes."

She smoothed down the side of her skirt and Joshua noticed the uncertainty in her eyes.

"You look wonderful, Eleanor," Joshua insisted.

"Really? You don't think I look silly. You know, like a little girl whose playing dress up?"

"I doubt there are any little girls around who can hold that dress in place the way you can," Joshua commented with a wry smile.

Eleanor broke into shy, hesitant laughter. The sound made something warm unfurl in Joshua's chest. He removed a credit card from his wallet and casually passed it to the saleswoman. "We'll take the dress."

Eleanor's face slowly lit up with delight. "Thank you, Joshua."

Her simple, sincere gratitude hit him right in the gut. He felt a strong momentary impulse to sweep her up in his arms and taste the sweetness of her lips, wondering if he could make her tremble with the same desire and passion that had unexpectedly seized him. . . .

A NIGHT TO REMEMBER

Adrienne Basso

ZEBRA BOOKS
Kensington Publishing Corp.
http://www.zebrabooks.com

ZEBRA BOOKS are published by

Kensington Publishing Corp.
850 Third Avenue
New York, NY 10022

Copyright © 2000 by Adrienne Basso

All rights reserved. No part of this book may be reproduced in any form or by any means without the prior written consent of the Publisher, excepting brief quotes used in reviews.

If you purchased this book without a cover you should be aware that this book is stolen property. It was reported as "unsold and destroyed" to the Publisher and neither the Author nor the Publisher has received any payment for this "stripped book."

Zebra and the Z logo Reg. U.S. Pat. & TM Off.

First Printing: November, 2000
10 9 8 7 6 5 4 3 2 1

Printed in the United States of America

To Jeanne Marie Ryan,
for her inspiring title suggestions.

To Maureen Cooney and Carol Ann Wilson,
for teaching me that truth is indeed stranger than fiction.

To my friends and colleagues
at the Westfield Memorial Library
who answer impossible questions every day.

One

Eleanor Graham was late. Not a few minutes late, not fashionably late, not sorry-I-got-caught-in-traffic late, but hopelessly late. The sort of lateness that makes panic set in so that you trip all over yourself trying to save time and end up making things worse.

Incredibly, she had hit every single red traffic light since she'd left her apartment a half hour ago. And somehow managed to get stuck behind every geriatric driver within a fifty-mile radius, all of whom drove at a sedate twenty miles per hour regardless of the posted speed limit.

"Oh, for heaven's sake, will you at least stay to the right?" Eleanor muttered under her breath. She pulled dangerously close to the rear bumper of the late-model sedan in front of her, but the gray-haired driver neither moved out of the way nor increased his speed.

Taking a deep breath, she resisted the urge to lean on the car horn. Instead she maneuvered into the right lane and zoomed past the slowpoke, showing tremendous restraint by not sticking out her tongue at the elderly couple seated inside.

Making a sharp right turn without signaling, Eleanor pulled into the partially hidden driveway of the country club and gunned the engine. With a breathless smile and screeching brakes she halted at the guard shack.

"Hi. I'm here for the Hamilton, Barton and Jones company picnic. Which way do I go?"

The slender man posted at the entrance gave her a puzzled frown and nervously checked his clipboard. "That started three hours ago, miss."

"I know, I know. I'm late. Better late than never, right?" Eleanor tried another smile as the guard shuffled through the papers. He started shaking his head and clucking his tongue, and for a few heart-stopping moments she thought he wasn't going to wave her through.

Oh great, after all I've been through on this morning from hell, now I'm not going to get in? As her fear and frustration mounted, Eleanor briefly contemplated driving on without his permission. Realistically, what was the worst thing the guard could do? Throw his clipboard at her?

But years of ingrained respect for authority combined with an overactive sense of responsibility kept her itchy foot off the accelerator.

A final sigh from the guard had Eleanor thinking she was doomed. To her utter delight he lifted his hand in a classic gesture of resignation and pointed up the winding hill. "Take the second right. About a half mile down you'll see a parking area for picnic guests. I imagine you can find your way from there."

"I sure can." Eleanor smiled broadly. "Thanks."

She drove faster than she should have, but kept a sharp eye out for pedestrians. Her sense of triumph at reaching the parking lot vanished quickly, however, when she realized there wasn't a parking space anywhere.

Eleanor circled twice. On her second pass she saw an opening next to an expensive-looking Jaguar. It didn't exactly look like another parking slot, but if she was very careful she could fit her small car in the space. Inching her way in, she successfully parked the car and carefully opened her door.

Snatching up her purse and the large round tin off the passenger seat, Eleanor paused to get her bearings. She got out and slammed the door, then squeezed her way around the Jaguar and scanned the distant horizon. Her eye was immediately drawn to the sea of royal blue T-shirts in the clearing at the edge of the woods.

Tugging self-consciously on her own matching blue shirt with the company logo emblazoned on the front, she took a deep breath and started up the hill.

The noise increased as she approached. The steady buzz of numerous conversations, laughter, and good-natured shouts, the crack of a bat hitting a ball. A heated softball game was in progress on one end of the open meadow, gathering a large crowd of spectators and players.

A roar went up from the crowd. Eleanor twisted around and saw the softball shooting toward the outfield. It arched high as it sailed gracefully across the field, over everyone's head. Several players went scrambling toward it, but no one came close to catching the ball.

Eleanor squinted and lifted her arm to shield her eyes from the warm May sunshine and watched the hitter trot leisurely around the bases.

Even at this distance she could easily identify the home-run hero—tall, broad-shouldered, with muscular legs that moved with natural athletic grace and an air of confidence that set him apart from other males. He was wearing a baseball cap, but Eleanor knew well that beneath it was a head of dark hair, and a face that defined the word *handsome*.

Joshua Barton, the brilliant, young, dedicated managing partner of the firm. Eleanor's heart did its predictable somersault in her chest. It was a reflex reaction, something she couldn't control even though she had honestly tried. After all, it was utterly ridiculous that an intelligent, sensible, grown woman in her late twenties would harbor such a schoolgirl infatuation with a man who probably didn't even know her first name.

The thought brought an ironic smile to her lips. He was handsome as sin while she was ordinary as pie. Opposites might attract in the movies, romantic impossibilities might flourish in novels, but this was real life.

Fighting back a sigh, Eleanor turned away from the softball game and trudged toward the large catering tent. She smiled vaguely at the people she passed, grateful not to encounter anyone she knew. She needed a few moments to regain her perspective.

When Eleanor ducked under the low canopy and entered the food area, she saw the country club staff clearing away the remains of lunch. She watched silently for a moment as they disassembled the beautiful setup, complete with linen napkins and tablecloths, china plates and silver chafing dishes.

No hot dogs and burgers, corn on the cob, or barbecue chicken for the employees of Hamilton, Barton and Jones. These financial wizards dined on vichyssoise and poached salmon, asparagus in vinaigrette, and hearts of endive salad, even outdoors.

Eleanor's gaze strayed to the dessert table, which remained intact. Dessert would be served later, probably after the softball game was finished. The tradition of the employees bringing the desserts to the annual company picnic had started long before anyone could remember. Yet even that was not a simple assortment of homemade cookies, Jell-O molds, or pies one would expect to find at a picnic.

Over the years simple sweets had been replaced by

A NIGHT TO REMEMBER

more sophisticated, elaborate creations. It had become a subtle yet cutthroat competition as each year employees and their spouses vied to outdo each other and create the most unusual and delicious dessert.

Eleanor eyed today's offerings with a sinking feeling. This year's desserts easily topped last year's entries. There were fancy cakes and tortes of all sizes and shapes, delicate pastries and fruit tarts, even a confection spun out of sugar that resembled an old-fashioned ticker-tape machine.

Bet the guys in securities got a big charge out of that one, Eleanor decided with a mocking grin.

"Would you like some more lunch, miss?" a young female staff member asked politely. "I can ask the chef to deliver more freshly cooked salmon."

"No thanks, I'm fine."

Eleanor resisted the urge to run her hand over her thigh. She knew she didn't look great in this outfit. Her most flattering pair of white shorts had somehow gotten a stubborn red stain on the cuff, so she was forced to wear a slightly shorter pair. And the required company T-shirt was a little snug across her chest.

Still, just because she didn't have the emaciated waif-like figure of a model was no reason to assume she had come back to the tent looking for seconds. Deciding the last thing she wanted now was to be seen approaching the dessert table, Eleanor waited until the staff was finished.

The moment they left the tent she rushed the table. The dizzy, syrupy smell assaulted her as she got close, making her feel like she was drowning in a vat of chocolate, vanilla, and sugar. Hastily popping the cover off the tin she had brought, Eleanor slid her dessert offering on the end of the table . . . toward the back.

"Hello, Miss Graham," a deep male voice intoned. "Are you enjoying the picnic?"

The tin cover dropped to the ground but hardly made a sound on the soft grass. Eleanor whirled around swiftly. She let out the breath she was holding and smiled in genuine relief when she met the friendly eyes of a fellow financial analyst, Mark Robertson. For one bizarre instant she had imagined that it was Joshua Barton who stood behind her.

"Oh, Mark. You startled me." Eleanor stepped away from the table. She absently accepted the cover he stooped to pick up. "Have you been here long? Did Mary and Trevor come with you?"

"My son decided to take an early morning nap and Mary thought it was a good idea," Mark replied. "It never looks good when your kid starts acting like a brat in front of your boss. Still, we beat you by at least an hour and a half. Where have you been?"

"I had a complicated morning," Eleanor muttered. She made a move to leave the tent, but Mark blocked her retreat.

"We didn't think you were coming," he continued with a slow grin. "In fact we had a lengthy debate trying to remember if you had ever been late for anything. Mallery thought you might have been late to a meeting two years ago, but Jeanne insisted you arrived after breakfast was served but before the meeting officially began so technically you were on time."

"Very funny." Eleanor grimaced at her coworker. How reassuring to discover that her reputation as reliable, responsible, old Eleanor was safe.

For the most part she liked Mark and enjoyed his offbeat sense of humor. He was a pleasant-looking guy with wavy brown hair and glasses who was devoted to his wife, Mary, and young son, Trevor. He worked in a separate division but often relied on Eleanor's superior research and analytical skills to complete his reports.

Mark took a step toward the dessert table and leaned over, peering with obvious interest into the tin she had hoped to put in an unobtrusive spot. "I thought you were going to make those special layered mint brownies?"

"Change of plans," Eleanor replied with a wan smile, deciding it was those ridiculous brownies that had set off the chain reaction of disasters this fateful morning.

Actually the morning had started out fine. She had gotten up early, mixed the batter for her mother's famous double-fudge mint brownies, spread it evenly in the pan, and popped it in the oven. After setting the timer she had spent several minutes making corrections to her term paper before printing out a final clean copy.

Realizing she had nearly a half hour until the brownies would be done, she'd decided to indulge herself in a bubble bath. Feeling truly decadent she had taken a book into the tub with her, the latest release of one of her favorite romance authors.

And therein lay her downfall. Caught up in the adventure and romance of this marvelous page-turner, she had missed the buzzing of the oven timer. Only the smell of burning chocolate permeating the air had brought Eleanor's nose abruptly out of the book. Wrapped in a towel, still soaking wet, she had raced into the kitchen, skidded to a stop, donned an old oven mitt, and reached inside. Wet hands, thin potholder, burnt fingers.

Eleanor had screeched in pain and dumped the entire mess into the sink, where it had fallen on her favorite serving platter. The dish had promptly broken into several pieces. Now she had no dessert for the picnic, no nice serving platter to display it on, and no idea what to make instead.

"The brownies would have been great, but those look,

ummm . . . interesting," Mark commented. He poked his finger into the tin, then lifted his head and glanced at Eleanor. "What are they?"

"Rice Krispie treats."

"Those marshmallow things?" Mark furrowed his brow and looked back at the tin. "My mom used to make them when we were kids. I haven't eaten one in years."

Mark reached in and grabbed one. But as he lifted his single selection out, half the contents of the tin came with it. He glanced helplessly at Eleanor.

"Oh no." Eleanor laughed nervously. "The treats were still warm when I packed them in the tin. Now they're all stuck together."

She snatched the serving fork off a platter of perfectly arranged pastries and jabbed at the gooey marshmallow mess in Mark's hand. By exerting a fair amount of pressure she was able to pry away most, but not all, of the extraneous sweet. It dropped back into the tin with an unappetizing clunk.

Mark was left holding a large, misshapen mass. He looked in true confusion at the sticky chunk in his fingers, then with a philosophical shrug opened his mouth and took a healthy bite.

"Mmmm," he mumbled. "Looks like a wreck, but tastes just like I remember them."

The stiffness in Eleanor's bottom lip gave way as the incongruity of the situation hit her. There among the perfectly prepared gourmet selections of triple chocolate tortes and elaborate three-tiered cakes sat her contribution.

Basic, simple, unpretentious, and stuck-together—sort of summed up her feelings about her place in the firm. She was the Rice Krispie treat among the gourmet foods.

Eleanor waited until Mark finished chewing his pilfered sweet before they left the food tent. With Mark licking his fingers they started up the slight hill toward a group of Eleanor's coworkers.

"There's Mallery," Mark commented, pointing toward the softball game, which was still in progress. "Man, he really loves wearing that manager's shirt. Made us all feel like we weren't good enough to eat lunch with him now that he got his big promotion. What a jerk. Everyone knows that job should have been yours."

"Mark, how many times have I told you, I don't care about the promotion," Eleanor said truthfully. "George Mallery is a smart man and a hard worker. I thought he deserved to be promoted instead of me. The simple fact is, he wanted it more than I did."

"A whole lot more," Mark said with a trace of bitterness. "By rights it should be you wearing that shirt," he insisted, referring to the three-button collared sports shirts with the small, discreetly embroidered company logo on the breast pocket that all the managers and partners were wearing.

Eleanor shook her head. She wasn't going to start this discussion with Mark again. They had been having it for three months and neither had budged on their position. Eleanor had eventually realized it was just too difficult for Mark to understand why she wasn't bitter about the promotion.

The simple truth was that she was working hard toward making a drastic career change and didn't much care about the upper levels of management at the firm of Hamilton, Barton and Jones. If graduate school continued at the current pace she would be ready to make the move in another year.

Then perhaps the persistent feeling of not exactly fitting in would finally vanish. She would be doing the kind of work that she really loved, that made her feel useful and important, that made her happy. Eleanor sighed softly at the thought.

It had taken considerable strength to not only realize that she wasn't destined for life as a financial analyst but to do something to correct the situation. Eleanor might lack courage and initiative in certain areas, but she was determined not to spend the rest of her life filled with self-pity because she had initially made a mistake in her career choice.

Eleanor and Mark joined a group of coworkers relaxing near the pond. Everyone stepped back and made room for them. Eleanor received warm greetings along with a teasing comment or two about her extremely late arrival.

"We're so glad you are finally here," Mary said sincerely. "Trevor has been asking about you all morning."

"Hi, Trevor." Eleanor hunched down and met Mark and Mary's three-year-old son at eye level. Thanks to the story times she ran at the local library they were good friends.

"Hi, Nora."

Trevor hid behind his mother's legs, but peeped out to make sure that Eleanor was watching him. She smiled and wagged her fingers at him and he giggled loudly. Eleanor really enjoyed the little boy's company even though he tended to be a bit spoiled.

She had been around enough young children over the past year, however, to realize it wasn't really Trevor's fault. His parents, especially his mother, thought everything that Trevor did was truly wonderful. Mary would smile with misty-eyed maternal pride at his every action, even when he was yanking books off the library shelves and throwing them on the floor.

"Did you win any fun prizes today, Trev?" Eleanor asked, knowing that the organized games and activities at the picnic included gifts for all the children.

"A boat," Trevor announced proudly. He ran off toward the picnic table to retrieve his prize and show Eleanor.

"Don't get so close to the edge of the pond, dear," Mary yelled out anxiously. She turned with a smile toward Eleanor and concluded, "It will be a small miracle if he doesn't end up in that water by the end of the day."

"My boat, Nora," Trevor declared, holding up a sizable plastic boat for Eleanor's inspection.

"It's so cool, Trev!" Eleanor exclaimed to the little boy's delight. "And it's green. Your favorite color."

"Green boat," Trevor repeated solemnly, squatting near the edge of the pond. "Watch the green boat ride in the water, Nora."

"Oh no, don't let the boat slip too far away!" Eleanor exclaimed.

Since she was the closest adult, she lunged toward the bobbing toy, stretching her body far out over the water. With an audible grunt, Eleanor successfully wound her fingers around the plastic. She turned to straighten up and felt a stinging smack on her leg.

"Don't touch! That's my boat, Nora. Mine!" Trevor screamed, swinging his arm back and hitting Eleanor square in the back of the knees a second time.

It felt like slow motion. Eleanor could feel herself losing her balance, could feel herself falling toward the water. It seemed as though she had all the time in the world to right herself, but in fact it was only seconds. She struggled to move her feet, wildly waving her arms around like a frantic windmill, trying desperately to regain her balance.

For a split second Eleanor thought she might be spared, but she was too off-kilter. She landed in the water with a giant splash. As the cold wetness hit her, Eleanor could hear Mary's shriek of distress, could see Mark leaping toward her in a failed rescue attempt.

Eleanor landed hard on her rump, and for once she was glad of the padding. Thankfully her head didn't go completely under the water, but the back of her neck and the tips of her shoulder-length hair were submerged.

For several moments there was utter silence and then everyone began shouting at once.

"Are you hurt?"

"Can you move your legs?"

"Did you get water up your nose?"

Eleanor let out a short burst of laughter. And then another. Before long she was laughing heartily. Perfect. This was the perfect ending to the day.

She shook her head and laughed harder, pleased to hear the rest of the gang joining her. Several people moved close to the edge to offer assistance and make sure she wasn't injured.

"I can get out on my own," Eleanor stated with a grin. "Don't get too close to the edge or you'll be joining me for a swim."

Her comment brought another round of laughter, as she had intended. She made a move to regain her feet but the sudden, overwhelming silence stopped her. It was so quiet one could hear the proverbial pin drop. Eleanor lifted her head curiously.

The group crowding the edge of the pond stepped aside, parting like a zipper. A newcomer came into view, standing dead center at the end of the two neat rows of people.

Mr. Joshua Barton.

Eleanor's knees felt wobbly . . . even though she was sitting down . . . in a murky, scummy pond, with all manner of insects and microorganisms crawling over her flesh. Yet she made no move to rise.

Instead she hastily glanced away. It was sort of like pretending to be invisible. Maybe if she stayed really still and didn't move a muscle, he wouldn't notice she was sitting in the water.

Eleanor risked a quick glance toward Joshua to see if her strategy was working. Sunlight filtered around his head. Men weren't supposed to be gorgeous. But there were no other words that could adequately describe him. He had an incredible face with classically handsome features, a strong, masculine body that drove women crazy.

Well, any woman above the age of seventeen and below the age of eighty. Eleanor surveyed him from head to toe. Make that eighty-five.

He advanced, his eyes widening slightly as if he had just noticed she was sitting in the pond. He quickened his pace and made a move forward to offer his help. Panicking, Eleanor raised her hands to ward him off. "I'm fine, really. I don't need any help."

"Are you sure?"

"Yes. Thank you."

Eleanor hastily stood on her feet, sloshed out of the water, and scrambled up on the bank to prove her point. The murky bottom of the pond had stained her socks and sneakers, bits of stringy vegetation clung to her arms and fingers. The smell was rank, and she prayed fervently that she was standing downwind of Joshua.

"Can I get you anything?"

Eleanor's first inclination was to curl into a ball and slide back into the scummy pond. Instead she straightened her spine and told herself that people did not die of embarrassment. Unfortunately.

"I'm fine," she repeated with a forced smile. She tried but failed to hold his gaze. Her eyes swept down to his left hand, which rested casually on his hip.

Eleanor blinked. Then her face broke into a broad smile, and before she could control the impulse and swallow her words, she heard herself declare in obvious delight, "You're eating a Rice Krispie treat!"

Joshua Barton always prided himself on dealing well with the unexpected, the difficult, the crisis situation. He was known for having a cool head while others panicked, a quick, solid grasp of impossible circumstances, and the intelligence and courage to make the tough choices.

Yet as he stared down the table at the endless desserts displayed before him like some ancient tribute to the gods, he felt the beads of sweat start to gather on his forehead.

It was warm and crowded under the catering tent. Employees and their families jockeyed for position, but Joshua knew the heat wasn't causing his discomfort.

Every eye was trained upon him. He was used to the attention, accustomed to the scrutiny. It had existed for all of his life. In fact it was only recently that he no longer felt so defensive about his position, for even though his great-grandfather had been a founder of the firm, everyone acknowledged Joshua had earned his place as managing partner.

And now, as leader of the financial firm of Hamilton, Barton and Jones, the employees were waiting anxiously to see which dessert he would select. The irony of the situation was not lost on Joshua.

How utterly ridiculous to think that having him eat the dessert that they brought would somehow give them an advantage . . . an inside track toward advancement . . . an easier climb up to the next rung. Promotions were earned in this firm. Wasn't he the perfect example of that?

Joshua bit back a sigh. He knew the politically correct

decision would be to sample everything, but just the thought of eating all those sweets made his teeth ache.

"Would you like me to serve you something, Mr. Barton?" a helpful country club staff member volunteered.

Joshua smiled grimly at the young woman and shook his head. If only it were that easy. Relinquish the responsibility, let someone else make the decision.

It was times like this that he really missed his mother. She would have known precisely how to handle the situation so no one would feel slighted or snubbed. Even his father, a bullheaded man known for his outspoken attitude, would have been an ally instead of an adversary this afternoon.

But his mother had died five years ago and his father, forced into reluctant retirement by Joshua, was down in North Carolina with his new wife. Joshua was on his own.

This was ridiculous. Moving swiftly down the length of the table, he reached out to grab the first item he saw when he noticed a large tin at the back edge of the table. Nearly, but not quite hidden.

Rice Krispie treats? Joshua thought he recognized them, but they only faintly resembled the sweet cereal concoctions he and his mother had made together after school as they discussed the trials of his life as a third grader.

With a nostalgic smile he reached for one of the large squares. It stuck to his fingers. Joshua suppressed a laugh, hoping not to offend the poor soul who had made these treats. He squared his shoulders, preparing to turn and face his audience. Both his facial expression and body language were deliberately set to dare anyone to challenge his dessert choice.

However, he was spared the showdown. Suddenly there were loud shouts and yelling coming from outside the tent, followed by the resounding sound of a splash, and then more shouts.

"My goodness, what's happening?" a concerned female voice asked.

Joshua didn't wait to be told. He quickly exited the tent with a sizable contingency trailing behind him. It wasn't difficult to locate the source of all the commotion. There was a large crowd gathered at the edge of the pond. Thankfully he heard more laughter than cries of distress.

One by one his employees noticed his appearance. Like a ripple on the water, the laughter running through the crowd ceased. Joshua felt a strange sense of isolation, as though his arrival had sucked all the fun out of the moment.

"Is everything all right?" he asked no one in particular.

Nobody answered but, like the Red Sea, the crowd silently parted and Joshua finally got a look at the source of all the commotion.

And what a sight it was!

A woman was sitting in three feet of very dirty pond water. The wet ends of her brown hair clung to her shoulders and there was a smudge of dirt on her left forearm.

She was not a woman who would be labeled beautiful wet or dry. In fact, wet she resembled something that the cat dragged in, as his grandfather liked to say.

Yet Joshua's entire body reacted. There was color in her cheeks and her smile was radiant. Her hands were submerged somewhere behind her, presumably to keep her upper body from falling backward into the water. This awkward position thrust her generous breasts forward.

The sight of those lush, wet curves caused many thoughts to form in Joshua's head. All of them sexual and totally inappropriate.

Joshua tried, but couldn't seem to take his eyes off her chest. The wet fabric clung to her full, round breasts, leaving nothing to his suddenly very active imagination. He wondered how her round body would feel pressed up against his hard flesh. How the contrast of her soft feminine curves would feel against his solid male strength.

She was in no way familiar, so Joshua assumed she was the wife of one of his employees. Probably the guy with the glasses, whom Joshua did recognize. He was holding tightly onto a little kid clutching a green plastic boat. Joshua suspected the child was the reason the woman had somehow ended up in the water.

Most women Joshua knew would be in a serious snit over this predicament. Yelling, blaming others, searching for sympathy and help. But this woman did none of those things. Initially she appeared to be laughing heartily, but her smile had vanished upon his arrival.

Well, whoever she was, he was grateful for her assistance. Her unexpected dip in the pond had saved him from the dessert table. Judging from her reaction to the treat he had selected, he decided she must have made the sticky cereal bars. It somehow seemed fitting.

"Can I get you some dry clothes?" Joshua offered, feeling an urgent need to do something for this soggy woman even though she had refused all his other offers of assistance.

"No thanks." She attempted a smile. "I think I'll head home."

The man with the glasses moved closer, putting a supporting arm around her shoulder. She looked down at the ground and twirled the toe of her soggy sneaker in the grass. The little boy clutching the boat came up and patted her knee reassuringly. She reached out and ruffled his hair affectionately.

Belatedly, Joshua realized he was staring, almost rudely. It suddenly made him feel ridiculously guilty for having such carnal thoughts about this woman. Another man's wife. A little boy's mother.

Joshua cleared his throat. Not wanting to embarrass this poor woman any further, he turned and walked away, wondering why he felt such a sharp pang of envy.

Two

"Mrs. Jackson just called. She and Mr. Barton are on their way down here right now. She said they want to talk to you, Eleanor. *Pronto*. Eleanor? Eleanor? Are you in here?"

The bulky copy-machine door wobbled, then swung wide open. A disheveled mass of curly brown hair appeared first, followed by a plain, unsmiling face.

"That is not amusing, Jeanne." Eleanor shifted her aching knees and glared across the hot, stuffy room at her coworker. "I've been wrestling with this blasted machine for the past forty-five minutes and I'm in no mood for jokes."

"I'm not kidding, Eleanor," Jeanne insisted anxiously. "I was working on the quarterly reports you gave me this morning when your phone rang. Since I knew you were trying to fix the copier, I answered it. It was Mrs. Jackson."

"Uh-huh," Eleanor mumbled in a disbelieving tone. She crammed her head inside the copier and continued yanking on the accordion-mashed section of paper jammed into the inner workings of the machine.

Distracted, she listened with half an ear to Jeanne's rambling account of the phone call, certain that Jeanne had managed to bungle the message. As usual.

There was no earthly reason for Mrs. Jackson, executive assistant to the firm's managing partner, to contact her. Eleanor was a lowly financial analyst, one of thirty individuals who held that position in the company. In matters of business, she had never dealt directly with Mr. Joshua Barton, aforementioned managing partner, either. It had to be a mistake.

A mistake that nicely reflected the overall tone of this frustrating day, Eleanor decided. Her morning had started with an uncharacteristically late arrival at the office thanks to a stalled commuter train. Two members of her staff had called in sick, the already pressing deadline for her latest report had been moved forward a full week, she had missed lunch, and a small snag on her pantyhose was now a gargantuan run down the center of her leg.

Best of all, if she couldn't get the darn copy machine to function properly, she was going to be stuck at the office until late into the evening. Again.

Of course it wasn't as if she had any special plans or any special someone who would care that she spent the better part of the night at work, but toiling away at the prestigious financial offices of Hamilton, Barton and Jones rated a minus five on a scale of one to ten in Eleanor's humble opinion.

"Mrs. Jackson, you've found us," Jeanne squeaked. "Oh, my. Hel . . . lo . . . hello, Mr. Barton."

Eleanor ceased pulling on the jammed paper in midtug and instantly became alert. *Joshua Barton? Here? Now? Was it possible?*

Eleanor sunk a bit lower behind the large copier, thankful she was completely hidden from view. Her eyes darted frantically about the room, searching for a nonexistent back exit. There was no escape! She took several deep breaths, then slowly, cautiously lifted her head and risked a quick glance over the top of the machine.

Eleanor caught a fleeting glimpse of the stylishly attired, gray-haired Mrs. Jackson, then gasped aloud. *Ohmigosh!* He was really *here!*

Eleanor ducked down instantly. The subtle vibration that seemed to reach deep inside her anytime she was within five feet of him began, warming her insides, causing her pulse to quicken and her skin to tingle.

She hadn't even caught a glance at the back of his head since the company picnic four weeks ago. How she longed now to feast her eyes on those incredible features that would have been labeled pretty if they weren't so masculine. Thick, luxurious dark hair. Bold, straight nose. High cheekbones. Even a slight cleft in his chin.

In the six years she had worked for his company, Eleanor had spoken to him precisely fifteen times. Sixteen, if you counted the incident at the company picnic, but Eleanor stubbornly refused to think about that encounter.

Unable to resist, Eleanor lifted her chin and risked another peek. Joshua looked fabulous. With his hip braced against the edge of a small filing cabinet and one hand resting comfortably in the pocket of his navy pin-striped suit, he was the embodiment of a successful, sophisticated, wealthy businessman.

But that alone could not account for Eleanor's reaction. There was a quiet intensity about Joshua that drew her toward his deeply set dark eyes, an edge to his polished civility that touched her heart and called to her soul.

The problem was Joshua barely knew she existed. Except if he remembered her as the nut who fell in the water at the picnic. Hopefully he had forgotten that humiliating incident. Yet even if he hadn't, it wouldn't matter, wouldn't change anything.

Men like him were never interested in women like her. It was a difficult, distressing fact to accept, but Eleanor firmly believed she had . . . until she came in contact with him. Then the woman she was—the woman who possessed a head filled with common sense, not romantic dreams—vanished, and visions of impossible fantasies captured her imagination.

From her cocoon of safety Eleanor heard Mrs. Jackson's cultured voice ask, "Is Ms. Graham here?"

Now was the perfect time to make her presence known, but Eleanor felt paralyzed with dread and incapable of moving. There was a long, silent pause and in her mind she pictured a speechless Jeanne pointing toward the copy machine, revealing her outlandish location.

"Ms. Graham, may we have a word, please? I'm on a rather tight schedule this afternoon."

The deep, dark tones of Joshua's husky voice sent a delicious shimmer down Eleanor's back. *He must think I'm some sort of lunatic,* she reasoned as a small bubble of nervous laughter escaped her clenched lips. Hiding inside a copy machine. That was almost as good as falling into a pond. Talk about making a memorable impression!

Eleanor glanced down at herself and groaned softly. Her skirt was rumpled, her blouse untucked, the tips of her fingers were coated with black toner, and her suit jacket was back at her desk. She pressed her hands to her hot face, wishing she could crawl completely inside the machine and shut the door behind her. But retreat wasn't an option.

Eleanor pulled her head out of the machine, squared her shoulders, and stood on her feet, vowing not to make a total fool of herself. Somehow.

"Hello, Mrs. Jackson, Mr. Barton." Eleanor nodded her head politely, deliberately keeping her ink-stained fingers behind her back. "How may I help you?"

Staring at her, neither Mrs. Jackson nor Joshua could completely hide their shocked reactions to her sudden materialization. Eleanor swallowed hard and moved an unruly clump of dark curly hair off her face. *I must look a lot worse than I thought.*

Eleanor glanced nervously about the room, noting that Jeanne had vanished. Coward.

The seconds ticked away and the silence created a knot of tension in Eleanor's empty stomach. Just when Eleanor was beginning to doubt she would ever be able to breathe normally again, Joshua spoke.

"Don't we have repair people to handle this sort of problem?"

"Huh?"

Eleanor bit her tongue, scarcely believing she had just uttered that inane sound. Striving for a quick recovery, she launched into a hasty explanation.

"Actually we do have a service contract with the copy machine's manufacturer and for the most part the individuals they send to work on the machines are very competent. Not always punctual, however. I mean, we'll call the company and explain that our machine isn't functioning and that we need service ASAP but that doesn't always guarantee that a repair person will be here on the same day.

"Once we waited nearly two full business days before someone finally appeared. So when the machine jammed today, I decided instead of wasting more time waiting for a repair person that might or might not show up, I'd try to remove the paper jam myself. And I have. Almost."

Eleanor drew in a deep breath and stared triumphantly across the room. Mrs. Jackson's eyes widened in astonishment while Joshua's eyes narrowed in confusion. Terrific. Now she was babbling like an incoherent idiot. She should have stopped talking after her eloquent, opening *huh.*

"We have not come here to discuss *copy* machines,

Ms. Graham," Mrs. Jackson said in a frosty tone. "Mr. Barton has a very delicate situation that I thought you would be able to help him with, however I'm not sure my assumption was correct."

"I'll handle this, Edna," Joshua interrupted.

Mrs. Jackson bristled, but quickly deferred to her boss. Joshua flashed an utterly devastating smile at Eleanor, and she fought hard to keep her excessive eagerness to please from showing in her expression. After all, she did possess some pride.

"This is actually a personal matter, not a business situation," Joshua began. "I want it understood from the beginning, Ms. Graham, that you are under no obligation to help me. Okay?"

"O-okay," Eleanor stammered.

"My father has recently remarried. Mrs. Jackson thought you might be familiar with his new wife. Rosemary Phillips?"

"The children's author?"

"Yes." A faint suggestion of color brushed Joshua's strong cheekbones. "Apparently she is quite famous. Unfortunately I've never heard of her, nor have I read any of her books."

"They're wonderful!" Eleanor exclaimed. Her mind unfroze as she spoke on a subject near and dear to her heart: children's literature. "Rosemary is so gifted. I'm constantly amazed by her talent. She's written over fifty books and she illustrates as well as writes the text for each of her stories. Her characters are enchanting. They're funny and endearing and utterly charming. She's brought hours of reading enjoyment to children and adults all over the world. I adore her books."

"It's nice to know that Rosemary has such loyal fans," Joshua said diplomatically. "Do your children enjoy her stories as much as you?"

"I don't have any children," Eleanor said quietly, hoping the color of her face was merely beet and not fire-engine red. "I'm single."

"Single?" A muscle ticked in Joshua's cheek. "Actually that might make things a bit easier."

Eleanor's heart gave a thud that shook her entire body. She stared intently at Joshua, somehow managing to hold his gaze for one breathless moment before looking away. Unbelievably she felt his eyes still on her face, so she glanced back. He sent her an encouraging smile.

It suddenly became difficult to breathe. Maybe it was the fumes from the copier ink she had inhaled earlier? Eleanor told herself it was ridiculous for a twenty-eight-year-old woman to have such intense adolescent feelings for a man who had never and would never look at her as anything more than an employee.

Yet somehow that didn't matter. Apparently her heart didn't possess any common sense when it came to Joshua Barton.

"Easier?" Eleanor squeaked. "What exactly do you mean?"

"I'm going to be meeting Rosemary for the first time this weekend and I feel at a great disadvantage since I know so little about her and her work." Joshua shrugged his broad shoulders. "Do you think you could spare the time to give me a crash course on Rosemary Phillips's . . . um . . . literature?"

"Certainly," Eleanor said in her most professional voice, hoping to cover the sharp pang of disappointment that swept though her. *Well, what did I expect? A dinner invitation, a marriage of convenience proposal, a plea to bear his child? If I continue acting like a hopeless romantic around Joshua, then I fully deserve to be disappointed.*

"I appreciate the help, Ms. Graham," Joshua said formally.

"I'm glad to be of service, Mr. Barton," Eleanor replied with a forced smile, annoyed with herself for feeling an almost desperate need to prove her worth. Why did it matter so much?

Her smile eased away and she mentally pulled herself together. "I recently read an advance copy of Rosemary Phillips's latest book. It's sure to be another hit. She's introduced a new character, Pinkerton Pig. He's a riot."

"Pigs?" Joshua regarded Eleanor with a dubious expression. "Rosemary writes books about pigs?"

"No, not really," Eleanor quickly replied. "I believe Pinkerton is Rosemary's first pig. Her most famous characters are brother and sister rabbits, Alex and Allyson. Of course my personal favorite has always been Owen. He's a dog . . . well, a puppy actually."

"Fifty books filled with puppies? Pigs? Rabbits? I'm never going to be able to keep all this straight," Joshua muttered in a distracted tone. "I'm flying down to D.C. tonight for a bipartisan fund-raising dinner. I'll be staying in the capital for the rest of the week for congressional hearings on the current economic conditions of the Third World. These are very important meetings. I need to keep focused on that agenda."

"You're pushing yourself too hard, Joshua," Mrs. Jackson scolded. "You haven't left the office until after midnight for the past week and a half. You should really try to reschedule this weekend trip."

Joshua waved aside Mrs. Jackson's suggestions. "I've already accepted my father's invitation. I cannot cancel at this late date."

"Perhaps Ms. Graham can accompany you on the plane down to your father's on Friday night," Mrs. Jackson suggested. "The corporate jet can leave here with Ms. Graham at three o'clock, make a quick stop at the airport to pick you up, then continue south. The flight from D.C. to North Carolina is nearly an hour. Ms. Graham can brief you on the plane."

"I suppose that might work," Joshua said. "Congress tends to wrap things up early in the day on Friday."

"I can't possibly leave on Friday afternoon," Eleanor interrupted.

Joshua and Mrs. Jackson turned toward her in surprise, as if they had somehow forgotten she was in the room. Mrs. Jackson's hard glare made her momentarily flinch, but Eleanor valiantly continued.

"I have an appointment, a commitment really, on Saturday morning that I can't change." She swallowed hard. "I can leave anytime after 10:30 A.M. on Saturday if that helps."

The dour glare from Mrs. Jackson seemed to indicate it didn't help one little bit, but Eleanor doggedly waited for Joshua's response.

"Saturday will be fine. We'll return on Tuesday."

Eleanor felt her mouth open, but couldn't speak. She turned to Mrs. Jackson in confusion. The older woman looked equally shocked.

"I only meant for Ms. Graham to accompany you on the flight, Joshua," Mrs. Jackson corrected. "I certainly didn't expect her to spend the weekend at the estate with you as your . . . your . . . date?"

"Why not?" Joshua said casually. "I think it's the perfect solution. If Ms. Graham is kind enough to do me this personal favor the very least I can do is extend her the famous, or rather infamous, Barton hospitality."

"I couldn't possibly intrude on a family gathering," Eleanor said, hardly believing she was arguing. Wasn't this her dream come true? Four days and three nights with Joshua Barton.

"Nonsense. The house will be filled with at least thirty people. There will be additional functions with over a hundred attending. One more guest won't create any difficulties." He gave her a strange look, then leapt to his feet. "Since I'll have so little time to prepare for meeting Rosemary I'll feel more comfortable having you by my side, Ms. Graham."

"I . . . um . . . well," Eleanor stammered. Coherent speech was impossible as her mind took a wild fanciful flight, light years beyond reality.

"It's settled. I'll return home Friday night and we'll leave on Saturday. At eleven A.M. Mrs. Jackson will make all the arrangements and provide you with a schedule of the weekend's events so you'll know what to pack. I believe there is some sort of formal party Sunday night."

Joshua held up a hand as Mrs. Jackson started sputtering objections. She quieted instantly, pressing her lips into a thin line. She didn't look very happy.

"You know where to reach me if anything unusual comes up while I'm gone, Edna. Call me immediately, regardless of the time," Joshua instructed his assistant. Turning toward Eleanor he added, "Thanks again for your help. I'll see you on Saturday, Ms. Graham."

He strode purposefully out the door, taking all the excitement with him. Eleanor's head was spinning. Was this really happening? Was she going to spend a weekend with a man she had dreamed about for untold hours? A man who was totally beyond her sphere, completely unobtainable, so far out of her reach it was almost laughable?

She exhaled a quiet breath, trying to regain her wits, and realized for the first time that she hadn't actually *agreed* to accompany him. But, of course, she would.

And then the reality of the situation hit her full force. Biting her lip in nervous frustration, Eleanor pondered the question that plagued women throughout the ages. *What in the world am I going to wear?*

Joshua walked swiftly through the carpeted hallway. He had a pain behind his eyeballs that was rapidly forming into a tension headache. Thinking about his father usually had that effect on him, probably because they had been at odds with each other for most of the thirty-two years of Joshua's life.

Growing up, the elder Barton had wielded his parental authority like a sword, and Joshua had rebelled at every turn. His mother had provided a much-needed barrier between the volatile father and son, but with her death five years ago the chasm had split wide open.

Joshua's mother had bequeathed her interest in the family business to her son, giving him a controlling majority. Joshua had made an honest effort to work with his father, but when that failed, he forced his father to retire, driving another wedge in an already unstable relationship.

With each passing year they drifted further apart, until eventually they were nothing more than polite strangers. Joshua had not attended his father's private wedding ceremony earlier this year, pleading an unavoidable business obligation.

He realized it was a mistake the night of the wedding, but it was too late. There had been no communication between father and son until a short, handwritten invitation arrived two weeks ago. The significance of this unexpected olive branch was not lost on Joshua. His father was reaching out. And Joshua was determined to do everything within his power to make up for his earlier slight.

"Hello, Mr. Barton."

A breathless, sexy female voice invaded his thoughts.

He glanced up and saw a long-legged golden vision gliding toward him.

Joshua's patented smile came automatically. "Good afternoon, Ms. Colter. I hope you're having a pleasant and productive day."

Ms. Colter's eyes widened with unconcealed excitement, probably because he remembered her name even though she had only worked at the firm a few months.

Ms. Colter slowed her steps noticeably, eager for an opportunity to chat, but Joshua nodded his head dismissively and kept walking. He had learned long ago to protect himself against feminine wiles, especially when the woman in question was an employee. In an age of sexual harassment lawsuits it made good business sense to maintain a professional distance.

Besides, the last thing he needed right now was the complication of a relationship. Past experiences in that area of his life were not among his finest accomplishments.

"Joshua, wait!"

He stopped, turned at the sound of the familiar voice, and watched Edna race toward him.

"It is a major mistake bringing Ms. Graham to North Carolina," Edna stated without preamble. "With a little effort I know we can devise a much simpler, far more efficient plan."

Joshua shook his head and smiled. Edna's forthright, no-nonsense manner was one of the qualities he admired most about her. Even if it did make him nuts sometimes.

"I've already made my decision. She's coming with me."

They reached the elevator. Joshua stabbed at the button, then held the door and politely waited for his assistant to precede him. The moment the doors shut, Edna spoke.

"I'll have Ms. Graham write a summary report for you, emphasizing the highlights of Rosemary's career. I can fax the report to your hotel the moment it's done. You'll have the remainder of the week to familiarize yourself with the details. I'll also purchase an assortment of Rosemary's books so you can read them before you arrive. They must be short if they're written for children. You can probably read at least a dozen of them on the plane."

Joshua watched Edna hastily scribble notes on the small memo pad she always seemed to have in her hand. He gave her a curious look.

"Why are you so negative about Ms. Graham? I thought she was the perfect solution to my problem."

"You've got to be kidding!" Edna nearly dropped her memo pad. "She's a disaster. A totally inappropriate companion for you. She babbles, Joshua. And her appearance! There was a hole in her stocking the size of a moon crater, her hair looked like it had been combed with an eggbeater, and her face was smudged with black ink. I heard a rumor that she fell in the lake at the company picnic. I can't even begin to imagine what your father will think when you walk into his home with Ms. Graham on your arm."

"Don't be such a snob," Joshua said, unexpectedly annoyed by Edna's judgmental tone. "Ms. Graham will be fine. Besides, her complexion is flawless. I'm sure she'll clean up very nicely."

Edna's response was a huffy snort and a raised eyebrow.

The elevator doors opened, saving Joshua from further arguments. But Edna matched his long strides and marched with him step for step to his office.

"I am through discussing this," Joshua stated emphatically. He closed the office door after them. "I want to show my father that I care about him and that I'm interested in his new wife. Ms. Graham can help me do that, Edna."

The older woman sighed in frustration. "I know I can't budge you once you've made up your mind. But for the record, I want my objections noted."

"Fine."

They stared at each other for a full twenty seconds before Edna turned on her heel, breaking the impasse. The door shut behind her with a forceful bang. Joshua expelled a heavy breath. He closed his eyes and rubbed the lids. His headache was getting worse.

He really hated it when Edna was right. The simpler solution to this problem would be a detailed report from Ms. Graham. There was no logical reason for her to spend the weekend with him.

Yet he wanted her with him, standing beside him. He thought he had recognized her as the woman who had fallen into the pond but he wasn't sure until Edna had mentioned it. In his opinion she had shown grace and humor under the most difficult of circumstances. Perhaps that was exactly what he needed this weekend—a little comic relief.

He was inordinately pleased to discover she was not an employee's wife as he had first suspected when he had viewed her lush wet form. There was an indefinable, intangible *something,* strangely appealing, about her that intrigued Joshua. He was so used to female interest that it rarely affected him, but the naked admiration in Ms. Graham's warm brown eyes had given his masculinity a raw jolt.

Dry, she didn't inspire wild, sensual thoughts . . . exactly. Physically she was shorter, plainer, and rounder than any other woman he had ever dated. Although he had thought about that wet T-shirt clinging to her chest more than once these past few weeks.

Still, she was hardly a brilliant conversationalist, although their meetings thus far had been too brief and under such bizarre circumstances it was impossible to make a fair judgment. So he couldn't logically determine where his interest in her was coming from.

Maybe it was just a reaction to the anticipated tension of meeting his father again. Or perhaps he was simply acting rebelliously true to form by bringing a clearly unsuitable companion with him. Whatever the reason, he had made his decision and he fully intended to stick by it.

Unfortunately he had forgotten to ask Edna a few things about the inappropriate Ms. Graham. Like what the devil was her first name? And why did she know so much about children's literature and his recently acquired stepmother Rosemary Phillips? However, given Edna's current mood, Joshua wisely elected to let those two items remain a mystery for a bit longer.

Three

"I don't see my mommy anywhere."

"That's okay," Eleanor said in a deliberately bright tone. She smiled encouragingly and glanced down at Jennifer. "I'm sure she's here somewhere. Let's go look for her together."

The little girl sniffled and took a shaky breath, but held back her tears. Eleanor winced silently as Jennifer clutched her hand, squeezing Eleanor's fingers in a vise-like death grip. She was awfully strong for a four-year-old.

Hand in hand they traversed the crowded children's department of the library, dodging kids with armloads of books, stepping over a pile of puzzle pieces strewn on the floor, and detouring around a group of energetic toddlers.

"Do you see her?" Jennifer asked, ending her question with a woeful hiccup. "Do you see my mommy?"

"Not yet," Eleanor replied, turning up her cheerfulness another notch.

She scooped down and picked up a stuffed yellow bunny that was lying in their path, handing it to Jennifer.

"You hold onto this," Eleanor instructed, hoping to distract the little girl. She suspected if Jennifer's mom didn't appear soon there were going to be a few tears and a lot of panic. Eleanor felt ill equipped to deal with either.

"Mommy!" Jennifer lit up with enthusiasm. She dropped the stuffed rabbit and Eleanor's hand and raced toward her mother. "Where were you? I've been waiting forever and ever for you to come."

"Is story time over already?"

"We just finished," Eleanor replied, hoping to ease the guilty flush from Jennifer's mom's face. The poor woman seemed exhausted and looked about nine-and-a-half months pregnant.

"Thanks so much for staying with her." Jennifer's mom rubbed her bulging stomach distractedly. "She's been very clingy these past few days. I think she's feeling a bit insecure."

"No problem," Eleanor said reassuringly. "She was very brave." Eleanor patted Jennifer's shoulder. "I'll see you next Saturday, Jen."

"Bye, Miss Graham."

Peace restored to her world, Jennifer happily trailed her mother out of the library, chattering every step of the way. Eleanor felt a strange, funny ache as she watched them leave. Mother and daughter, comfortable and happy with each other.

Was this something she wanted for herself? A little girl to spend time with and share a few special and even some not-so-special moments? Eleanor had never thought of herself as a particularly maternal person before but lately she had experienced some unusual stabs of yearning whenever she was around children.

Even the annoying ones.

Dangerous thoughts, indeed.

Shaking off her odd mood Eleanor once again scooped up the rabbit and put it away in the toy box, then glanced around the children's room of the Somerville County Library. It was the usual Saturday morning bedlam. Parents and kids everywhere, working at the computer terminals, huddled together at low tables, scrambling among the stacks searching for books. Eleanor loved every wild, crazy minute of it.

"I've picked up the puppets and put away most of the books from your story time, Eleanor. I can have someone straighten out the rest of the story room later. What time did you say your ride was coming?"

"Eleven." Eleanor smiled in appreciation at the young library assistant. It was one of the things she liked best about working at the library. Everyone always lent a hand, without being told or asked.

"I'm going to get my tote bag and purse out of my locker," Eleanor said, checking her watch. "If someone shows up asking for me, let them know I'll be right out."

"Sure."

Eleanor hurried out of the department. Her gaze moved beyond the clusters of kids and parents, then stopped abruptly on the solitary man standing in the entrance arch. He was looking around curiously, as if he had never seen the inside of a library before.

Joshua!

Eleanor halted in her tracks. For a split second everything inside her went still. His perfectly creased khaki pants, pressed blue oxford button-down shirt, polished loafers, and expertly tailored navy blazer should have made him look totally out of place in this bastion of suburbia. But they didn't.

Eleanor remembered a friend once saying that a man who's comfortable in his own skin is comfortable anywhere. That expression certainly defined Joshua. He had that easy confidence that people have when they are successful at what they do and a relaxed grace that made you want to watch him and him alone.

"Ms. Graham?"

"Hello, Mr. Barton." A stray brown curl fell across Eleanor's face. She quickly looped it behind her ear. "I wasn't expecting you. Mrs. Jackson said she would send a car to take me to the airport."

"My driver is waiting out front. No doubt double-parked." Joshua frowned. "The parking lot is a madhouse."

"Sorry." Eleanor dipped her head. "It's always crazy around here on Saturdays, especially in the morning. I'll go grab my things. I promise it will only take a few minutes."

She leaped away before he had a chance to protest, returning in record time.

"Ready?" Eleanor asked in what she hoped was a confident voice. Her palms were sweaty and her stomach was fluttering like she had swallowed a bird, but she was steadfast in her determination to conquer her nerves.

This was really happening. Fate had mysteriously placed her in the path of her most secret desire and she had spent every night of the past week vowing to make it a memory that would last a lifetime. Of course the real trick would be to make it a *positive* memory.

A few moments later they were safely inside Joshua's chauffeur-driven Bentley. Eleanor was trying hard to act as though it were a common occurrence to be driven around in such luxury and failing miserably.

The car was incredible. The leather seats felt as soft as silk and she could see her reflection in the polished wood accents of the car's interior. It even smelled luxurious.

Eleanor took a deep breath, scrunched her shoulders, and snuggled back into the leather. It was heavenly.

"Do you spend a lot of time at the library?"

Startled, Eleanor jumped up. Lost in the unexpected

sensual enjoyment of her environment, she had nearly forgotten Joshua was sitting beside her. She looked over at him and smiled timidly.

"I'm at the library every Saturday morning doing children's programs. Story times, arts and crafts, holiday events, whatever is needed. I even did a puppet show one morning. I was a terrible puppeteer, but the kids didn't seem to mind. They laughed along with me at all my mistakes."

"You work there?" Shock widened Joshua's piercing dark eyes. "As a second job? Do I need to seriously evaluate the pay scale for my employees and make some adjustments?"

"Of course not," Eleanor answered. She nervously plucked off a piece of lint from her skirt. "The only reason I can afford to work part-time at the library is because I have a real job at Hamilton, Barton and Jones."

Joshua cocked his head. "Why do you work there if you don't need the money?"

Eleanor squirmed, then lowered her head. She willed herself not to blush. "Because I want to be a children's librarian, not a financial analyst," she murmured.

"Excuse me?"

Her head shot up in defiance. "I said I want to be a children's librarian."

"Really?"

"Yes." She folded her arms across her chest. "I attend classes two nights a week and have already successfully completed more than half the required courses. If I continue at this rate, I should have my degree by next spring."

Joshua lifted one eyebrow. "You have to go to school and take special classes to work in a library?"

"Yes," Eleanor replied frostily as he hit a nerve with his all-too-familiar question. "In fact you need an advanced degree to be a librarian." She regarded him pointedly. "A master's degree."

"Uhmm. I guess there is more to being a librarian than learning how to *shhhhhh* people."

Eleanor opened her mouth to issue a scathing retort to Joshua's condescending comment but halted when she noticed the glimmer of amusement twinkling in his eyes.

She broke into a small smile. "Well, there is an exciting course on buying sensible shoes I can't wait to take. The class fills up fast, but I'm hoping to snag a space next semester."

He laughed. "So that's how you know so much about Rosemary's books. I asked Edna how she knew you would be knowledgeable about children's literature but I never got a straight answer."

"Mrs. Jackson must have seen a copy of my continuing education request for reimbursement form. When I started my graduate program I took mostly business reference and computer technology courses and the firm willingly paid for them. However once I ventured into kiddie lit, I was on my own."

"Why don't you like working at my company?" Joshua asked quietly.

Joshua's face revealed mild curiosity, but his voice had an almost forlorn tone. Eleanor's throat constricted. She suddenly felt terribly disloyal.

"It's not your company," Eleanor insisted. She bit her lower lip. How could she possibly explain to a man whose entire professional life was based on making huge sums of money that his type of work brought her no joy?

"I just don't want to spend my days crunching numbers and writing reports," Eleanor said carefully. "I've discovered a career that brings me real pleasure and I plan on pursuing it."

"What about financial security?"

"Have you been talking to my mother?"

He laughed again. Eleanor immediately decided it was a sound she could listen to all afternoon. She grinned hesitantly, hardly believing the personal direction in which the conversation had been heading. She wasn't used to such genuine male interest. It was, unfortunately, something she could quickly learn to enjoy. Especially if it came from this particular man.

"Your mother doesn't approve of your new career choice?" Joshua asked.

Eleanor shook her head. "She thinks I've lost my mind giving up a promising career in the corporate world of finance to be, as she calls it, 'a modestly paid public servant.' "

"Ummm, parental objections." Joshua grimaced knowingly. "Something I've had a bit of experience with."

"Gosh, who'd ever look at the two of us and believe we have the same problem."

"Who, indeed?"

Their gazes met in merry understanding. Joshua's eyes were so warm and inviting, his smile achingly sensual. Eleanor felt herself sway toward him ever so slightly, wondering dreamily if she closed her eyes, would he kiss her?

"We should be at the airport in twenty minutes, Mr. Barton."

The chauffeur's deep voice shattered the spell. Eleanor pulled herself back abruptly. Her heart began beating at a maddening pace while her cheeks began to heat. She cast her gaze out the darkened car window.

Pull yourself together, Eleanor lectured herself sternly. *He's just making polite conversation. He is not in any way, shape, or form interested in you. As a woman. And it's certainly bordering on the pathetic when you interpret good manners and innate kindness as sexual interest.*

But how in heaven's name was she going to cope with her perfectly understandable and completely inappropriate attraction to him?

Eleanor pondered this question in gloomy silence, but as the car sped past a large strip mall she sat up in alarm.

"Oh goodness, I almost forgot. We need to make a quick stop before we reach the airport." She turned toward Joshua apologetically. "I have to pick up my dress. For the formal dinner on Sunday evening."

"No problem."

Joshua lowered the privacy partition and Eleanor hastily gave the chauffeur directions. In ten minutes the car pulled up to the front curb of the small dress shop.

She opened the door without waiting for the chauffeur, committing what she felt sure was a major breach of the rich-and-famous etiquette, judging by the driver's startled expression.

"I'll be right back," Eleanor shouted, making a mad dash for the store. The last thing she wanted was to walk into this small shop with either Joshua or his chauffeur. It would simply be too mortifying for either of them to know that she was in fact renting a formal gown for the weekend instead of buying one.

Eleanor expected to be in and out of the store in five minutes or less. However, she ran into a rather sticky problem. They couldn't find the dress she had spent three agonizing hours selecting.

"Are you absolutely certain that my dress isn't here?" Eleanor cried in frustration. "It's dark blue, with silver trim around the neck and sleeves. I specifically told the salesclerk I would be in this morning to pick it up and pay for the rental."

"I already checked twice," the young salesgirl declared in a bored voice. "It's not here."

"Well, please look again," Eleanor insisted in a firm voice. "I absolutely must have that gown. Now!"

The girl flipped her hair over her shoulder and stalked away in a huff.

"What's the delay?"

Eleanor silently groaned in frustration when she heard Joshua's deep, sensual voice.

"Apparently they've lost my dress," she finally admitted, certain that this sort of thing never, ever happened to people like Joshua.

He glanced about the shop curiously. "Don't they have another one?"

"I doubt it," Eleanor muttered under her breath. "My luck is never that good."

The salesgirl returned with a superior smirk on her face and empty hands. Eleanor didn't bother saying anything. What was the use? She turned around in defeat and left.

Once back inside the car, Eleanor huddled in the corner of the Bentley and fought against despair. Maybe she should stay home and forget the entire weekend. Or perhaps she could fly down on the plane with Joshua, give him a detailed briefing on Rosemary's books, then fly back home. Alone.

A wistful feeling caused Eleanor's throat to tighten. She really, really wanted to spend this time with Joshua but how could she possibly attend a very formal occasion without the proper clothing? In her heart Eleanor knew that even if she was dressed correctly she would most likely still feel out of place. Yet if she was dressed right she could at least blend into the crowd. Pretend, just for an evening, that she belonged.

"Change of plans," Joshua announced to his driver. "We have to make another stop. I need to buy a dress for Ms. Graham. I'll phone our pilot and tell him we'll be late."

Joshua turned his head in Eleanor's direction and asked, "By the way, what is your first name?"

"Eleanor . . . but I really—"

"I'm Joshua."

"Yes, I know. But as I was trying to say before, I really can't allow you to buy me a dress."

"Why?"

"It isn't proper."

Joshua's eyebrows drew together. "I'm not trying to be improper, I'm trying to be expedient. There's a dress boutique next to the shop where I have my suits made. I'm assuming they will have the right type of dress you require for this party.

"The boutique is on the way to the airport, so we won't be driving miles out of our way. The prices at this store are sure to be exorbitant and I certainly don't expect you to go into debt purchasing an article of clothing you need in order to help me.

"Therefore, I only feel it's fair that I pay for your dress. However, if there is someplace else you would rather shop, please inform my driver. Immediately."

Eleanor's mouth opened and closed. She couldn't think of anything to say that didn't sound peevish and immature, so she kept silent. She realized she shouldn't really be surprised by his actions. Joshua was a man who solved a problem by taking control.

Well, she had a few surprises of her own. Knowing it would be foolish to make an issue of it now, Eleanor wisely decided to wait and sort out the details of paying for the dress later.

All too soon they arrived at the elegant, staid women's store Joshua had selected. It reminded Eleanor of a church. Hushed, quiet, reverent.

A reed-thin salesclerk in a sleek black shift drifted toward them. Eleanor's heart sank. She looked down in distress at the mushroom-colored short-sleeved cotton knit top with matching calf-length skirt and flat-heeled pumps she was wearing. This was by far the trendiest outfit she owned and it didn't measure up to the clothes the saleswoman was wearing. She definitely didn't belong in this shop.

Eleanor would have turned and run in a second, but Joshua must have sensed her panic. He clutched her elbow firmly and began urging her forward.

"May I be of assistance?" The saleswoman asked in a low, cultured tone. Although the words were meant for Eleanor, the saleswoman never took her eyes off Joshua.

"I need a dress," Eleanor mumbled, feeling gauche and unsophisticated as the saleswoman finally turned her attention on her. "A formal dress."

"I'm certain we can find something for you. We have a variety of styles, something for every taste. However, the best selection of dresses are size ten and under." The saleswoman's eyes moved quickly over Eleanor. Then she leaned over and inquired sweetly, "Can you wear a size ten, dear?"

"Only if it's mismarked," Eleanor muttered under her breath.

Joshua made an odd noise that sounded suspiciously like a laugh. Eleanor felt the blood drain from her face. This was simply too embarrassing to be believed.

"Well, I'm not sure . . ." the saleswoman began, making a clucking noise with her tongue.

"If you don't have anything suitable, we'll happily take our business elsewhere," Joshua told the salesclerk in a cold voice.

The saleswoman practically snapped to attention. "I

can assure you, that won't be necessary, sir," the clerk said, her voice rising in dismay. "Please, come this way."

Within minutes, Eleanor was nearly drowning in a sea of dresses.

"Do you have a style or color preference?" the clerk asked, glancing anxiously between Eleanor and Joshua.

"Not really," Eleanor said, clearly overwhelmed. She had never seen so many pretty, outrageously expensive clothes. Some didn't even have price tags. She turned instinctively toward Joshua for guidance.

"I prefer simple styles, but Eleanor looks good in everything," Joshua declared.

Eleanor's jaw dropped. *What did he just say?* Her eyes met his and a mischievous smile curved across Joshua's mouth. A warm, wonderful feeling spread through her heart. She found herself grinning back at him, relaxing for the first time since they had entered the shop.

"I'd like something in dark blue or black," Eleanor said firmly. She skimmed her hand over the generous curve of her hip. She would not be ashamed of her body. "In size twelve, please."

Joshua settled himself in a pink-and-white striped armchair that was surprisingly more comfortable than it looked and waited. Eleanor and the snobby saleswoman had disappeared behind the mysterious dressing-room doors moments before, and he doubted they would be returning anytime soon.

Normally he disliked shopping, especially with a woman. But being with Eleanor made it feel like more of an adventure than a chore.

Who could have guessed that her initial timid manner and plain appearance hid a quirky sense of humor? What a delightful surprise. Joshua also appreciated how

Eleanor managed to avoid a scene at the store where they had lost her other dress.

He detested incompetence and rarely tolerated it, but gave Eleanor credit for realizing demanding satisfaction from the young clerk would only have resulted in an unpleasant confrontation that would not have changed the outcome of the morning. They still would have left that shop without her dress.

A soft, rustling noise caught Joshua's attention. He looked up just as Eleanor, swathed in a cloud of black taffeta, emerged from the fitting room with the saleswoman close on her heels. The ball gown Eleanor wore was fitted at the waist and hooped out like a large bell. It made a swishing sound each time she moved.

Over it she wore a sheer jacketlike black top that covered her from her neck to her wrists. The dress didn't look bad on her, but remembering well how that wet T-shirt had hugged her chest, Joshua decided he wanted to see more of Eleanor's lovely white skin.

He jerked himself upright. Now where in the world had that unexpected thought come from?

Joshua shook his head. Despite the fact that he was starting to like Eleanor, it was totally ludicrous to imagine her as a romantic partner in his life. For one thing, she worked for him, and he never dated his employees.

In so many ways, on so many levels, they were mismatched. He was a passionate, headstrong, adventurous type while Eleanor was a more conservative, proper, reserved person. Of course, aside from the vast differences of their pasts, there were also the expansive differences of their futures.

Hell, Eleanor's biggest goal in life was to be a librarian while he thrived in a hectic, cutthroat business environment. Talk about different lifestyles. How could he possibly relate to a woman who found contentment reading stories to little kids and shelving books?

Feeling irritated, Joshua strode over to the women, determined to end this little shopping spree immediately and put the morning back on its proper business course.

"All set?" Joshua asked curtly. He stood near the saleswoman and practically glowered at her.

She gave him a brief, cursory glance. Eleanor didn't even raise her eyes. Joshua's irritation escalated.

As the salesclerk fussed with the skirt of the dress, Joshua stared hard at Eleanor, rocking back on his heels and waiting impatiently to catch her eye. She was averting her eyes from the three-way mirrors and making funny little strangling sounds each time the clerk said anything.

"Do you like that one?" the saleswoman inquired politely. "It's a classic style and very flattering."

Eleanor sighed. "I look like a Civil War widow."

Joshua's mouth quirked. He tried, but failed to hold on to his annoyance.

"Remove the jacket," he suggested in a quiet voice.

Eleanor's face paled, as if she had just noticed he was standing so near. She raised her eyes and gave him an indecipherable look, then slowly peeled off the gauzy top. The dress had a low-cut strapless neckline that emphasized her impressive bosom and showcased lots and lots of smooth, creamy white skin.

Joshua's gaze flicked to Eleanor's bare shoulders, wondering if they were as satiny soft as they looked. Swallowing hard, he forced himself to look away, sternly reminding himself they were completely wrong for each other.

"You look great."

Eleanor managed a crooked smile. "Oh, sure. I was born to wear designer clothes."

She smoothed down the side of her skirt and Joshua noticed the uncertainty and vulnerability in her eyes.

"You look wonderful, Eleanor," Joshua insisted.

"Really? You don't think I look silly? You know, like a little girl who's playing dress up with her mother's clothes?"

"I doubt there are any little girls around who can hold that dress in place the way you can," Joshua commented with a wry smile.

Eleanor broke into shy, hesitant laughter. The sound made something warm unfurl in Joshua's chest. He removed a credit card from his wallet and casually passed it to the saleswoman. "We'll take the dress."

Eleanor's face slowly lit up with delight. "Thank you, Joshua."

Her simple, sincere gratitude hit him right in the gut. He felt a strong momentary impulse to sweep her up in his arms and taste the sweetness of her lips, wondering if he could make her tremble with the same desire and passion that had unexpectedly seized him.

Instead Joshua did the only sensible thing possible. He turned on his heel and fled.

Four

"Is your seat belt securely fastened?" Joshua asked in a deep voice. "The pilot just informed me that we've been cleared for takeoff."

Eleanor glanced across the aisle. They were seated in the first row of seats in the small, luxurious plane cabin. She didn't immediately answer his question. Instead she stared at him, realizing that she was surprised to discover he was going to be riding back there with her for the flight. For some odd reason she had expected him to be flying the plane.

That image was more in keeping with her perceptions of him—Superman and James Bond all rolled into one. Eleanor honestly never doubted for a moment there wasn't anything Joshua Barton couldn't do, if he set his mind to it . . . including flying a plane.

"Seat belt is fine," she eventually murmured.

Joshua leaned over and tugged on her belt, just to be certain. The movement startled her and she jumped. Recovering quickly, she schooled her features into a blank expression, but he never lifted his head. As he withdrew, Eleanor caught a gentle whiff of his subtle cologne—clean, crisp, masculine, and oh, so sexy.

She bit her lip to keep from sighing. Her mind started spinning in slow circles as a strange, wicked thrill came to life inside her. She imagined Joshua turning toward her, giving her a lazy, sexy smile, then drawing her close and covering her mouth with his.

How would it feel? Would there be bells and whistles and explosions of colors behind her closed eyelids, a swift-beating pulse at her throat, the sensation of the earth moving under her feet as they kissed?

An image flashed through her mind, of her body sprawled beneath his as they embraced, hungry flesh straining and pressing tightly together, but she instantly pushed it away.

Get a grip, Eleanor demanded of herself. This was not a date, this was business. She needed to be certain to remember that—at all times. Joshua was a dangerous man, inspiring sensual, romantic fantasies. But they could never become a reality.

"All set," Joshua muttered briskly. He turned away and she saw him press a button on the wall near his seat. She supposed it was a signal to the pilot.

Eleanor pulled herself back from her romantic daydreams. She reached down and retrieved several picture books from her heavy canvas tote bag, deciding she desperately needed something to focus on during the flight. Or else she was going to make a total fool of herself before they even cleared Philadelphia air space.

Thanks to the fair weather and a competent pilot it was a smooth takeoff. The plane climbed steadily for several minutes, then leveled off. Fortunately so did Eleanor's stomach. She wasn't the best of flyers and had been concerned about the potential for a turbulent flight in the small aircraft.

Yet as she held the books in her lap in a near death-grip, she realized her fears had been groundless, because her stomach felt fine. Except when she was on the receiving end of one of Joshua's piercing glances.

The moment Joshua was given the signal from the pilot, he released his seat belt and instructed Eleanor to do the same. Once free of the constraints he prowled about the cabin, removing his briefcase and laptop from a storage bin. He arranged a variety of official-looking papers on a movable table, turned on the computer, and positioned the table in front of his seat so he could easily access these items.

Then Joshua fixed himself a drink—Scotch and water—after Eleanor declined one, downing it in several quick gulps.

He eventually settled back in his seat, but paid no attention to the work he had so studiously arranged. With an audible sigh, he leaned his head back and thrust out his long legs, crossing them at the ankles.

The space Eleanor initially thought was so large seemed to shrink. She tried to stop herself, but couldn't help an occasional glance in his direction. He seemed unaware of her scrutiny, or perhaps he was so accustomed to subtle as well as blatant stares he didn't even notice hers.

"This is normally a short flight. With clear weather and the unusually low amount of air traffic today we should arrive at the airstrip in North Carolina in about an hour," Joshua announced in a flat tone. "We need to spend that time discussing Rosemary's work."

He spoke without looking at Eleanor. His head was lolling lazily against the high seat back, his gaze pinned out the small plane window. He sounded so weary and unenthusiastic she thought his eyes might also be closed, but couldn't be certain since she was unable to see his face. Yet it was only an illusion of relaxation, for she noticed the tightness of his white-knuckled fingers as they gripped the armrest.

"I've brought a number of Rosemary's books with

me," Eleanor replied, rooting about in her tote bag. "A few I borrowed from the library, but most are from my personal collection."

"Excellent." He turned toward her, and she could see the muscles flexing along the square line of his jaw.

Wordlessly Eleanor thrust several books in his general direction. His mood was strange and unsettling. Not precisely rude, not precisely brooding, but a far cry from the charm she knew he was capable of bestowing.

She shuffled the remaining books she held on her lap, then gave up the pretense and stared openly while he read, trying to judge his feelings, identify and understand the emotions that seemed to be bubbling and churning inside him. Clearly something was bothering Joshua and she desperately hoped it wasn't her.

"That's my very favorite story," Eleanor blurted out when Joshua finished the first book. "It only won an Honor Medal in the Caldecott competition that year, but I think it should have taken first place. I'm sure it didn't win because Rosemary had already won the award two years prior and the Caldecott committee doesn't like repeat winners."

Joshua glanced at Eleanor, looked down at the cover of the book he held, then back up at her. "So all of these small round silver and gold symbols on the book covers represent some sort of award?"

"Yes." Eleanor ran her finger lightly over the book jacket. "Rosemary has won countless awards over the course of her career, but none more prestigious than the Caldecott Medal," she explained with enthusiasm. "That award is given annually by the American Library Association to the artist who has created the most distinguished picture book of the year. The only restriction is that authors must be citizens or residents of the United

States, but obviously that encompasses a great many writers."

"And Rosemary has won this coveted prize?" Joshua asked slowly. He seemed to be digesting that information as though he didn't quite believe it.

Eleanor's spine stiffened. "She has won once, but has also had six titles named as Honor Books. They are sort of the runner-up prize, although no one refers to them precisely in that manner. Still, in a competition of this size and scope, when literally hundreds of books are considered, being a runner-up is a big deal."

"I see," Joshua replied, yet his puzzled expression suggested otherwise. With a slight shake of his head he turned to the books she had given him and began reading.

Eleanor felt a twinge of dismay. Apparently she hadn't clearly conveyed that Rosemary Phillips was an exceptional children's author and illustrator, greatly admired by peers, professionals, and readers of all ages. Deciding it would be best to let Rosemary's work speak for itself, Eleanor waited anxiously while Joshua read the other two books.

"Would you like to read a few more stories?" Eleanor asked politely when Joshua was finished. "I have a whole bag full of picture books."

He offered her a sharply frowning expression. "Are they any different from the three I just read?"

Eleanor's heart sank. He didn't get it. No wonder he seemed so surprised that Rosemary's stories had received awards.

Although picture books were designed and written as a visual experience for children, many adults, herself included, appreciated the whimsy and humor in the stories. In Eleanor's humble opinion, Rosemary Phillips's books were marked by excellence in both artistic technique and story themes. Yet Joshua had obviously failed to notice that fact.

"There are many layers to Rosemary's books," Eleanor said quietly. "Naturally she has to show respect for a child's understanding and abilities when she writes, since kids are her principle audience. Still, there is much here that an adult can savor, especially the subtle traces of humor. I think you need to look at these books with a slightly different perspective to fully appreciate their impact."

Joshua shrugged his shoulders, but dutifully opened the book again. Eleanor let out a small breath. She wasn't exactly sure why, but she felt it was important that Joshua at least acknowledge and attempt to comprehend the magnitude of Rosemary's genius.

"So I'm supposed to be looking for funny stuff, right?" Joshua sat up straighter and peered intently at the open book. "Things that a kid would laugh at? Like the flower pot on the puppy's head and how the little rabbit isn't wearing pants, just a shirt?"

Eleanor shook her head. The rabbit wasn't wearing pants! He thought that was supposed to be funny? "You must have been a real handful as a child," she declared, as she plucked the book off Joshua's lap and began reading the story out loud.

By the second page her nerves had dwindled enough to allow her voice to remain steady and strong. By the fourth page she was enjoying herself so much that she no longer felt self-conscious. Consequently by the fifth page Eleanor was in full storyteller mode, varying the volume and pitch of her voice for each character, making appropriate sounds and gestures, alternating the speed and delivery of her words.

She finished with a triumphant crescendo. Closing the

book gently, she turned her head and smiled smugly at Joshua.

There was a blank expression on his handsome face, but his eyes held a hint of true astonishment. Eleanor cleared her throat nervously. The roar of the jet engines suddenly seemed overpoweringly loud. She could feel the tips of her ears begin to heat as a wave of embarrassment washed over her entire being.

What in heaven's name came over me? She had only meant to demonstrate the whimsy of the book and instead acted out the entire story as though he were a three-year-old. *Dear God, where's a parachute when I need one? Better still, I should probably jump without one and spare myself the agony of surviving the fall.*

Just when Eleanor thought she had reached the end of her capacity to endure humiliation, Joshua's lips moved. He broke into a wide, genuine smile and said softly, "Read it again."

The last time someone had read Joshua a story he had been seven years old. An elderly baby-sitter had kept him company in his lonely sickbed while his parents attended an important business event. He remembered being angry that they had left him and petulantly had refused the kind woman's offers to cheer him up.

He had declared loudly that being read to was for babies, but she had been persistent. And he remembered being oddly comforted by the familiar words of his favorite story, patiently read and reread by the caring sitter.

Eleanor's spirited rendition of this comical tale brought that memory to life. And other memories, too, of his mother sharing books with him and those rare occasions when his father would read him a story before bed. Impulsively Joshua wondered what had happened to the substantial book collection of his childhood favorites.

"I'm glad that you enjoyed the book," Eleanor said stiffly. She pressed a hand to her hair, nervously smoothing back a stray curl. "Some . . . sometimes these stories are better received when read aloud."

"Apparently." He grinned mischievously.

She cast her eyes away from his and Joshua felt a stab of regret. Obviously she was embarrassed by her spirited performance, but he had thought it was immensely entertaining. He found himself remembering how pretty she had looked while she was reading, with her head tilted to one side and a smile on her face and in her voice. For a few moments she was quite irresistibly attractive.

"Perhaps we should look at another book," Eleanor suggested.

"Sure." Joshua quickly flipped through the volume she handed him. It seemed similar to the others, with bright colorful drawings of various friendly-looking, cuddly animals. The pictures were charming to view and cleverly humorous in a childlike way. Yet he still failed to see what was so incredibly unique about them.

He was about to say just that, but one look at Eleanor's expectant face changed his mind. Apparently there was something special about this story and he had about three minutes to figure it out. Feeling like he was cramming for a final exam, Joshua gave it another try.

"I can see that this book is meant to be a bedtime story," Joshua began slowly. "And I also noticed there are more pictures in this one and not nearly as many words."

Eleanor nodded approvingly. "Exactly. Spare in text but long on action, much of it related through these cleverly expressive pictures. In essence, the very definition of a picture book. To write and illustrate a story which cannot be understood by reading the text alone."

"So that's the big challenge with this type of book?"

"Yes. And believe me, it isn't easy to achieve this kind of balance." Eleanor leaned closer. "Try to imagine telling the story to someone over the phone. It doesn't work, because they can't see the pictures."

Taking that into account, Joshua reread the three stories. He saw now that the slapstick wit of the illustration moved beyond the story to enrich it. His appreciation for Rosemary Phillips's talent went up a full ten degrees.

Still, he wondered privately about his father's choice of wife. Rosemary seemed far more creative and cerebral than any of the women his father had dated after Joshua's mother died. Joshua hadn't really expected his father to remarry, but if that happened he assumed his stepmother would be more of a society type.

The kind of woman who pestered the interior decorator about paint colors and material swatches, worried about her charitable fund raisers and doing well in the country club golf tournament. Certainly not a woman famous in her own right, successful in a highly competitive, creative field.

Joshua accepted another pile of books from Eleanor. He read them carefully and, as the plane flew steadily through the bright afternoon sky, they discussed the originality of Rosemary's artwork and her gift for fitting the artwork to develop the story.

"You know a lot about this business," Joshua concluded. "Have you ever considered writing your own children's book?"

"Well, I did have an idea for a picture book that I thought would be great," Eleanor admitted, with a telltale blush of color in her cheeks. "I worked on it for nearly a year, even had a friend who is a graphic artist do a few illustrations for me. When I thought it was perfect, I sent it off to several different publishers."

"And . . ." Joshua prompted, fascinated by the risk she had taken.

"And . . ." Eleanor replied, elongating every sound in the three-letter word. "As I said before, writing a good picture book isn't nearly as easy as it seems. My story was rejected by every publisher who saw it. And rightfully so." Eleanor gave him a self-deprecating smile. "I was initially crushed, so I put the manuscript away. Then I read it six months later and had no difficulty pinpointing the major flaw in my work. Bottom line, the book had everything—except a plot."

Joshua's eyes met hers. She was laughing. He told himself there was nothing inherently funny about failure or rejection, yet Eleanor chose to remember her foray into the world of publishing with humor instead of bitterness. Admirable.

As he helped her put the books away Joshua realized that some of the apprehension he felt over meeting his father's new wife had eased. He wouldn't be a complete outsider. At least now he could converse intelligently about Rosemary's work. He felt slightly calmer, more in control, dreading a bit less the events of the upcoming weekend.

He smiled at his teacher. She really did understand this stuff and was sensitive and knowledgeable enough to teach others. Despite the odd moments of inappropriate and completely unexpected sexual jolts he felt for Eleanor, Joshua decided taking her along on this trip had been the best decision he'd made all week.

"Thank you, Eleanor," he said sincerely.

Impulsively Joshua reached for her hand and brought it to his lips. It was a courtly gesture, an old-world, time-honored custom that somehow seemed appropriate for this old-fashioned woman. He placed a single, gentle kiss on the top of her delicate knuckle.

And got the surprise of his life.

Who would have ever imagined that such a simple act could turn into a truly intimate moment? Her skin felt smooth and unbelievably soft beneath his sensual caress. As his lips brushed against its silkiness, he detected a faint scent of lemons.

It was more enticing than any exotic perfume he had ever inhaled. His body tightened, his blood pressure climbed.

He heard her breath catch, felt her skin heat beneath his possessive grip. Leisurely he stroked the valley of her palm with his thumb. The pulse at her wrist jumped and Joshua smiled faintly. Amazingly this casual contact was exciting him more than any kiss he could remember. Feeling bewildered and restless, Joshua lifted his head and stared at her.

Eleanor looked as startled as he felt. Her eyes widened, then narrowed, and for a moment she seemed frozen in place. Suddenly the plane dipped and Joshua wasn't sure if the sharp pang in his stomach was due to the sudden loss of altitude or the contact with Eleanor's soft, warm flesh.

The plunge effectively broke the mood. Eleanor pulled her hand out of his and turned away, hunching her shoulders and wrapping her arm around her waist.

The red signal light near his seat began blinking. Joshua answered the call from the pilot automatically and reality returned in full force.

"We should be landing momentarily," Joshua stated, in a voice that came out gruff and deep and husky. "I made arrangements for a car to be left at the airstrip so we can drive directly to the house."

"Okay."

Her voice was breathy, but steady. A difficult feat considering how rattled she had been by his actions. That little episode seemed to affect her almost as much as him. With effort Joshua managed to avoid looking at Eleanor as the plane continued its descent.

Not that scrutinizing her would provide any of the answers he craved. But since she was the cause of his discomfort, she was the logical place to start looking for explanations.

He busied himself by putting away his briefcase and computer and fastening his seat belt in preparation for landing. Yet all the while one thought kept nagging at his brain.

If kissing Eleanor's hand got him so worked up, how the hell would he feel if he kissed her on the lips?

What in the world had happened on that plane?

While Joshua drove the car that was waiting for them at the airfield, Eleanor sat primly in the passenger seat, knees together, hands folded in her lap, and tried to figure it out. It was impossible.

One minute they had been discussing picture books and Rosemary Phillips and Caldecott awards and the next Joshua had been kissing her hand. It was without question the most romantic, and oddly erotic thing that had ever happened to her. Her toes curled inside her shoes at the memory.

It must be all the leather, Eleanor decided with a grim appraisal of the car interior. That rich, subtle odor was turning her brain cells to mush. First the Bentley, then the plane, now the inside of a Porsche. A Porsche! When Joshua had mentioned that a car would be waiting for them she assumed it would be a rental car. A boxy sedan, solid, safe, dependable.

Instead there had been a black Porsche. Sleek, sexy and fast.

Joshua drove it commandingly and way too fast. But it took the turns in the road smoothly and the straight stretches like a bullet. Eleanor had always appreciated the thrill of speed, but mixing it with nerves, silent tension and Joshua Barton was almost too much sensation.

She glanced at him. He was focused on the road, so she studied his profile. Straight nose, square jaw, sensual mouth, strong chin. His pure male beauty nearly took her breath away.

This time he must have noticed her scrutiny. He turned his head, flashed her a quick smile, then returned his attention to the road. Eleanor's pulse quickened. She struggled to regard him in a rational, cautious manner, but it was difficult.

Ever since he had taken her hand and kissed it, all she could think about was kissing his lips. Being held tightly in his arms, bodies pressing, tongues caressing while the world exploded into passion.

Eleanor sucked in a breath. Was the hot sun getting to her already? Frying her common sense and heating up her vivid fantasy life? Not that it needed much heating. When it came to Joshua, her romantic, sensual, and sexual flights of imagination quickly took on a life of their own.

Eleanor took a mental breath and crossed her ankles. Time to regroup and refocus. She turned her attention to the passing scenery, admiring the bright blue sky, brilliant sunshine, and beautiful green slopes rolling out toward the horizon. She had never been in this part of the country and she found it very pretty.

Joshua made no attempts at conversation. The silent tension built slowly, but Eleanor decided she preferred it to stilted conversation. Besides, by keeping her mouth shut she was able to avoid saying something totally inappropriate. Like, what kind of underwear do you wear, boxers or briefs? And would you be so kind as to show me?

The road narrowed but Joshua didn't adjust the speed of the car. Still, she felt safe, trusting his judgment and ability to handle the powerful automobile. Eleanor concentrated on the ever changing view, wondering if they were getting close to the house. She caught a fleeting glimpse of a large building in the far distance, towering trees with Spanish moss draped romantically in the branches, and a spot of blue ocean.

"Reflections," Joshua announced as he turned into the end of the long gravel driveway. He punched a code into the security panel and two huge black wrought iron gates slowly swung open.

Eleanor craned her neck back and watched the majestic gates in awe. Then she firmly pulled up her jaw and murmured, "Excuse me?"

"Reflections," he repeated, enunciating each syllable separately. "Home sweet home, sugar."

The *sugar* threw her, so it wasn't until she read the engraved brass plate discreetly located on the brick wall surrounding the estate that she realized Reflections was the name of the property.

Was he kidding? The house had a name?

Panic whispered along Eleanor's spine. She wasn't sure if she was ready to deal with all of this. And he really didn't need her help anymore. She had already given him a crash course in Rosemary's books and explained the basic philosophy of picture books.

Maybe if she asked very nicely he would turn the car around and bring her back to the airstrip. Or drop her near a pay phone so she could call a cab. They must have cabs in North Carolina, right?

"Is this where you grew up?" she asked, when intense curiosity helped her find her voice.

"No. We spent summers here when I was a kid and Thanksgiving once in a while. My father's family were genuine carpetbaggers. They came south after the war and built this place with—"

"The war?" Eleanor interrupted. "You can't possibly mean the Civil War?"

"The War Between the States," Joshua corrected with a smile. "You're below the Mason-Dixon Line now, so you'd better watch your tongue, sugar."

His imitation of a slow Southern drawl turned her insides to mush. She leaned back into the comfortable car seat and briefly shut her eyes. Maybe she could call for that cab after they arrived at the house.

Joshua waited until the gates closed behind them before proceeding down the driveway. As they approached, she sat up and clutched the door handle. Then the house came into view and for the first time ever while in his company, there was something other than Joshua that claimed Eleanor's complete attention.

The house was huge. At least five stories and more Victorian or Gothic in style than the traditional white-columned Southern-style mansion she was expecting. There were turrets and rounded edges, gabled roofs, soaring towers of pale gray stone and shutters of dark green. Window boxes overflowed with blooming annuals beneath the upper floor windows.

Wide, sweeping verandas edged the house, complete with white wicker furniture artfully grouped in conversation clusters. Lush dark-green-striped cushions added graciousness and a romantic flavor of by-gone days.

The lush green grounds seemed to stretch all around until they were finally stopped by the blue ocean. The only other structures in sight were made with the same stones, clearly part of the estate. It was all so vast, private, and secluded, with an atmosphere that exemplified the very essence of grandeur.

She had envisioned taste, elegance, and wealth, but this went one step beyond. Every blade of grass in place, every flower in perfect bloom. Even the air smelled crisper, cleaner. The entire picture spread before her eyes looked like a magazine layout. Eleanor couldn't imagine anyone actually *living* in this beautiful place.

"It's magnificent," Eleanor said with sincere awe. "Unbelievable. Like something out of a movie set. Or a fairy tale."

"No need to romanticize it," Joshua said sharply, as he switched off the ignition. "It's just a house."

Eleanor flushed. "Sorry," she whispered, feeling like a complete idiot.

Joshua sighed loudly. "No, I'm sorry," he said as a flicker of regret marred the perfect symmetry of his handsome face. "My remarks were rude and totally uncalled for. Please forgive me."

"Okay." Eleanor turned the car handle and scrambled to climb out of the car. Anything to put some distance between herself and Joshua.

Then she felt the pressure of his strong grip on her forearm, forestalling her exit. She raised her head to stare at him and instantly saw regret darken his eyes.

"The house is beautiful. I guess I had forgotten." He ran his fingers impatiently through his hair. "I'm feeling very unprepared for this visit and it isn't fair taking it out on you." He opened his door and got out, making his way around to her side.

Eleanor couldn't begin to understand why he felt the need to be *prepared* to meet his father and his father's wife, but she appreciated his apology.

"Well, if you're feeling unprepared you can only imagine how I feel," Eleanor replied lightly, picking up the thread of conversation as Joshua assisted her out of the Porsche.

He paused and tilted his head. A small, sexy smile tugged at his lips. "I have no doubt that you'll impress the hell out of them."

Eleanor groaned at the outrageous flattery and fell in step beside him. "You have no idea how much I want to believe you," she whispered softly, as they walked to the wide entrance doors.

Five

They didn't get very far. After taking only a few steps toward the house, they saw those gorgeous wide double doors suddenly open. A couple stepped outside. Eleanor immediately recognized the woman as Rosemary Phillips. If anything she was prettier than her publicity photo, which Eleanor thought was most remarkable, since she had walked past many an author at a book signing because she had naïvely expected her to at least resemble her photograph.

Rosemary was probably close to sixty years old but certainly didn't look it. Her hair, a frosted blond, was cut short and full and framed her slender face artfully. She had large, expressive eyes, high cheekbones, very few wrinkles, and the most beautiful complexion Eleanor had ever seen.

Standing beside her, hovering in an almost protective manner, was Joshua's father. Although he was a handsome man, Eleanor could discern little resemblance between father and son. The older Barton's face was longer and narrower than his son's, his features sharper and more angular. Yet upon closer inspection she noted that physically the two men were very similar—tall, broad-shouldered, and well built.

Though their faces were not alike, there was more than

a hint of masculine pride and confidence in their expressions that *was* so similar it spoke of the blood ties between the older and younger man.

There was no welcoming smile on Warren Barton's face. He watched their approach silently, with brows drawn together over sharp, shrewd eyes. Eleanor thought longingly of the smothering hugs and kisses she always received from her widowed mother and vowed to call her mom the moment she returned home.

Beside her, Joshua walked rigidly. His obvious tension made her even more nervous. Taking a deep breath for courage, Eleanor forced one foot in front of the other while her eyes darted anxiously between the two people standing so imposingly together.

Rosemary and Warren made a very attractive pair, fit, trim, tanned, and dressed in elegant, casual clothes that said *wealthy* in a rather understated fashion. Yet Eleanor couldn't help but think, *Where is that famous Southern hospitality you always hear about? Honestly, would it kill them to at least smile?*

"About time you got here," Warren Barton suddenly bellowed. "I expected you two hours ago. We've been holding luncheon, but who knows what it will taste like now."

Joshua stopped dead in his tracks. "Hello, Father," he said coolly. "Sorry about lunch. We've already eaten. And if I remember correctly, I told you we'd arrive sometime before three. Since it's only two-ten, we're technically early."

Warren Barton huffed his reply. Eleanor watched Rosemary reach over and give her husband's hand a reassuring pat. The older man answered his wife's gesture of comfort by squeezing her hand. Then he stiffened his spine and glared down at his son.

Their eyes clashed. Neither man moved, nor blinked.

Their expressions held such an identical look of stubbornness it might have been comical, if it weren't so tense and uncomfortable. It reminded Eleanor of a wildlife program she had seen last month on her favorite cable station. Two bull elks, squaring off for territorial rights. Any minute now she expected Joshua and his father to hunch their shoulders and start banging their heads together.

Eleanor glanced at Rosemary and saw the same feeling of helplessness she was experiencing reflected in the other woman's eyes. Both women understood this was not their battle. They could only wait and silently witness the struggle between father and son.

Just when she thought her wobbly knees were going to give out, Joshua took a small step forward. Eleanor latched onto his arm. She felt the immediate tension that rippled through him, but was determined to keep him moving at all costs, figuring if this unexpected stress didn't get to her she would probably die of sunstroke out here in the blazing June heat.

Joshua's arm felt stiff beneath her fingers, but he gave no outward sign of emotion. She tried to imitate his unemotional mask—after all, these two people were strangers to her—but it was difficult. She had no experience with family members who treated each other so coldly and formally. Eleanor felt like she was walking through a minefield. Just one wrong step and everything was going to explode.

After what seemed like an eternity they reached the veranda. Joshua took two steps up, but halted on the third. Warren Barton blinked at his son and his lips curved upward in a ghost of a smile.

"It's nice to see you, Joshua," Warren said, advancing toward them. The two men shook hands briefly. Neither seemed comfortable with the physical contact.

"This is Eleanor," Joshua said simply by way of introduction.

Eleanor smiled tentatively and held out her hand. "Hello, Mr. Barton. It's very nice to meet you."

"Welcome, Eleanor. Please, call me Warren. I'm glad you were able to join us this weekend." Warren turned and gestured toward the woman standing at the threshold. "I'd like you both to meet my wife, Rosemary."

The older woman smiled fleetingly and came forward. Eleanor deliberately thrust her free hand behind her back, forcing Joshua to greet his new stepmother first.

"I'm delighted to finally meet you, Joshua," Rosemary said sincerely. "Warren has told me so much about you."

"Hello, Rosemary," he replied somberly as he shook her hand.

Rosemary looked startled for a second. She made a slight move forward and Eleanor could have sworn she intended to hug Joshua, but one glance at his stony expression must have effectively squashed that impulse.

Eleanor's mouth tightened. She had seen warmer greetings at an IRS audit. Determined to do something, anything, to shatter the impossible tension, Eleanor followed her instincts.

"I'm thrilled to meet you, Rosemary," she said enthusiastically as she embraced the older woman in a quick, friendly hug.

After a slight hesitation, Rosemary quickly recovered and hugged Eleanor in return. When the two women separated, Eleanor swore some of the uncertainty in Rosemary's eyes had been replaced by a spark of hope.

With the introductions over, a heavy, awkward silence descended. Eleanor could feel a small trickle of sweat roll down the center of her back. She, who was seldom at a loss for words, struggled to find her voice. *What an odd family!* Stiff, formal, outwardly polite, inwardly hostile. It was becoming increasingly more uncomfortable watching this strained interaction between them.

"Well, there's no need to be standing outside in all this heat," Rosemary finally said. "Why don't we all go in and have a drink? I know you've already eaten lunch, but I'm sure you're thirsty."

"A cold drink sounds wonderful," Eleanor replied. "A tall glass of iced tea or lemonade would really hit the spot right now." She didn't dare look over at Joshua, knowing she should have waited for him to respond. After all, this was his home, his family. But frankly she was too terrified of what he might say.

"I'll call Robert to bring in your luggage," Warren declared.

"No need for that," Joshua insisted, walking back to the car. "There aren't many bags. I can manage."

Warren's eyebrow shot up. "Remarkable. Leave it to my son to find the only woman in the Northern Hemisphere who travels light. Looks like your luck with girlfriends has finally changed, my boy. For the better."

The older Barton gave Eleanor a quirky smile. She swallowed hard and turned to Joshua for support. His girlfriend? Not in this lifetime. Yet her palms grew damp and a restless wildness rose inside her as she waited for Joshua to correct his father's outrageous mistake.

But Joshua wasn't paying any attention to her. His father had followed him down to the car and now stood with outstretched hands, offering assistance with the luggage. After a slight hesitation, Joshua handed off one of the bags.

"Wow, this is heavy," Warren exclaimed. "What do you have in here? Rocks?"

Joshua laughed. "No rocks, just books. Eleanor is a big fan of Rosemary's."

"Really?" This time Warren's smile was warm and

genuine. "It's nice to meet a woman with such good sense. Better not let this one get away, son."

Everything inside her went still. Surely *now* Joshua would correct his father.

Instead he grinned broadly at her. A dimple formed on his cheek and she forgot entirely what she had been thinking.

The men joined the women on the porch and they entered the house with Rosemary leading the way. Eleanor tried not to openly gape at the opulent surroundings as they walked into the formal living room, but it wasn't easy: a sweeping ocean view, soaring twelve-foot ceilings with detailed, molded plasterwork, priceless antiques, museum-quality artwork, heavy, expensive carpets over shining hardwood floors, numerous bunches of fresh flowers arranged in silver or crystal or porcelain vases.

The sunlight poured through the long French windows, reflecting off the rich wood accent pieces, giving an inviting glow to the peach and soft green fabric designs on the cushions, rugs, and spare window treatments.

"What a lovely room!" Eleanor exclaimed.

"I just finished the redecorating this week. I wanted everything ready in time for the party." Rosemary twisted her hands and glanced anxiously at Joshua. When he didn't say anything, she wandered across the room, straightening a pillow on the love seat, then brushing a speck of dust off the edge of an exquisite Pembroke table. "I hope you like it. I know you don't get down here often, Joshua, but this is still your home."

"Very nice," Joshua muttered, but his set face gave away none of his inner feelings.

Eleanor bit her lip. Once again the undercurrent of tension reigned supreme.

"It's a beautiful room," Warren boomed out. "You did a superb job, Rosemary. Didn't she, Josh?"

"Superb," Joshua repeated stonily.

They were saved from the strain of trying to make further conversation by the arrival of an older woman carrying a silver tray of drinks. Judging by the warm greeting Joshua gave her, Eleanor assumed the woman, Martha, had worked for the family for many years.

Martha blushed and protested, then grinned proudly when Joshua took the heavy tray from her and carried it the rest of the way to the sideboard.

Although both lemonade and iced tea had been brought as Eleanor had requested, she recklessly decided to join everyone else and have a vodka tonic. If the first half hour was any indication as to how the rest of the visit was going to be, Eleanor suspected she was going to need something a whole lot stronger than iced tea.

Everyone settled awkwardly on the beautiful furniture and gave their complete attention to their drinks. The moments of strained silence steadily ticked away. Eleanor searched her mind frantically for a neutral topic of conversation to introduce but was unable to come up with anything.

Well aware that with this crew any topic posed the threat of alienation or all-out war, Eleanor prudently decided it might be smarter to keep her mouth shut. She realized she had landed herself in a situation that was way over her head and the only thing she could do was hope that someone else possessed the courage to start a civilized discussion.

"Did you have nice flight down?" Rosemary finally asked, breaking the awkward silence.

"Very pleasant," Eleanor jumped in quickly. "The flight was very smooth and the plane was so comfortable."

"Does the company still own that gas-guzzling corpo

rate Learjet I advised you to sell three years ago?" Warren Barton asked his son.

"Yes, it does," Joshua replied steadily. Although his posture remained relaxed, there was no mistaking the hard, challenging glint in his eyes. "As a matter of fact, I'm seriously thinking about buying a second one so the partners don't have to share."

"Waste of money." Warren snorted with disapproval. He walked over to the bar and freshened his drink. "Didn't you read that article I sent you about fractional ownership of private aircraft? For a much smaller initial investment, reasonable management fees, and competitive hourly rates you can be guaranteed a jet with as little as four hours' notice."

"Our profits have exceeded all predictions for the past three years," Joshua said forcefully. "The firm can easily justify the cost of owning a second corporate plane."

"Just because you can afford it, doesn't mean you should buy it," Warren insisted. "Didn't I teach you anything?"

"Oh, I learned plenty from you." Joshua rose from the couch. "Warren Barton, the famously frugal millionaire."

"Now, what the hell is that supposed to mean?"

"It's a compliment, Father." Joshua sighed heavily. "Without fail, I hear it at every board meeting."

Eleanor saw Warren cast his son a puzzled look. Joshua squared his shoulders and lifted his head. "It's been a very long day. If you'll excuse us, Eleanor and I would like to relax before dinner."

"Of course." Rosemary jumped up from her chair like a scalded cat. "How rude of us not to realize how tired you might be. Traveling can be so draining."

"It would be nice to freshen up." Eleanor struggled to summon up a reassuring smile, knowing it was hardly a secret that it wasn't the traveling that was so exhausting.

"We'll see you at dinner, seven-thirty in the dining room," Warren said in a tired voice. "Maybe you'll have time for a walk on the beach or a swim in the pool before we eat. I remember when you were a youngster we could never keep you out of the pool."

Warren Barton's wistful gaze strayed to his son, but Joshua didn't notice. There was something so sad and troubled lurking in the depths of those eyes that Eleanor immediately forgave the older man's belligerent attitude toward his child.

"I've had Martha prepare your usual room, Joshua. And Eleanor is in the blue room," Rosemary said. "I hope that is all right."

"That's fine." Joshua held up his hand. "Please, don't trouble yourself. I know the way."

On cue Eleanor rose from her seat while Rosemary sat back on the sofa. Joshua grabbed Eleanor's arm and steered her through the wide, arched doorway. She barely had time to cast an apologetic smile at her hosts as she was whisked away.

The older servant, Martha, joined them as they climbed the enormous grand staircase to the third floor. Their luggage was nowhere in sight. Someone, perhaps Martha or the aforementioned Robert, had apparently delivered it to their rooms, confirming Eleanor's initial impression that this place was more like a four-star hotel and less like a real home.

"I know you haven't eaten since we left Philadelphia," Joshua said when they reached the third-floor landing. "You must be starved. Would you like me to have a tray sent up from the kitchen?"

"No thanks. I'll just wait until dinner."

Eleanor was surprised to realize that her early hunger had indeed vanished. Amazing. After years of searching she had finally discovered the perfect diet. If this sniping between Joshua and his father kept up for the next four days she would never be able to swallow anything past the lump of tension firmly lodged in her throat. For once it would be very simple to lose some weight.

"I'll come to your room at seven-twenty so I can escort you down to dinner."

The sound of Joshua's deep, male voice startled her. She had been so caught up in her jumbled thoughts and feelings she was paying little attention to her surroundings. Eleanor lifted her head to reply, but Joshua was already gone. Only the smiling Martha remained.

The servant held open a heavy wood door and respectfully stepped aside. Feeling more than a little uncomfortable, Eleanor entered the room. Martha quickly followed. She crossed to the windows and pulled back the heavy drapes. Bright sunlight filled the large room.

Martha started moving around the room, showing her the closets, the television and CD player cleverly hidden inside an antique armoire, how to switch on the various ceiling fans, how to adjust the room temperature, how to call down to the kitchen if she wanted something.

"The room is very pretty," Eleanor muttered, not sure what else to say. "I'm sure I'll be very comfortable. Thank you, Martha."

After extracting a promise from Eleanor to ring immediately if she needed anything, Martha left.

The moment the door closed behind her, some of Eleanor's tension eased. She flopped onto the enormous four-poster bed and wondered if it would be possible to hide out in this enchanting room for the rest of the visit. She had a lovely, comfortable room, a suitcase full of books, a marvelous view of the ocean, a kitchen at her disposal probably twenty-four hours a day. What else could she possibly need?

Well, maybe a bathroom. Eleanor rolled onto her stomach and glanced around her spacious quarters. There were several doors. Martha had opened most of them during her tour, but Eleanor had felt too uncomfortable to pay close attention. Dimly she remembered a glimpse of pale yellow tile and an old-fashioned bathtub with claw feet that looked big enough to swim laps in.

Curious, she walked to the far side of the room and pulled open a door. Closet. With all her clothes already unpacked and hanging neatly inside. Flushing, Eleanor opened a second door. Another closet. Spare blankets, extra pillows, even a woman's bathrobe.

Eleanor smiled. Heck, this was even better than a four-star hotel. Getting into the spirit, she contemplated the remaining two doors.

"Hmmm, let's see." She tapped her index finger impatiently against the side of her cheek and then lunged for the door of her choice. Gleefully she yanked it open.

And discovered a half-naked Joshua Barton on the other side.

Eleanor's hand dropped away from the door handle. A shiver ran down her spine, but she stood very still, not daring to move. He was in the process of getting dressed and hadn't noticed her invasion. Perhaps if she backed away very slowly, very quietly, she could leave before he even detected her presence.

She tried putting one foot behind the other. Honestly. But movement suddenly became impossible as every ounce of her attention became riveted on the man in front of her.

He had changed into a pair of cut-off jean shorts and was shrugging on a well-worn light blue oxford shirt. His hair was tousled, his feet bare, and a fair part of his naked chest was in plain view. Eleanor's heart started thudding. She told herself sternly it was the shock of discovering him on the other side of her bedroom door.

It was not, she insisted, the fact that he looked so outrageously handsome in such a disheveled state or the realization that they were going to share *connecting rooms* for three nights.

He turned away and bent at the waist, probably to pick up his shoes. The seat of his shorts tightened over his rump. It wasn't fair. Even the man's butt was beautiful.

The world began to shift around her. At a loss for words, feeling more and more like a voyeur, Eleanor finally cleared her throat. Loudly.

Joshua whirled around. His eyes flew to her face, and Eleanor was jolted by the impact of his sexy, assessing gaze.

"Hi." Eleanor took a deep breath and worked hard to swallow. Determinedly she kept her eyes above his waist. He had rolled up his shirtsleeves, and her gaze lingered there. His forearms were strong and solid and tanned, with a light dusting of dark hair.

"Eleanor? Are you all right?"

"What?"

"You're just standing there. Staring." He rested his hands on his hips. The shirt gaped open, revealing more of his chest. "Is something wrong?"

She could feel herself blushing. Well, of course she was staring. He was the most physically perfect male on the planet. And he was waiting for her to answer him.

"Our rooms connect." It was a totally obvious statement, but the best she could come up with at the moment.

Joshua straightened and his eyes locked with hers. "Connecting rooms is about as far as my father's Victorian sensibilities will go. I hope you don't mind."

"I don't mind," Eleanor whispered. The words were barely out of her mouth when she caught her breath. How in the world was she going to get any sleep knowing he was lying so near? "I'm a bit surprised, that's all. And confused. Apparently your father is under the impression that we're a couple."

Joshua sank down on the edge of his bed. "Is that a problem?"

She shook her head, then frowned. "I realize that you and your father have some unresolved . . . issues."

"Issues, huh?" Joshua snorted and slapped a sock onto the bed. "I suppose that's one way of putting it."

Eleanor shoved her hands in the pockets of her skirt. Both his tone and attitude told her loud and clear he didn't want to discuss this with her, but she plunged ahead anyway.

"Listen, Joshua, I feel like I've walked into a movie right smack in the middle of the film and I don't have any idea what's happening. I'd really appreciate a little clarification." She lifted her left foot and rubbed the side of her right ankle with the tip of her shoe. "Are you telling me you want to pretend that we are a couple for the entire visit?"

She saw the tendons in his neck tighten. He waited so long to answer that she feared he wasn't going to.

"It would make things a whole lot simpler if we didn't bother to correct my father's initial impression of our relationship. Unless you have a problem with that," he added, almost as an afterthought.

The very idea makes my stomach queasy. Yet for once her thoughts mercifully did not reach her tongue. Eleanor tried to weigh the pros and cons rationally, but that was impossible. He was offering her the chance to live out her deepest, most forbidden fantasy by pretending to be his girlfriend. Who could it hurt?

"If that's what you really want, then I won't volunteer any information to correct the impression your father and Rosemary already have about our relationship."

"Great." He smiled at her. "Oh, and one more thing.

I'd appreciate it if you wouldn't mention that you work for the firm."

Eleanor blinked. "You want me to lie about my job, too?" she asked, still reeling from the notion that they were going to pretend to be a couple for the next few days. And nights.

Joshua flinched. "Not lie, just omit some of the details. I'm sure my father is going to want to know why you are so interested in Rosemary's books and how you've come to know so much about them. I figured we could tell them that you work in a library, in the children's department. That's not a lie."

Eleanor's eyes darkened with wariness. "This is starting to get rather complicated. And I must confess, I have the distinct impression that you aren't telling me everything."

Joshua flushed and averted her gaze. She experienced a grim sense of satisfaction, knowing she was right. Eleanor leaned against the doorjamb and waited for an explanation.

She watched him slip his bare feet into a pair of well-worn Topsiders. Then he stood up and came toward her. She couldn't help but notice how his physical perfection was still intact, even in these ultracasual garments. He stopped a few feet in front of her and for a moment Eleanor wasn't sure what to do. Move forward or step back?

"One of the first policies I enacted when I took charge of the company was the rule that employees were not permitted to date each other," Joshua said. "It hadn't been much of an issue until then, since we hired so few females, but we were making a conscious effort to hire a more diverse work force and that included actively recruiting minorities and women. In an age of sexual harassment lawsuits the no-dating policy seemed like a sensible and prudent way to protect the firm. My father thought otherwise."

"He didn't agree?" Eleanor's feet shifted from side to side.

"That's putting it mildly." Joshua sighed and rubbed the back of his neck vigorously. "We argued about it for a solid week, then had a showdown at the monthly board of directors meeting. The board sided with me. Two days later, my father retired from the firm."

"Oh." The bleakness in his voice touched her heart. "So if your father and Rosemary believe that we're dating, then I definitely can't be working for Hamilton, Barton and Jones. It would be a gross infraction of the rules."

"Precisely."

Eleanor crossed her arms protectively across her chest. "I know I already said it, but it bears repeating. This is starting to get very complicated. And I think it is only fair to warn you, Joshua, I'm not a very convincing liar."

Joshua grimaced slightly. "Don't worry, you won't have to be. My father won't be asking you many personal questions about our relationship."

"How can you be so sure?"

"Frankly, he really doesn't care very much about what goes on in my life."

Six

Joshua had his emotions under control by dinnertime. A long walk on the warm beach, along with some contemplative moments on the dunes, had forced him to reevaluate his motives. He had come to North Carolina to make peace with his father. Not to start another war.

Consequently at dinner he kept the conversation focused on neutral topics and was rather proud of himself for completely ignoring two of his father's jibes. Of course Eleanor's concerned looks and anxious expression helped keep Joshua focused on his goal.

Eleanor was turning out to be a strong ally. He appreciated her quiet acceptance of the situation and her gracious compliance with his request for help. And as dinner progressed he came to realize more and more how lucky he was to have her with him this weekend.

Both his father and Rosemary seemed very taken with Eleanor. Joshua rubbed his fingers on the stem of his wineglass and smiled. Hell, it didn't take a genius to see that they probably liked her a whole lot more than they liked *him*.

He took a bite of his crab cake and gazed across the table at her. Despite the formal dining room setting where the four of them sat beneath two Waterford crystal chandeliers at a table that could easily seat twenty people, it was a casual dinner. There were no hovering servants, no complicated table settings, no elaborate courses with dramatic presentations.

Instead all of Joshua's favorite childhood foods had been served, and he wondered briefly who had been responsible for the selection. The family cook?

"Tell me a little bit about your books, Rosemary," Joshua said as one of the younger maids cleared the dinner plates. "Where do you get your story ideas?"

Rosemary's eyes widened in astonishment. She swallowed the food in her mouth and gave him a weak smile. "Actually, many of my books are inspired by moments from my own childhood. I was never blessed with children, so when I first started writing my editor suggested that I take the deepest, darkest, most embarrassing secret about myself and put a humorous twist on it.

"Naturally it was hard to choose just one." Rosemary's smile widened. "However, I eventually decided to write a story about sibling rivalry and I realized that being honest about my actions, reactions, and emotions to the unexpected arrival of a baby sister gave the story the one element my manuscript ideas had been missing. Total honesty."

Rosemary looked directly at him as she spoke, and Joshua had to struggle to resist squirming in his seat. She was speaking about her books, yet it was as though she realized how fraudulent he had been with *his* actions, reactions, and emotions toward his father.

Joshua smiled at Rosemary, trying to demonstrate how cool and unaffected he was by her words, but it wasn't easy. Her perceptive writer's eyes saw far too much for his comfort and her comment held just enough truth to make him feel guilty.

"Did you always want to be a writer?" Eleanor jumped in eagerly.

Joshua sighed with relief. Eleanor to the rescue once again. Clearly she had been waiting for the opportunity to start asking her idol Rosemary all sorts of questions about her books but had been too polite or shy to introduce the topic.

Rosemary turned away from him and smiled pleasantly at Eleanor. "I had no interest in writing of any sort when I was a college student. My dream had always been to be an artist. I studied fine art for years, but after unsuccessfully trying to support myself by painting, I ended up designing and selling greeting cards to pay the rent. My work was brought to the attention of a book publisher by a good friend and I was invited to try my hand at illustrating a children's book.

"It was a lot more difficult than I thought it would be, but the publisher was very pleased with the results. I was given steady work and continued doing the drawings for three different authors. Eventually I was offered the opportunity to create my own story. I struggled quite a bit, but truly enjoyed the challenge.

"The book received encouraging reviews, so I wrote a second, then a third. Gradually I discovered that writing and illustrating these picture books was a far more fulfilling career than I had imagined. So instead of a portrait artist, I became a children's author and illustrator."

"You make it sound deceptively easy, my dear," Warren said, regarding his wife fondly. "And it certainly isn't."

A hint of color flooded Rosemary's cheeks and she blushed like a teenager. "You're biased."

"My father's right. People who don't really understand the process think it's so easy. Just throw a few cute, colorful sketches on the page, slap on a sentence or two, and suddenly you have a children's book." Joshua added sugar and a dash of cream to the hot coffee he had just been served and stirred it energetically with a silver spoon. "I was truly astonished when I read your books and saw not only literal but metaphorical references. I guess most adults don't expect to find that level of sophistication in a story written for children."

"You've read some of my books?" Rosemary asked with surprise. She exchanged a delighted glance with her husband. "Your father was very embarrassed when we first met because he had never seen any of my work."

"It's not like I have any grandchildren to read your books to," Warren defended himself gruffly. "Not yet, anyway."

Joshua dropped his spoon. It clattered loudly onto his dessert plate. Grandchildren? Since when did his father's thoughts start encompassing grandchildren?

"I'm pleased to say my influence has rubbed off on Joshua," Eleanor said with a nervous smile. "Though he doesn't share my passion for these wonderful books, he is definitely learning. I have high hopes he'll come around one day."

"Somehow I have trouble imagining Eleanor reading you a bedtime story, son," Warren said with a sly grin.

Eleanor made a short, strangled sound and blushed purple. Warren shot her an odd look.

Rosemary frowned pointedly at her husband and dabbed her mouth with her linen napkin. "Dare I ask if you have a favorite picture book, Joshua?"

"Well, I am partial to General Explorer."

"Ahh, one of my few human characters." Rosemary sat back in her chair, as a faraway, pensive look lit her eyes. "General Explorer was originally modeled after my late husband, but then Jerry got sick and I couldn't concentrate on the story. After he died I found it impossible to work on the book without bursting into tears, so I threw out all my original sketches and started over.

"But for the first time in my career, I couldn't draw,

couldn't write, couldn't create. Every decision I had to make seemed so monumentally important that I became totally frozen. I was incapable of making a choice and sticking with it."

"Writer's block," Eleanor diagnosed sympathetically.

"Perhaps." Rosemary pursed her lips. "But at the time all I felt was ineptitude."

"It's a terrific book, so we know that you managed to finish it," Joshua said. "How did you *unblock* yourself?"

"I forced myself to work," Rosemary said simply, but Joshua could tell there was nothing simple about it. Clearly this had been a big professional hurdle. "My editor was wonderful. Very patient and supportive. Each morning I would work on my character sketches and then fax my drawings to New York. By the time I started working the next morning, I'd have a page of notes and suggestions. It kept me grounded and focused and helped me believe I could somehow write the book.

"After almost three months of working that way both the editor and I felt we were finally getting close to expressing the essence of General Explorer. Then miraculously one day it all seemed right. I made a few more adjustments, faxed the changes to my editor, and he called me right away. To say he loved it. What a relief."

"So you were happy with the book?" Eleanor inquired.

"It was a milestone for me in many ways," Rosemary replied. "I remember the lovely party my publisher generously threw to introduce the book. I flew to New York and had a fabulous time. There were book signings all over Manhattan. It was very exciting.

"My editor came with me to most of them. It was delightful having an opportunity to meet him at long last. We even had a chance to work together, in person, instead of by phone and fax, on a few future story ideas. I found him to be a very talented and creative young man."

Rosemary folded her napkin and placed it on the edge of the table. "I also understood why at last, after so many months of drawing and revisions, he finally liked the drawing of General Explorer so much."

"Why?" Joshua asked.

"Well, I realized after spending so much time with him that the final drawing of General Explorer looked exactly like my editor."

Everyone laughed. Joshua glanced over at his father. The older man's eyes twinkled with merriment, but there was something more in his face. Real happiness and contentment. An easygoing, relaxed element that in Joshua's opinion was almost foreign to his father's personality.

Joshua's eyes shifted between his father and his father's wife. Rosemary glowed with good humor. She gave her husband a sly look that spoke volumes. Warren returned her teasing glance with a wink.

Joshua suddenly felt like an intruder, witnessing this private, almost intimate exchange. He could clearly sense the glimmer of passion beneath the surface of those glances and it made him very uncomfortable.

Eleanor's soft voice distracted him. She was asking Rosemary additional questions about her books and her writing. Astonishingly, his father answered one, sounding very knowledgeable. Rosemary smiled approvingly at her husband.

The older man appeared to blush. It had to be a trick of the light, Joshua instantly decided. His father blushing? He stared harder at the older man, then jerked his head over to look at Rosemary.

Though separated by the considerable length of the dining room table, Rosemary and Warren seemed to touch, to connect with each other. The knowing glances, the comfortable smiles, the affectionate expressions all spoke of their deep feelings and commitment. They were a couple, a team.

An unexpected knot of resentment tightened inside Joshua. He knew his parents had loved each other deeply, knew his father had grieved at Joshua's mother's untimely death. Yet clearly his father had recovered from his sorrow, had successfully gone on with his life. Had apparently forgotten all about the woman who had been his wife for over thirty years and had given birth to his only son.

The resentment confused Joshua. It made him feel petty and small. But it wouldn't go away. He looked at his father's smiling face one last time and knew he needed to leave . . . quickly, before these odd feelings overwhelmed him, took control of his tongue. Forced him to say things that were best left unsaid.

"If you'll excuse me, I believe I'll stretch my legs," Joshua announced to no one in particular. He stood up abruptly and his chair, pushed off the lush Oriental area rug, scraped loudly against the hardwood floor. Making no further explanations, he escaped the room.

The silence seemed outrageously loud behind him. But Joshua didn't pause to consider it. He kept walking. Through the sitting room, the sun room, past the maid tidying up in the library, then finally out the French doors at the rear of the solarium, into the blessed cool air of the night.

He strolled aimlessly along the lower veranda, trying to move the direction of his thoughts. His feelings were childish and downright ridiculous. His father was a grown man. He had been a widower a long time. It was only right that he move ahead with his life, try to find some joy and happiness. In his heart Joshua knew he didn't want his father to spend the rest of his life alone.

Yet somehow knowing that his father had found a terrific woman, a soul mate, made Joshua feel lonelier than he ever had.

He continued walking toward the back of the house, stopping when he reached his favorite observation spot. He leaned forward, bracing his elbows on the wide railing. Taking a deep, full breath Joshua stared off into the distance, his eyes drawn to the dark vastness of the ocean. The steady lull of the tide and pounding of the surf set up a soothing rhythm in his head. Gradually he felt his body's muscles begin to unclench.

"Is everything okay?"

The gentle, female voice broke through the stillness. He didn't have to turn his head to know the moment Eleanor reached his side. He could feel her nearness.

"I hope I wasn't too rude before, but I really needed some fresh air," he said.

"Hmmm. Did you drink too much wine at dinner?"

Joshua forced his head around. Her words were flippant, but her tone was steely.

"I needed some fresh air," he repeated. "All that laughter and good cheer and cozy feelings were starting to give me a headache."

"Of course." Eleanor's lips grew thin and taut, but she didn't say anything else. Yet the hint of challenge in her eyes spoke loud and clear.

Joshua lazily straightened himself. He tried to stare her down, but this time it didn't work. Perplexed, he rubbed his chin with the back of his knuckles. "I'm acting like a real jerk, right?"

The challenge in her eyes was immediately replaced with understanding. "I know this must be difficult, accepting Rosemary as part of your family. But time goes on. Circumstances change and people are forced to go forward, to adapt. Nothing stands still."

Her words were not especially original, but they struck

a sympathetic chord inside him. "You want to know the strangest part of this whole situation? I like Rosemary. She's classy, smart, gracious, funny. And she's crazy about my father. He's a very lucky man."

"But . . ." Eleanor prompted.

He smiled enigmatically. There was no hiding anything from this woman. Joshua had never been big on sharing his feelings, especially ones he didn't understand, but the urge to talk was almost irresistible.

"But I resent the hell out of the fact that it isn't my mother sitting at that dining room table." Joshua hung his head in disgust. "Which is a completely moronic emotion, since my mother has been dead for years."

"My father died nearly ten years ago and I still miss him," Eleanor admitted. "Time helps dull the pain, but some of the sadness always remains."

Joshua lifted his head. "I'm sorry about your dad," he said softly. "I didn't know."

Eleanor shrugged, but the gesture didn't erase the sadness in her eyes. "He had a massive heart attack in the middle of the night, when I was a sophomore in college. There was nothing anybody could do to save him."

"It must have been very rough on you."

"It wasn't easy." She turned her gaze to the horizon, staring out at the moonlit sea. "Like you, I'm an only child. Suddenly it was just me and my mother and she completely fell apart. My dad had a decent life insurance policy, but college is expensive and my mother hadn't held a job in twenty years. Her lack of skills, education, and experience forced her to take a fairly demeaning, low-paying position that I know she must have hated. Yet somehow we managed."

"So you studied business hoping that you wouldn't ever find yourself in the same circumstances as your mother," Joshua remarked, as a big piece of the puzzle fell into place.

Eleanor shook her head. "The business degree was definitely my mother's idea. I always had a knack with numbers and she felt it was really important for me to be prepared for a growing, financially secure career with a lot of opportunities for women. I wasn't sure what I wanted to do, and she felt very strongly about it, so it seemed logical to follow her advice. Besides, I couldn't disappoint her after she worked so hard to put me through school."

"And now?"

Eleanor straightened her spine and raised her chin. "I paid off all of my student loans, helped her buy a beautiful condo in Florida, which is where she always wanted to live, and I'm paying for graduate school."

Joshua liked the way her eyes glittered with determination. "Time to take charge, huh? How does it feel?"

"Terrifying." She laughed lightly. The musical sound carried out to the waves and was swallowed up by the night-shrouded sea. "Yet, as the saying goes, better late than never. What about you? Did you always want to work in the firm? Or was it expected?"

Joshua considered her question. "I suppose it was always assumed that I would become involved in the family business, but I was never pushed in that direction by either of my parents. They weren't the types that wanted me to spend my life fulfilling their dreams. Luckily my ambitions and abilities coincided with the goals of the company. I've enjoyed taking charge of the firm. My biggest regret has always been that I was never able to work with my father."

"Different management styles?" Eleanor inquired sympathetically.

"That's one way to put it." Joshua laughed harshly.

"We disagreed on everything from how to invest the employee pension fund to the color of the carpet in the executive suites. It's bad enough we lock horns on a personal level, but at the office it was a war zone.

"In the end I felt I had no choice but to force my father's retirement, and I'm sure he still resents it. My mother was always the peacemaker in our family. It's been a rocky few years not having her around to run interference between me and my father."

She squeezed his shoulder. "Maybe it's past time to forge your own link with your father. Isn't that the real reason you're here?"

There was no need to answer such an obvious question. Joshua took a deep breath and realized with surprise that it felt strangely cathartic to discuss these emotions so openly, honestly, without fear of censure or judgment. He decided a female perspective was one thing that had been missing from his life for too long.

"I'm beginning to wonder if it has gone too far for a real reconciliation," Joshua said, almost afraid to voice his deepest fear. It made the possibility of failure seem alarmingly real. "Now that my father has a new wife, in essence a new family, perhaps the most I can hope for is a polite, pleasant relationship. Not exactly ideal, but certainly an improvement over the endless tension we now share."

Eleanor clutched his forearm tightly. "You can't give up so quickly, Joshua. It will get better. You just need to try a little harder, and be patient."

He listened to the certainty in her voice and realized how much he wanted to believe her. "It's that simple?"

"No, it isn't simple." She exhaled slowly. "We both know it's not easy. But it is worth working toward. I know you feel that way, or else you wouldn't be here right now."

She was right. He had come down here expecting the

worst, thinking he was prepared to cope with it. Things hadn't precisely worked out as he expected, except for the worst part, but he wasn't ready to quit yet.

Joshua inhaled the balmy air, marveling at how a little discussion could so radically improve his outlook. Thanks to Eleanor. He moved toward her, feeling a deep need to share a physical closeness with her while he thanked her . . . for listening, for understanding, for caring.

Her eyes grew large and round as he neared. He saw her throat move as she swallowed hard, swayed a little, and glanced away. Still, he came closer.

His intentions were noble, pure, nonsexual. Yet as he drew near he instantly became aware of two surprising facts. She was incredibly nervous, and he found that oddly exhilarating. Sexually exciting. He hesitated, almost afraid to touch her. Out here in the moonlight she looked different, almost delicate, with fragile limbs and wide, innocent brown eyes.

He continued to stare at her, studying the way the soft moonlight played over her face. His gaze traveled down to the swell of her breasts, which were full and tempting. She was a lush creature, not provocatively sexual, yet feminine and alluring in a unique way.

Knowing he wouldn't be able to rest until he touched her softness, Joshua lifted his hand. He caressed her cheek lightly, then moved his fingers along her jaw, back and forth against the smooth skin.

"It's getting late," she croaked out. "I should probably go inside."

"Probably," he whispered thickly, sliding his fingers under her hair until he found the nape of her neck.

She tilted her head into his caress and sighed with pleasure. He felt a burst of desire that was entirely improper given the circumstances. Joshua struggled to keep himself rigidly restrained, but it was difficult. A strange need that could not be easily ignored rippled through him.

He continued to move his hand slowly and gently along her slender neck, trying to ease the tension he felt in her. Yet his touch served to heighten, not diminish the sizzle between them.

For several long moments neither of them moved. Indecision and common sense dominated Joshua's thoughts, but he deliberately shut them down. This was not a moment for thinking. This was a moment of feelings and emotions . . . and actions.

Joshua shifted his position so that he was standing directly in front of Eleanor. Slowly, carefully, he pulled her closer. She gave a startled gasp, but didn't resist. Within seconds, she stood between the span of his muscular legs, her eyes wide. He could feel her slight trembling. Her nerves put his on edge, building the excitement, heightening the anticipation.

He leaned toward her and a hint of color bloomed in her cheeks. For the first time he noticed her full and well-shaped lips. Lovely. Her tongue darted out nervously and she licked those pouting lips. They glistened with moist invitation and filled him with sudden, hot urgency.

Joshua knew he probably shouldn't. But he did it anyway.

His mouth came down over hers swiftly, dominating all thoughts. She made a tiny sound. Of surprise? Of pleasure? Of encouragement?

For an instant it seemed as though time stood still. Then her lips parted beneath his. He took her deeply with his tongue. She tasted like moonlight and mystery. Eleanor made a small, whimpering sound and pressed her hands into his chest. He could feel her fingers clenching and unclenching as he deepened the kiss further.

Heat and need sank into his belly. Acting instinctively,

Joshua moved his hands to her shoulders. He held her tightly, keeping her body pressed against his. She felt delicious. Willing, exciting, and oh, so womanly. Her nipples were brushing against the thin cotton of his shirt, making his body pound and throb.

He could feel his control begin to fracture, as the urge to slip his hands beneath her dress and caress her soft, womanly curves became unbearable. It would have been so easy to progress to the next step, to completely throw caution to the wind and act on this heady thrill of sensual power.

Yet Joshua pulled back just in time, before passion completely obliterated all his senses and he started tugging at buttons, wrestling with bra clasps, exploring those beautiful, full breasts and tight, puckered nipples.

With great reluctance, he gently ended their kiss. Eleanor shuddered and listed to the right, clearly wobbly on her feet. He steadied her within the circle of his arms and then regretfully stepped back.

His sexual frustration was acute, yet he tamped down his own desires. This was not the time, nor the place, nor the woman to be doing this with. Was it?

A slash of moonlight illuminated her face. Her hair was mussed, her lips swollen, her eyes still darkened with unfulfilled passion. Joshua hesitated, not certain what to say.

"I . . . ah . . . um . . ." Eleanor tried to speak. Failing, she turned her head away. The uncertainty he glimpsed on her face filled him with unexpected tenderness.

"I'm very glad that you're here with me this weekend," he finally whispered. "Good night, Eleanor."

Taking a deep breath, Joshua turned and walked away, discovering, to his great surprise, it was far more difficult than he ever would have imagined.

Seven

Eleanor awoke to the muffled, distant sound of deep, male voices. Momentarily disoriented, she tried sitting up, but got herself tangled in the soft cotton sheets. With a growl of frustration, she twisted and turned, then kicked away the light covering. Her furious efforts left her winded, but she paused only a moment before swinging her legs over the edge of the high bed and sliding down to the floor.

She paused to listen, but all was quiet. Eleanor shook her head to clear the cobwebs, then lifted her arms and stretched, working out the kinks in her lower back. The room felt warm, the air heavy. She wondered what time it was, but the ornate antique clock was on the far side of the room and she couldn't read the delicate gilt face from this distance.

Eleanor sighed and pushed the heavy mass of hair off her face. Damp tendrils remained plastered against her neck. The sticky heat of the room seemed to seep into her bones and Eleanor realized that turning off the air-conditioning last night so she could open the window and listen to the ocean might not have been the best idea.

Of course she hadn't exactly been thinking clearly last night when she'd tried falling asleep. For the first hour she had sat up on the high four-poster bed, her eyes trained on the connecting door between her room and Joshua's.

She had strained her ears listening for the creak of the bed or a rustling of sheets or the sound of footsteps approaching, trying to convince herself she didn't hold a faint glimmer of hope that he was going to knock on that door. And ask to come into her room.

It was a foolish notion and yet, who would have ever believed that he would have taken her in his arms and kissed her? And that the reality of those kisses would have been even more magical, more exciting than the fantasy she had weaved?

Eleanor willingly conceded she had a rather fanciful imagination, but there was no denying the rush of excitement, the flash of desire that their moonlit kiss had sparked. Still, the most remarkable discovery was the knowledge that the passion had been mutual.

Their bodies had been pressed close, close enough that she could easily feel Joshua's readiness to take the embrace far beyond a few kisses. But he had stopped. And she had let him.

So for the second hour after retreating to her lonely room last night, Eleanor had lain on her back and stared up at the ceiling, reminding herself again and again of all the reasons a romance between her and Joshua was nothing more than an unrealistic fantasy, born of some deep, impossible dream.

Rather like the notion that someone could create great-tasting, nonfat, no-calorie chocolate ice cream.

By the start of the third hour, Eleanor had been thoroughly depressed and completely disgusted with herself for feeling that way, so she'd opened the window to listen to the ocean, hoping the sound of the waves would drown out her melancholy. Thankfully nature's gentle sea noises had helped lure her to sleep.

Morning had brought sunshine, more heat, and a healthy dose of much-needed reality. It took only the light of day and a glance at the elegant splendor of her bedroom furnishings for Eleanor to remind herself that she was an ordinary woman and Joshua was an extraordinary man. And never the twain shall meet.

Deciding a cool, refreshing shower was the best way to prepare for the day, Eleanor headed toward the bathroom. But she stopped upon hearing the deep male voices again. She frowned, thinking she might have conjured them up, but the volume grew louder. Not loud enough for her to distinguish actual words in the conversation, but enough to realize that she hadn't been dreaming when she'd heard them before.

Barefoot, she padded over to the window and carefully pushed aside the sheer curtain. Immediately she spied Joshua and his father walking side-by-side toward the terraced patio directly below her window.

Both men were wearing wet bathing trunks. Obviously they had just been swimming, either in the pool or the ocean. Together? Eleanor crossed her fingers, hoping that was the case.

They reached the edge of the patio and turned to climb up the steps. Eleanor sucked in her breath and pressed the palm of her hand to her chest. *Be still my heart.* Warren was wearing a white T-shirt over his wet bathing suit, but Joshua was shirtless, with only a towel draped nonchalantly around his neck to cover the perfection of his broad shoulders, naked chest, and flat abdomen.

With a small sigh she realized there wasn't an ounce of fat on his lean, athletic body. She reasoned he was at least six inches taller than she was, so he had to weigh more than she did. All in all, a minor comfort.

The impact of his male virility hit her, even at this distance. Yet while his sexual magnetism might have captured her attention, it was the other stuff that truly fascinated her.

She liked the glimpse of insecurity she had seen last night when they talked about his relationship with his father. She liked how he had acted so commandingly with the snobby sales clerk in the expensive dress shop. She liked his intellect and humor. She didn't even mind his moments of brooding intensity.

Still, all the liking or disliking wouldn't make much difference for the future. But it could make this weekend far more interesting.

More voices interrupted her thoughts. Eleanor craned her neck to gain a better view of the patio. A small group of people entered her line of vision. Joshua and his father both moved forward to greet this merry band. Three men and five women, of indeterminable ages. All she could really tell from this vantage point was that they were slim, tanned, and expensively dressed.

With a sinking feeling, Eleanor remembered Rosemary mentioning at dinner last night that house guests would be arriving early in the day, in anticipation of tonight's formal party. Disheartened, she let the curtain fall back into place and stepped away from the window.

Oh, goody. Just what she needed. A group of rich, sophisticated people challenging her already fledgling self-confidence.

Her earlier idea about spending the remainder of her visit hiding out in her room took on even greater appeal. This was hardly the crowd for her. After all, she was a woman who would willingly wear slimming black in the middle of an August heat wave instead of torturing herself by doing a single sit-up.

Eleanor sat on the edge of her bed, distractedly picking at the minuscule pieces of lint on the spread. It was no use sulking. She had agreed to be Joshua's *date* for the weekend and was committed to keeping her word. There really wasn't much she could do about her uncomfortable feelings except chalk them up as one more consequence of the weekend that she hadn't exactly thought out.

After her cooling shower, Eleanor felt a little better. She put on a one-piece bathing suit and terry cloth cover-up that fell to her knees. The key to survival was having a plan. If the beautiful people were still outside on the patio, she would pop over for a quick introduction and then head for the beach.

She walked slowly down the steps of the grand staircase and through the house, encountering no one. With each step Eleanor gave herself a much-needed pep talk, reiterating that although her current social life was dismal, she was usually good at making light conversation, even under awkward circumstances.

Besides, these people were all strangers that she would in all likelihood never see again. Making a good impression was not essential. All she really needed to do was prevent herself from making a disastrous one.

Eleanor paused at the French doors to glance again at the group gathered on the patio. From this distance they looked even more intimidating. Resolutely she opened the door and stepped outside.

No one noticed her. She took another small step. Despite the warm sun, Eleanor shivered, then realized the chill came from the fear inside her. Not only was the prospect of meeting all these unfamiliar people making her nervous, but she was greatly concerned over how she was going to face Joshua again without letting her embarrassment about last night's kisses show.

It wasn't easy, but she somehow managed to get her feet to move. Rallying her waning courage, Eleanor walked out onto the patio with a smile plastered on her lips that felt as though it was threatening to crack her face in half.

Again, no one seemed to notice her arrival. They were all too busy greeting and preening for each other. Eleanor sighed with hope. Maybe she could just glide past them with a casual wave and a friendly hello.

"Eleanor, come over here," Warren boomed out. "I have some old friends I'd like you to meet."

Effectively caught, Eleanor reluctantly drew closer. Her sensitive nose inhaled the scent of expensive perfumes, and her tension increased.

The introductions were a flurry of odd-sounding first and vaguely familiar second names. Names she recognized as companies traded on the stock exchange or appearing in the society and gossip columns of national newspapers. This was indeed a select crowd.

Eleanor struggled to keep everyone's identity straight. It was difficult not only trying to match the odd-sounding first names with the correct faces, but trying to recall how they were all connected.

"I didn't catch your name," a tight-lipped woman said. "Who are you again?"

"I'm Eleanor," she answered, lifting her chin and forcing herself to look directly into the woman's condescending eyes. "Joshua's friend."

"Really?" The woman studied her with more interest. "I wasn't sure I had heard Warren correctly. Joshua is usually switching girlfriends so fast it's hard to keep up."

"Not anymore," Eleanor replied with an artificial smile, deciding she didn't like this woman very much. What was her name again? Mitsy? Muffy? Eleanor only remembered it was something that ended with a *y* and was better suited for a dog than a person.

In fact, this haughty woman was a tiny, compact creature that reminded Eleanor of a small breed dog, the little yippy kind that barks at anything in a challenging, ferocious manner.

"Good morning."

For one brief instant, Eleanor's brain reeled at the sound of that familiar male voice.

"Hello, Joshua." Eleanor smiled bravely. Her momentary annoyance over the snotty woman vanished as Joshua gave her one of his heart-melting smiles. She fully expected him to walk away after his greeting, but he stayed near. They moved from group to group together, making small talk. Eleanor couldn't help but notice she was on the receiving end of many open, curious stares.

She put on a confident front, yet was ever alert to the opportunity for escape. All this attention was more than her nerves could handle.

"Ready for that walk now, Eleanor?"

Although he was standing right beside her, Joshua's voice sounded like it came from a great distance away.

"I'd love a stroll on the beach," she replied steadily, conscious of the stares being thrown her way.

Joshua took her arm and led her down to the white sandy beach. She told herself to ignore the sensual heat that traveled up her arm at his touch, deciding it was high time she learned to conquer this impressive power his physical nearness had on her body.

When Eleanor judged they had walked far enough to be out of sight, she took a deliberate step away from Joshua, just to prove to herself she could. Besides, it seemed safer.

If Joshua was aware of her withdrawal, he made no mention of it. They walked for what seemed like hours, but must have been only minutes. Yet the farther they went, the more relaxed Eleanor grew. It was a bright, sunny day, and the hot sun felt wonderful on her head, neck, and shoulders.

The warm ocean breeze was invigorating, and the fresh, tangy smell of the sea along with the rhythmic pounding of the waves gave her an odd sense of peace. Eleanor was content to merely follow Joshua's lead and they strolled for quite a distance before stopping.

Joshua placed his hands on his hips and stared out across the water toward the endless horizon.

"Do you like to surf?"

Eleanor gulped. "You can't possibly mean on a board?"

"A board?" Joshua turned toward her and grinned. "No, I meant body surfing, but that's an even better idea. I haven't been on a board in years. Would you like to try it? I bet I could find one or two if I looked around the beach cabana."

"There's no need to go to such trouble on my account." Eleanor fumbled for the sunglasses tucked inside her beach bag and slapped them over her eyes. To hide the fear. And panic. "I'm sure we can have just as much fun body surfing."

Had those insane words actually come from her own lips? The girl who had been constantly teased by her father whenever the family had ventured to the shore for merely "dipping" into the water, and never attempting to swim?

Eleanor actually did enjoy the water. She had even taken swimming lessons as a child in a pool. But she had never swum a stroke in the ocean, just bounced around in the waves.

"The water looks great. I can't wait to get in," Joshua enthused.

She cleared her throat several times as she watched him throw off his towel and head for the shore. Joshua entered the water in attack mode, running into the surf and diving into a huge wave just before it broke. He surfaced on the other side, laughing, shaking the droplets of water off his head like a shaggy dog.

Eleanor felt an odd mix of fear and envy as she watched him frolic in the waves. He looked like he was having a great time. How she wished she could be so bold and daring, so totally reckless. Feeling challenged, she walked purposefully to the edge of the shore. When the next wave broke and washed near, she experimentally dipped her foot into the foaming surf.

Eleanor shivered. The water was freezing! How could he stand swimming in it?

"You have to jump right in!" Joshua shouted.

"Right." She smiled weakly, hanging back. "I think I'll watch you for a while until I figure out what to do."

He shrugged and swam out farther. Eleanor retreated to where Joshua had dropped his towel. Knowing he wouldn't be able to see her very well, she courageously removed her cover-up and spread it on the sand. She positioned herself comfortably on the thick terry cloth, leaned back on her elbows, and settled in to enjoy the view.

Joshua swam as he did most things—with power, command, and near perfection. Squinting into the bright sun despite her sunglasses, she enjoyed every moment of staring at him. But before too long the sun started making its presence known. Eleanor could feel the sweat trickling down her back, her arms, her legs. Even the back of her knees were getting damp.

It was really hot. She had slathered on sunscreen and brought a wide-brimmed hat, so she wasn't too worried about getting a sunburn. Heat stroke, however, might be a possibility.

She shifted her position, but there was no shade, no relief from the heat. Finally conceding defeat to the elements, Eleanor stood up, removed her hat and sunglasses, brushed the sand from her hands, and walked cautiously to the shoreline.

The water was still shockingly cold. Big surprise. But after a few moments of standing in the water, her feet no longer felt cold. Gingerly, she ventured out a few more steps, until the foamy, sea-green water reached her knees. Then her waist.

"Great. You're finally coming in."

Startled, Eleanor lifted her head and saw Joshua swimming toward her. Hell! Panicking that he was going to come close enough to get a really good look at her in her *bathing suit* she pitched herself forward.

Her feet came out from under her as she fell. The shocking, frigid water disoriented her momentarily and she couldn't find the bottom. Kicking her feet wildly, Eleanor felt herself being pulled under by the strong current. Real fear clutched at her. *Oh Lord, I'm going to drown. All because I was too vain to be seen in a bathing suit.*

Just when it felt like her lungs were going to burst into flame from lack of breath, Eleanor's feet touched solid ground. With a sob of relief she pushed her shoulders and head out of the water.

"Are you all right?"

Eleanor nodded her head. A strong pair of warm arms encircled her. Grateful for the solid human contact, Eleanor wrapped her arms around Joshua's back and drew close. Her cheek rested against his wet chest and the steady thump of his heart assured her that she was fine now. Just fine.

They bobbed in the waves together and Eleanor let herself float along, held securely in his safe embrace. She regained her breath and her heart reverted to a normal rhythm.

"Are you sure you're okay? You gave me quite a scare."

He tucked a portion of her wet hair behind her ear and she felt his fingers linger on her cheek. She lifted her head.

"I think I swallowed a live fish."

Joshua chuckled. "I think you swallowed half the ocean." His finger brushed the tip of her nose playfully.

Eleanor's heart started thumping. His gaze was so sweet, so full of genuine concern. She tried to swallow and realized the tightness in her throat wasn't caused by the gallon of seawater she had just ingested. "That was a real graceful entrance, huh? Would you believe I've been asked to show the Olympic diving team my moves?"

His smile broadened. "Do you want to go back and rest on the sand?"

Eleanor bit her bottom lip. "No. I'd like to try the body surfing. Will you teach me?"

"Sure."

His eyes twinkled with admiration and Eleanor basked in the glow of his approval. It was a ridiculous choice really, considering her weak swimming skills, but something about being near Joshua made her feel compelled to take a few risks.

Besides, if she really started drowning, she had every confidence he could save her, and in the process he might just have to administer mouth-to-mouth. Now, how awful would that be?

Eleanor swam-walked to a shallow area and watched Joshua closely as he timed his approach, caught the top of the next large swell, and shot past her, curling on the wave. He rode it almost to the dry sand. Eleanor whistled in appreciation. It really did look like fun.

"Ready?" he asked, swimming back toward her.

"No, but I'm going to try it anyway."

"Good for you."

Bravely she followed him farther out. The pull of the

current was strong, but she could still touch the sandy bottom if she stood on her toes.

"I want to try it," she declared again. "What do I do?"

"You have to face the shore, look over your shoulder, and wait for a big swell. Timing is essential. Swim out too soon and you'll get buried under the surf. Too late, you'll miss the wave."

Eleanor hunched her shoulders and prepared herself, running Joshua's instructions over and over in her head. No matter what else she did today, she was determined to "catch" at least one wave, even if it took all afternoon.

Squinting into the sunlight, she watched the green, foamed wave rise and come closer . . . and closer . . .

"Now!"

At Joshua's command, she began paddling furiously, but her timing was off and she missed the first wave. The same happened for the second and third wave. But somehow she managed to catch the fourth. Again her timing was lousy and she got buried in the strong surf, but for a few wonderful moments she felt like she was flying through the air.

The wave carried her to shallow waters. Eleanor came up sputtering, certain there was seaweed and all other sorts of muck clinging to her hair. But she didn't care.

"Wow, this is wild," she announced.

Joshua held out his hand and she automatically reached for it. They jumped a breaking wave and headed out to deeper waters.

All was still and quiet as they waited for a good wave. The saltwater stung her eyes, but felt cool against her hot skin. Though hardly a person who embraced strenuous physical activities, Eleanor was surprised to realize this was the most alive she had felt in a very long time.

The cool ocean waves lapped against her back, nudging

her aside, but Eleanor held her position, treading water. Until a sudden, frightening thought entered her head.

"Hey, Joshua, there aren't any sharks in this area, are there?"

"Not usually." Joshua smiled and looked around. "I saw a few fins earlier, but I'm sure they were dolphins. It probably is a good idea to keep alert, though, and if something attacks you, smack it directly on the nose."

Eleanor's sarcastic retort was lost on the howling wind. They rode a few more waves and she smugly acknowledged she was getting better at it. But she was also starting to get very tired. This time when Joshua suggested a rest on the sand, Eleanor agreed.

Joshua gallantly spread his towel on the sand and they shared it.

"It is magnificent out here." Joshua sighed loudly. " 'I must go down to the seas again, for the call of the running tide . . . Is a wild call and a clear call that may not be denied'."

"Longfellow?" Eleanor guessed.

"No, John Masefield. From his poem 'Sea Fever.' Actually the opening line is more famous: 'I must go down to the seas again, to the lonely sea and the sky, And all I ask is a tall ship and a star to steer her by.' "

"Masefield? I'm impressed. I thought most guys viewed poetry as a medieval form of torture."

"I've always liked poetry." Joshua bowed his head and for an instant Eleanor swore he looked embarrassed. "The beauty and simplicity of the phrases, the power of the words and images, all that intense desire and emotion."

"Emotion?" Eleanor wrinkled her nose. "It has always been my experience that men are generally uncomfortable expressing anything that even resembles an emotion."

"Expressing them and reading about them are two entirely different matters."

"Mmmm." Eleanor lazily swirled her index finger in the dry, warm sand. "Speaking of emotions, I noticed you and your father walking together earlier this morning. Did you have a chance for some meaningful conversation?"

"Let's just say he talked, I listened and struggled to hold my temper in check." Joshua shook his head. "My old man is damn opinionated."

"From what I've observed it doesn't take very much effort to get a rise out of you," Eleanor commented dryly.

"Okay, I admit it. I overreact to my father's comments sometimes." Joshua picked up a broken shell and tossed it into the ocean. "I'm working on it."

"Really?" Eleanor lifted a disbelieving eyebrow.

"Really."

"My advice is to work harder."

"Yes, ma'am." Joshua smiled. He took a deep breath. "It's hot out here. Come on, let's cool down."

She didn't have time to answer. He stood up, hauled her to her feet and they ran to the water, hand in hand. Eleanor's body felt a little stiff from their previous exercise, yet she willingly followed.

They opted not to body surf this time, but were content to float lazily in the water, allowing the waves to take them on a gentle journey.

"I usually swim out here alone," Joshua commented. "It's nice having company along."

Eleanor glanced back at the deserted beach. "That is a very foolish idea. It isn't safe to swim alone, especially in the ocean."

"There's never anyone I want to take," he insisted.

"It still isn't smart." She cleared her throat. "But I

suppose I should feel honored that you invited me along today."

"Do you?" Joshua swam close, circling around her. She held her breath as he drew nearer. She wondered if he could tell how her pulse was racing, how her body suddenly felt alert, alive, because he was so close.

"Do I what?"

"Feel honored?" He clasped her shoulder and drew her forward, toward that beautiful bronze chest.

"Naturally," she whispered, struggling to fix a nonchalant expression on her face.

"Good." He cupped her face in his hands, then pressed his lips to hers and initiated a slow, coaxing kiss.

A wave lifted them gently upward and her shoulder bumped his, but Joshua didn't break off the kiss. Instead he twined his hands around her neck and tipped her head sideways so he could deepen their contact.

She felt the gentle thrust of his tongue and a sense of wicked satisfaction filled her soul. *Last night wasn't a fluke. He really does find me desirable!*

For a second she was so overwhelmed with sensations and emotions, she couldn't react. Then his tongue slid heatedly over her bottom lip and she came to life.

Eleanor returned his kiss ardently, her mouth sure and firm as it caressed his. She leaned into him, pressing her breasts against his bare chest. Below the water she bent her leg and rubbed it along his outer thigh, then boldly shifted her position, pressing her upper thigh against the hard ridge of his arousal.

He felt incredible. Firm, muscular, solid. She couldn't seem to keep her hands off him. She caressed his dark brown nipples until they grew erect, then boldly let her hands travel down his chest and across his flat, muscular abdomen.

Joshua groaned. He pulled her even closer, initiating a

suggestive rhythm with his hips that made her feel hot and carnal and incredibly sexy.

"Inside, sugar," he whispered harshly in her ear. "Put your hand inside my suit and touch me."

Oh, Lordy. A part of her brain commanded that she cease at once, stop this foolishness before it careened completely out of control. Yet floating out here together in some strange, erotic way seemed to separate her from reality.

She moved her hand down and grasped him. Inside his bathing trunks. Carefully, she curled her fingers around his rigid maleness. The former somber hesitancy she had felt was tempered by the look of pure male satisfaction that came over his face.

She moved her hand, stroking and soothing, brushing and gliding. Joshua arched against her and muttered something harsh under his breath. Eleanor felt the tremor that shivered through him and she kissed him, absorbing his passion. He feasted hungrily on her mouth, sucking her tongue until she felt dizzy.

She had read about couples making love in the shower, but this was even better. There was something primal and seductive about the water that sensitized every nerve ending. Eleanor felt as if her entire world were centered on this man, this moment in time.

He kissed her again. She tasted the tang of the salty ocean on his warm lips, and then on his skin as her mouth made a wet trail down the side of his neck to the hollow of his throat. His pulse raced against her lips. With a smile of triumph she felt the urgency in his body grow even larger.

"That feels so damn good, but this ocean water is just too cold." Joshua's voice held a trace of resigned desperation. With obvious reluctance he pulled her hand away and brought it up to rest on his shoulder. "In this instance, being a woman puts you at a decided advantage."

Eleanor was only beginning to comprehend his meaning when he bent his head and traced her left earlobe with his tongue. Then he slipped his fingers inside the top of her bathing suit and brushed his fingers across her bare breasts, her tight nipples.

She sank into the sensations. He lifted her out of the water, high enough so he could bend his head and reach the tips of her breasts with his teeth and tongue.

"Joshua," she whispered, as the bright, hot excitement shimmered through her.

"Do you like that? Does it feel good?" he asked thickly.

She whimpered and rocked against him, straining her body to get closer and closer to his heat.

"I want you to come, Eleanor," he said hoarsely. "I want to bring you real pleasure."

His shocking words should have brought her firmly back to reality. Instead they made her already taut desire tighten and ache. Her body seemed so synchronized to his, her need so strong, she doubted it would take much more than a few more soul-melting kisses and tender caresses until she climaxed.

"I only pray that we don't drown," she whispered.

The cold of the water surrounding them contrasted sharply with the heat of their bodies. They rose and fell together gently with the swell of the waves. Somehow the weightless floating seemed to intensify the need pounding through her.

At Joshua's urging, she straddled his thigh. His hand reached between their bodies and slipped inside the elastic leg of her swimsuit. She held her breath as his questing fingers explored up to the top of her thigh, across her stomach, through the crisp curls that guarded her innermost secrets.

Eleanor gasped at the splendid invasion, and he swallowed her reaction with a deep kiss. His hands never hesitated. One finger probed deep inside her warmth, while his thumb caressed her most sensitive spot. With swift, sure strokes Joshua expertly brought her to the edge, then gently held her as she fell over.

Shyness and embarrassment quickly followed her climax. *What in the world have I just done?* Her sexual experience had been limited to two long-term relationships where the most adventurous thing she had ever done was make love on the couch instead of in a bed.

She felt his hands move to the back of her spine, to keep her from slipping under the water. She could hear their shallow breathing in the quiet stillness of the water. It was almost as loud as her thundering heart.

For what seemed like an eternity they simply stared at each other, bobbing in time to the rhythmic waves. Then Joshua broke into a wide grin.

"You are one incredible woman." He kissed her tender lips softly. "Race you to the shore."

He vanished in a flurry of movement. Eleanor took a deep breath, conjured up a weak smile, and obligingly followed in his wake.

Eight

"Eleanor? Are you almost ready? My father and Rosemary thought we could share a quiet drink before the party began. I told them we would meet them in the solarium at seven."

"I'm sorry, I don't think I'll be dressed by then, Joshua," came the muffled reply from the other side of the closed door. "Why don't you go ahead without me?"

Joshua pivoted on his heel, paused, then turned back to the door that connected their bedrooms. "I'll go down and make our excuses. Then I'll be back to escort you to the party."

The faint humming noise of a hair dryer instantly ceased. "You'll be back? Well, I . . . ummm, I'm not sure how much longer I'll need. Are you sure you want to wait?"

"Yes."

"Oh." She cleared her throat. Twice. "Great. Guess I'll see you soon."

Joshua smiled. Eleanor's voice held all the enthusiasm of a woman facing a firing squad. He felt bad knowing she was so reluctant to attend the party, but happy realizing her feelings meant she wouldn't leave the room without him. Which was exactly what he wanted.

Ever since their erotic escapade in the ocean this morning, Joshua had been feeling restless and edgy and filled with an almost unbearable need. For Eleanor. He hadn't wanted to go anywhere without her by his side, and tonight was no exception.

It was a surprising, yet not completely unhappy discovery. This strange, unexpected sense of awareness he had for her seemed to burn a little hotter each time he was near her. The house had been too crowded when they returned from the beach to afford them any privacy, any chance to slip away unnoticed.

So instead, they had mingled with his father's guests, chatting amicably about a variety of inconsequential topics. Yet in truth what Joshua was really doing was anticipating the time when he could again be alone with her.

He didn't know exactly when his feelings toward Eleanor had changed. Maybe his attitude had first. He no longer saw her as a means to an end, a way to learn about his father's new wife, but as a person in her own right. Intelligent. Funny. And surprisingly sensual.

It was a remarkable revelation. Like suddenly discovering the gentle kitten you brought home from the pet store had a ferocious, feline streak hidden deep inside. It wasn't precisely a bad thing, just an unexpected notion.

Joshua checked his watch. It was nearly seven. He paced the room for a few moments, feeling unaccountably restless. He was confident that he could control his wayward desires around Eleanor, but more and more he was starting to believe that it wasn't necessary. That thought alone brought on hot chills.

Deciding it would be prudent to return quickly, Joshua hustled out of his bedroom. It took him less than twenty-five minutes to race down to the solarium, toss off a quick drink with his father—who was also without female companionship since Rosemary was still dressing—and return upstairs.

On the way back, Joshua snagged a chilled bottle of champagne and two crystal goblets, reasoning a drink or two before the party might help Eleanor relax.

He popped the cork and poured the sparkling nectar into two crystal flutes. The moment Eleanor stepped into his room, he handed her a glass.

"Thank you."

She stood awkwardly in the middle of the room, one hand clutching her flute of bubbly champagne, the other a tiny black evening bag. She looked lost and fragile and a rush of pure male protectiveness seized his heart. No matter what else happened tonight, he was determined that Eleanor was going to have a wonderful time. A memorable time.

He raised his glass and tapped it gently against hers. "To moonlit nights in North Carolina. May they always be this enchanting."

Her eyes grew big and round. For a few seconds she simply stared at him, then hastily lowered her eyes and took a quick sip of her drink. "It tastes lovely."

He watched her tongue glide sensually along the rim of the crystal and a flicker of anticipation shot through him. She looked gorgeous. Even though he had seen her wearing the dress in the shop, he was stunned by her radiance tonight. It nearly stole his breath away.

He wondered how he had ever thought her plain, ordinary. The exposure to the hot sun earlier in the day had given her skin a pink glow, softening the creamy whiteness of her shoulders to a delectable color. She wore more makeup than usual, but it was discreetly applied, highlighting her eyes and cheekbones. Her hair was swept up and pinned atop her head, displaying a graceful neck with a sexy nape that looked ripe for kissing.

"Shall we sit?" he asked, indicating the cozy love seat near the picture window that looked out on the ocean.

"I can't sit!" Eleanor exclaimed. "I'm afraid I'll wrinkle my dress."

Joshua bit back his laugh when he realized she was serious. "Okay, let's lean." He topped off her champagne glass, then rested his shoulder against the closet door frame. "Better?"

"Much." She imitated his action, positioning herself on the opposite side of the door frame. She gave him a hesitant smile and sipped her champagne.

He saw the uncertainty in her eyes and realized she was waiting for his reaction. To her appearance? Probably.

"By the way, you look beautiful tonight," he said in a soft, seductive tone. "Simply stunning."

Eleanor promptly choked on her drink.

Alarmed, Joshua reached over to help, but she waved him away. "I'm fine," she rasped. "The bubbles just went down the wrong way."

"Most women just say thank you after they receive a compliment," he said teasingly, waiting until she had stopped choking before refilling her glass. "That's one thing I'm starting to admire about you. This incredible need you seem to have to be different."

"That's me all right. Different."

She took another sip of her drink and this time managed to swallow without incident. She raised her glass mockingly, as if daring him to comment. Joshua grinned appreciatively.

Her sense of humor was one of the things he found oddly endearing about her. Whoever would have imagined that laughter could be an aphrodisiac? Certainly not him. He felt oddly humbled to have been unwittingly taught this simple truth.

His eyes traveled again over the lovely expanse of bare shoulders she displayed. Yes, there was no denying there was an extra sparkle about her tonight. Possibly from excitement, but Joshua decided he knew her well enough to determine it was partially nerves that brought on that additional glow.

"Nervous?" he asked with a gentle smile.

"You have a real talent for stating the obvious, Joshua." Eleanor pursed her lips. "I'm a wreck at the thought of meeting all these high and mighty people. What I really need from you is a little practical advice on how to conquer those nerves. And I'm warning you right now if you tell me to picture everyone in their underwear, I'm going to pinch your arm as hard as I can."

Joshua chuckled. Her honesty and lack of artifice were something else he was quickly coming to appreciate. "The trick to dealing with nerves when encountering a group of strangers is learning how to fake it," he instructed.

"What?"

"Fake it." He shrugged his shoulders. "As you circulate around the room, remember at all times to give everyone a wide, carefree smile."

Eleanor obediently grinned, wet her lips, then grinned again. "I can't do it," she sighed, turning away in defeat. "I feel like an idiot. And I'm certain I look like one, too."

"You've got the wrong approach." Joshua put his hands on her shoulders and swung her toward him. "It's not only the smile, but the attitude behind it. You've got to start grinning and smirking as if you know something that everyone doesn't."

"I know I don't belong at this party. Does that count?"

He dipped his chin to his chest and peered at her from beneath his lashes. "You need a serious attitude adjustment, Eleanor."

"I thought I was supposed to smile."

Joshua exhaled slowly. Her teasing grin and flirtatious manner were doing a number on his already overheated libido. The temptation to kiss her was really strong and getting stronger by the minute.

When an enchanting blush raced upward from her throat to her cheeks, Joshua realized a trace of his desire must have been evident on his face. She took a hasty gulp of champagne and angled her head to observe him.

Eleanor kept her eyes hidden, but her hands gave away her sudden agitation. Her knuckles were white as she clutched the goblet and for a moment he feared the glass might shatter in her hands.

Maybe it would be best to wait until later in the evening before the kissing between them started. To heighten the anticipation, to build the excitement, to stoke the fires of passion that were shimmering just below the surface.

"I can hear the orchestra tuning up," Joshua said, removing the nearly empty glass from her nerveless fingers. "Shall we go downstairs and join the party?"

Eleanor took an exaggerated breath, then placed her hand on top of his. " 'Lay on, Macduff, and damned be him that first cries, "Hold, enough!" ' "

"Shakespeare, right?"

"Who else? I find it comforting knowing I can usually count on the bard to provide the appropriate phrase, no matter what the occasion."

Joshua leaned close, until his breath brushed gently against her cheek. " 'Two households, both alike in dignity, In fair Verona, where we lay our scene, From ancient grudge break to new mutiny.' "

Eleanor's smile finally relaxed. "Stop. There's no need to get carried away with the melodrama of *Romeo and Juliet*. I'm nervous enough already."

"Sorry, I thought I was distracting you. Let's talk about something else. How about John Milton? Just mentioning *Paradise Lost* practically puts me to sleep."

Eleanor pinched his arm. Joshua barely felt it. He was

enjoying himself too much. He had forgotten how much he liked English literature and was amazed at how much he had remembered from those few college courses he had sandwiched between the barrage of business lectures.

Yet another example of the difference he had teased Eleanor about earlier. No other woman of his acquaintance could get him to think about literature . . . and like it. She truly was different from any other woman he had known, but in a unique, refreshing way. He felt like a real idiot for not having realized that sooner.

The first floor of the house was bustling with noise and guests. Within minutes Joshua and Eleanor were standing in the foyer, participating in an informal receiving line beside his father and Rosemary.

"Now, who might this pretty lady be? I don't believe I've ever had the pleasure of meeting her."

Joshua turned just in time to see Adam Hughes, an old golfing buddy of his father's, lean suggestively toward Eleanor and practically drool over the perfectly shaped curves of her breasts. Mr. Hughes's eyes looked too bright and anxious as he appraised her creamy shoulders like a greedy child looking at a luscious dessert, poised to take a bite.

A primal burst of jealousy shot through Joshua. Damn, the mangy coot was old enough to be her grandfather.

"Good evening, sir." Joshua thrust out his hand, grimacing when he realized he had to nearly wedge his arm between Eleanor and the old geezer, because the man was so close. Hell, he was almost standing on her toes. "It's nice to see you again."

Adam Hughes raised a bushy gray eyebrow and gave him a hard, speculative glare. Joshua immediately took a protective step closer to Eleanor.

"So that's the way the wind is blowing," the older man

said with a sly smirk. He squeezed Joshua's hand firmly. "About time you found yourself a good woman."

His boisterous, cackling laugh turned a few heads, but Adam Hughes either didn't notice or didn't care. Joshua strongly suspected the latter was true.

"What a character," Eleanor whispered in Joshua's ear, as Adam Hughes shuffled off.

"He's a dirty old man," Joshua retorted, still struggling with his temper. "The old lech was trying to look down the top of your gown."

"Really?"

"Yes."

"Wow. I'm glad I let you talk me into buying it. And wearing it tonight without the sheer jacket. This really is a great dress." Eleanor craned her neck forward to catch a glimpse of her admirer. As if sensing her gaze, Adam Hughes turned around and gave her a suggestive wink.

Joshua made a low, disagreeable sound in his throat.

Eleanor must not have noticed. She grabbed Joshua's arm excitedly. "He winked at me! Did you see? My first conquest of the evening. What a hoot. How old is he, seventy-five, seventy-six?"

"He's pushing eighty and not likely to make it if he keeps acting up."

"Oh, he's harmless." Eleanor linked her arm with Joshua's and patted his hand in an absent manner.

"You're wrong."

"I am?" Eleanor's head whipped around in surprise.

"Absolutely." Joshua leaned over and pressed his lips against hers in a caress that was both sensuous and tender. He thought the dreamy, faraway expression on her face when he finished was a good sign. A most encouraging sign. "That old codger definitely isn't your first conquest of the evening. That honor belongs to me."

* * *

Eleanor dredged up what she hoped was a confident smile. Which wasn't easy, considering how the butterflies in her stomach were doing a major war dance. When the evening began she had been feeling too terrified to leave the safety of the bathroom, and when she finally had emerged, Joshua had been patiently waiting for her.

Dressed in a designer black tuxedo, he'd looked more gorgeous, more perfect than any human being had a right. They had shared a bottle of champagne, some witty banter, and a newly discovered intimacy that made breathing a definite chore.

But the stunner of the night had come later, when he claimed to be captivated by her. Eleanor swore if she hadn't been holding onto his arm when he made his little announcement, she might have easily tumbled to the floor.

Three hours later, he was still at it, acting like she was the most fascinating, interesting, exciting woman in the room. And quite frankly, it scared the hell out of her.

She had spent the afternoon playing and replaying their sexy swim in the ocean and had rationally concluded that it had been all about desire. Raging hormones. A natural, physical reaction between a man who had been too long between partners and a woman who carried a secret longing for him deep in her heart.

But tonight, tonight it was different. The desire was there. Heightened, she supposed, by the forbidden taste they had already sampled, yet not fully experienced. Yet there was more. Possessiveness, protectiveness, and a genuine feeling of affection. Coming from Joshua. Toward her.

She resisted the urge to pinch herself, admitting a part of her wanted to stay asleep if this really was a dream . . .

to pretend, just for this magical night, there would be a chance to explore these incredible physical and emotional feelings.

She was sure the food served at dinner was superb; yet though she had eaten a fair amount of the artfully presented delicacies on her plate, Eleanor had tasted nothing.

Among her dinner companions, who thankfully included Joshua, the conversation was witty and cultured, and incredibly she contributed a word or two without looking like a total fool. A part of her was having a wonderful time. Living the fairy tale as the enchanting Cinderella while the handsome prince danced attendance on her.

Yet another small, insecure self was watching with wary eyes, reminding her not to get too comfortable, too at ease. Because handsome princes didn't really fall in love with incredibly ordinary women. And it was only a matter of time before Joshua woke up to the fact that she was precisely that—an ordinary woman.

Eleanor knew that Joshua's discovery of her true self would be inevitable, but tonight her more immediate concern was the rest of this high and mighty company. So far she had been lucky, yet she was too much of a pessimist to believe her luck would hold.

She was waiting for the moment of denouncement. The gasps and stares, the shouts of fraud when someone in this glittering crowd of beautiful, wealthy, sophisticated people took a closer look at her and realized that she didn't belong here.

She was an obvious outsider among people who made business decisions that affected the lives of entire communities, whose families had founded companies that formed the cornerstone of today's global economy, who had bank balances larger than the net worth of some small Third World countries.

Perhaps Joshua had not been too far off the mark when he'd quoted Shakespeare earlier. Perhaps they were a bit like Romeo and Juliet, star-crossed lovers separated by distances that were difficult and treacherous to breach.

"May I have this dance?"

She stared down at the open palm thrust just below her waist, at first too surprised to answer Joshua. She was a horrible dancer, awkward and clumsy, forever tripping over her own feet and treading on the toes of her partner. So when she opened her mouth, it was with the express intention of refusing his invitation.

Yet miraculously she found herself being gently coaxed onto the dance floor, following trustingly in Joshua's wake. He held her hand tightly and pulled her through the crowd to a secluded corner of the dance floor.

Her entire being trembled as he took her in his arms, but at the same time being held so tightly gave her a sense of enpowerment, making her believe she could do anything. Here within the circle of his strength, anything truly did seem possible.

Eleanor sighed with pure pleasure and closed her eyes, resting her cheek against the fine wool lapel of his jacket. It felt cool and comforting.

Joshua moved in time to the music with an easy grace she envied, but Eleanor soon discovered if she relaxed and let him lead they could glide easily about the room.

It was, however, impossible to completely relax. Being held in his arms, so close to all that hard masculine strength and solid muscle, made all of her senses come alive.

They slowly revolved around the edges of the dance floor. As they rounded a corner, she looked up directly into his eyes. He smiled softly and deliberately pulled her closer. An expectant thrill shot through Eleanor as her hips met his. She could feel the hard proof against her thighs that he desired her.

She was suddenly swamped by a host of sensations, all of which she found disturbingly pleasant. Fearing he would see her emotions clearly, she turned her head, but for a few forbidden moments allowed her imagination free rein.

Yet, it was just all . . . too much. The room was ablaze with candles, and there was music playing softly in the background, supplied by a talented group of musicians. The pleasant scent of roses mingled with the cool sea breeze wafting through the many sets of open French doors.

Everything within the room sparkled, from the gilt-trimmed walls, to the low-lit chandeliers and the many priceless gems adorning the necks of most of the female guests. Even outside, Eleanor could see the crystal white moonlight spilling over on the veranda, illuminating the shadows of the night most invitingly.

"Are you having a good time?" Joshua asked. He skimmed his hand lightly over her bare shoulders.

"Are you?"

"I'm with you. How can I help but enjoy myself?"

Eleanor shuddered. The steady stroke of his fingers rattled her completely, and she unthinkingly sputtered out the first thought that popped into her head. "This is the most remarkable affair I've ever attended. I'm just so relieved that I managed to get through dinner without saying something completely appalling or getting a fleck of pepper stuck in my front teeth, I haven't had the energy to focus on much else."

His gaze sharpened, and Eleanor felt her stomach sink. *Was it humanly possible to have said anything more idiotic?*

Then she saw the light of humor flare to life in his eyes, and noticed the sexy way his upper lip twitched.

"I'm glad you're having fun," he muttered. "I'd also like to point out that I would have immediately let you know if there was something stuck in your teeth. And I sincerely hope you would have done the same for me."

She flashed him a relieved smile. Well, at least he enjoyed her quirky sense of humor. Not everybody did.

The slow, romantic music ended and the band quickly launched into a fast-tempo tune. Eleanor shot Joshua a pleading look that fortunately he understood.

"Would you like to get a drink?" Eleanor asked.

Joshua shook his head, leaned close, and pressed his lips against her ear. "Let's take advantage of this beautiful evening and take a stroll in the moonlight," he murmured.

Eleanor nodded her head, not trusting her voice. He ushered her toward a pair of open French doors on the opposite side of the room. As they walked across the room, several people called out greetings, but Joshua merely nodded or waved at them politely, not bothering to stop and chat with these acquaintances.

Out of the corner of her eye, Eleanor saw Warren and Rosemary clustered with a group of folks directly by the exit. Joshua must have noticed them, too, because he quickly veered away. Putting his arm firmly around her waist, he steered her to another set of open doors.

Eleanor caught only a fleeting glimpse of Warren's thoughtful expression before she and Joshua disappeared into the moonlight.

"I think we're dressed a little formally for the sandy beach," Joshua decided. "Would you like to see some of the grounds of the estate?"

"Sure."

They walked in silence for a few minutes, with only the bright moonlight slanting through the trees to illuminate the way. Soon the sounds of music and laughter faded, and the twinkling lights of the mansion grew small.

A gentle breeze whispered across Eleanor's face. She took a deep breath, savoring the clean scent of dew-wet grass and the pungent sweetness of blooming night lilies. Joshua took her hand as they crested a small hill, so she wouldn't slip in the wet grass.

When they reached the top, Eleanor paused to draw in a breath of surprise. Dominating the valley below was a small structure. It seemed like an otherworldly apparition, a round little house, complete with columns, a domed roof, stone veranda, and long, narrow windows. It was lit from the inside, and it shone through the still, dark night like a glittering glass lantern.

"It's a summerhouse," Joshua informed her. "My mother saw one years ago on a trip to England at some fancy estate and always talked about constructing a similar structure here. My father had it designed and built the year before she died."

"It's beautiful," Eleanor said with genuine awe. "Like something from a fairy tale."

"Wait until you see the interior. Mother spent months choosing all the items she placed inside. She even brought an artist down from New York to paint frescoes on the walls."

Joshua led the way. As they drew near and entered, Eleanor realized that the diminutive size of the structure was really an illusion. The interior space was a single large room, airy and welcoming. It was tastefully furnished with charming gilt furniture reminiscent of the romantic Victorian age, beautiful Chinese silk drapes and a lively patterned rug, in pastel shades of pink, blue, and cream.

The room was lit by brass-and-crystal antique wall sconces, positioned in discrete locations. The walls did indeed tell a circular story, a chivalric fantasy that began in a meadow of spring flowers. A medieval knight in armor and his gaily caparisoned horse marched boldly toward the castle and then single-handedly assaulted the great stone walls to rescue the fair maiden imprisoned inside.

"This place is truly magical," Eleanor whispered. She reached out and touched the velvet petal of a white rose, part of a generous bouquet that adorned one of the tables. It felt soft and silky, and the delicate scent clung to her fingers.

"Would you like stay here for a while?"

There was an extended, charged silence. Eleanor knew very well what he was asking. She had seen the day bed hidden in an inviting alcove, covered in lace-edged, fluffy pillows. This place was a sensual feast, missing only a pair of lovers. Her and Joshua?

Did she dare?

Eleanor thought suddenly about all the things she had missed in her life. The times she had played it safe, approached life with almost religious caution, never daring to let herself dream beyond the staid and expected course of action.

Yet tonight was different. She *felt* different. It wasn't just the beautiful ball gown that made her feel special. It was everything. The dinner, the dancing, the moonlight. It was Joshua looking impossibly handsome in that tuxedo, looking at her with eyes that seemed to want her.

Tonight was a night for testing the fates, for dreaming the impossible. A chance to reach out and grab excitement, rather than let it pass by.

Eleanor raised her eyes to his. She feared too much of what she was feeling was being exposed in her eyes, but she refused to lower them.

She felt caught by the force of his gaze. His heated

look seemed to be trying to break through the wall of pent-up emotions she had suppressed for so long.

She opened her mouth to speak, then swallowed, trying to ease the tightness of her throat. Her eyelids fluttered closed. She felt neatly split in two by her warring desires: to follow, as always, the safe path, or to finally take a risk.

Did she dare? She opened her eyes and gazed once more into his steel-gray eyes. A bittersweet pang struck directly at her heart. How could she not?

Nine

Eleanor didn't say a word. She merely stared at Joshua. Gradually a slight smile appeared on his handsome face. She reasoned he assumed her silence meant she wanted to stay with him. Wanted to be with him.

Eleanor nearly laughed out loud at the thought of his reaction if she had instead declared she was going to leave. What would he have done? Become speechless with shock, no doubt, since it probably had never happened before. He wasn't the sort of man women ever said no to.

Eleanor decided she didn't want to go down that road. Thinking about the women in his past wasn't a good idea. She was insecure enough without imagining herself being compared, unfavorably, to all the other females with whom he had ever been intimate.

Eleanor bowed her head and gripped the chair in front of her. Now was not the time to succumb to an attack of nerves. As the television commercial advised, never let them see you sweat.

Resolutely she lifted her head. "I was surprised to see all the lights were turned on inside the summerhouse before we even entered. Is that usual?"

"I instructed the groundskeeper to put them on the moment it got dark." Joshua shifted closer to her. "I was really hoping I'd have an opportunity to bring you here tonight."

He had planned all of this? Was that true? Her eyes flashed up at him, anxiously looking for some sign of his inner emotions. Triumph briefly glinted in his eyes, but it left so quickly she was uncertain she had seen it.

He took another step toward her and Eleanor's breath caught. With a most tender expression he reached for her balled fist, straightening her fingers slowly. He did the same thing with her other fist, then sandwiched her hands between his larger ones.

He held them firmly yet tenderly. Eleanor could feel her hands begin to tremble, but she didn't pull away. He gazed down at her, his eyes piercing. Joshua seemed to be searching her face, and she wondered briefly what he expected to find.

"How about a drink? This little hideaway should be stocked with a few treasures." He shifted, but held on tightly to her left hand, seemingly reluctant to let her go. Joshua moved to the antique sideboard, tugging her along behind him. He opened a cabinet. "Ahh, here we are. May I pour you a glass?"

"Yes, thank you." Eleanor sent him a wavering smile and pulled her hand away. She settled herself on a delicate powder-blue chair reminiscent of the Victorian era, that looked far more comfortable than it felt.

Perched on the edge of her chair, she followed his every move intently. The tempo of her heartbeat increased. Nothing in her experience had prepared her for the feelings that were churning inside her. Fear mixed with excitement, mixed with dread, mixed with elation.

She took the snifter of amber liquid he offered her with unsteady hands and drank a large swallow. Her eyes instantly starting tearing.

"This tastes like expired cough syrup! What in the world am I drinking?"

"A very rare Napoleon brandy. Vintage 1880."

Eleanor sniffed the drink tentatively, then recoiled. She shuddered and put down the glass. "It's no wonder that Napoleon died an unhappy, broken man. He was mortified knowing someone planned on naming this vile concoction after him. He must have spent his last days hoping that history would remember him as a great military leader instead of the poor soul associated with this horrendous drink."

"I suppose it is an acquired taste." Joshua smiled, his teeth even and white.

Eleanor wondered briefly if he had ever worn braces as a child, then quickly discarded the notion. Physical perfection such as his needed no human assistance.

She sighed. A relaxing warmth settled in her stomach, softening the edges of her nerves. *Must be from the brandy,* Eleanor thought. She contemplated taking another small sip, but realized she would probably have to hold her nose to swallow it. Not quite the sophisticated, romantic image she was hoping to achieve.

"Would you like something else to drink?" Joshua inquired, almost as if sensing her indecision.

She shook her head from side to side. The last thing she needed right now was more alcohol. Spending an evening with Joshua Barton required the complete attention of all her unencumbered faculties.

Yet her sober senses seemed to have a mind of their own, for they immediately started wandering. Her eyes went directly to his sensual mouth. Unwittingly she stared at his lips, remembering how wonderful they felt pressed against her own. The mere thought of kissing him again brought on that thready pulse, rapid breathing, and weakness in her knees.

She knew he was also observing her closely, for she felt his eyes move over her body with smoldering sexual regard. With a start, Eleanor realized she could get lost in that gaze. A slow pounding started deep in her belly. Shaken, she picked up her glass and ran her thumb back and forth over the rim.

His eyes remained pinned on her, and awareness of him coursed through her. Eleanor's discomfort grew. She jumped to her feet and restlessly paced about the beautiful room, making a great show of examining some of the small, unusual items on display.

"Would you please try to relax, Eleanor? I promise not to bite. Well, at least not at first."

His voice sounded very close. Too close. She turned and found herself captured neatly in his arms.

His lips met hers in a warm, arousing kiss. He nibbled on her lower lip for a moment, then pushed his tongue inside. She tasted the brandy he had sipped earlier. Funny, it now tasted marvelous. Smooth and rich and mellow.

He whispered her name and then kissed her again, with a deep, almost savage possession. Her lips clung to his and the heat of his mouth made her skin tingle. His tongue teased hers and she playfully answered his sensuous prelude to seduction by tracing the inside of his upper lip with her tongue.

Eleanor began to quiver with anticipation. She had never before felt such a hunger, a craving. It seemed as though she had been burning and aching for days for the taste of his lips, the feel of his hard muscular body. She whimpered softly and rose on her toes, desperately bringing herself closer.

"You're driving me wild, Eleanor," he groaned. "I've thought of nothing but you since we kissed last night."

His hands went to her breasts. Cupping her through the fabric, he teased the nipples into hard peaks. She arched against him excitedly, her body coming alive. He pushed down the top of her gown and somehow managed to free her left breast from the confines of her undergarments.

He ran his thumb over the nipple, stroking and teasing. Eleanor's eyes drifted shut under this expert assault of her senses. Then his mouth closed over the sensitive nipple. After a heartbeat of urgent anticipation, he sucked deeply.

She gasped loudly and her body began to tremble. Melting into his caresses, she twined her fingers through his hair. A score of emotions poured through her. The outside world ceased to exist and it was only the two of them, lost together in this sensual world.

"Joshua," she rasped out.

"Eleanor." He lifted his head and she could feel him smile against her skin. "Does that feel good?" He deliberately swirled his tongue around her aroused nipple. "How about that? Do you like that?"

Her throat tightened, making speech impossible. His touch was so extraordinary, so exciting. His hands seemed to be everywhere, heating everything he caressed. They traced the line of her body, the sides of her breasts, the curve of her waist, the roundness of her hips.

He shifted position and started nuzzling her neck. The light stubble of his jaw grazed her bare shoulder. His breath was warm, his heightened passion spurning her own. Through her haze of desire she felt him sliding down the zipper at the back of her gown. A wave of panic crashed over her. Abruptly, she slipped from his embrace.

"Goodness, it's bright in here. I never imagined such small fixtures could give off so much light." Eleanor's breath was coming in long, deep gasps and it was difficult to speak. She ran a hand absently through her hair and realized most of the pins were gone.

Heavens, she must look like a wreck. Hunching her shoulder, she discreetly rearranged herself back inside the ball gown.

Joshua's expression was fierce. Somehow during their embrace his tie had been lost and the top two studs of his shirt undone. The pulse at his throat beat strong and steady. She could see the longing in his eyes, that slow, steamy gaze that made her knees feel weak.

He took a few steps toward the edge of the room, reached out, and flicked a switch on the wall. The lights dimmed, casting the room in a warm pink glow.

"Better?" he asked, gathering her back into his arms.

Eleanor's throat constricted. She nodded her head. Once again their lips merged and without a second thought she succumbed to the urge to kiss him with all the desire that had been building inside her.

From the moment he had first spoken to her, Joshua had roused a strange restlessness in her that had long been dormant. This was her chance to finally explore that desire. She was a bit unsure, a bit nervous, yet being surrounded by his addictive male presence made Eleanor yearn for all the carnal pleasure they could share.

"Let's get more comfortable," he whispered suggestively.

Eleanor allowed herself to be guided to the lovely day bed. They moved awkwardly, taking short steps between long kisses. The back of her knees hit the brass frame. She must have swayed, but he caught her and gently set her upon the bed.

He loomed above her. She lifted her face toward him and he claimed her lips in another series of deep, soul-melting kisses. Kneeling over her, Joshua expertly peeled off the top of her ball gown. He unhooked her bra, attempting to take it off. Instinctively she tensed, clasping her hand over his.

A NIGHT TO REMEMBER

"Maybe I should leave it on."

Joshua gave her a confused frown, then understanding lit his handsome features. "I think you are beautiful, Eleanor." He ran his hand delicately along her cheek. "Sexy and lush. I want to see as well as feel you. All of you."

His hand went again to her bra, but this time she didn't stop him. She held herself rigidly still as he removed it, along with the rest of her underwear, bracing herself for a negative reaction.

She had always been self-conscious about her breasts. Sure, guys were supposed to be enamored of a large chest, but those perfectly sculptured plastic surgery creations were not like the real thing. Certainly not her real things.

He took hold of her wrists and slowly spread her arms. "Perfect," he said. "Even better than I imagined."

Eleanor felt herself blush. It seemed wildly erotic to be sitting before him naked, displayed like some wanton lover while he remained fully clothed.

"What about your clothes?" she inquired.

"No problem."

With a wicked grin he stood beside the bed, watching her intently while he undressed. Carelessly he dropped his shirt, unfastened his belt, lowered the zipper on his fly. In one fluid motion he pushed off both his trousers and his briefs.

The sigh started from her toes. She had always found him irresistible. Not only was he physically perfect, he was quite simply the most fascinating man she had ever known. Dressed casually in shorts and a sports shirt or a perfectly tailored business suit or looking like something from the deepest regions of a fairy-tale fantasy in his formal evening clothes. Yes, fully dressed he was mesmerizing.

Utterly naked, he was mind-numbing.

Joshua moved closer, placing one knee on the edge of the bed. She promptly lost what little breath she had left. His handsome features assumed an intent expression and for a split second she feared she was going to lose all control.

He captured her hand in his and placed it flat against his chest. "Touch me, Eleanor."

She didn't have to be told twice. Her hands glided over his body in long, sensual strokes, across his shoulders, and chest, along his arms and ribs. With his sleepy eyes and groan of delight encouraging her, she traced the muscles on his stomach, then played with the dark nipples buried among the crisp chest hair until they hardened into tight peaks.

Feeling bold, she moved her hand farther down, across his ribs and belly. She hesitated when she reached the top of his groin, then felt Joshua's quivering breath in her hair.

"Touch me," he repeated in a deep, silky voice.

A shudder went through her. Her hand slid down to his erection. She took him in her hands, smoothing her fingers down his hard length. It felt like satin over steel. Rock-solid and pulsing with life. He thrust against her hand and she tightened her grip. A drop of moisture covered the tip of his penis and she slowly massaged it into his hardness.

"Enough," he growled, pushing her hands away.

She felt herself being lifted, then lowered on her back onto the day bed. Eleanor waited with restless anticipation for him to cover her with his body, to press her into the softness of the pillows beneath her back.

Instead, he knelt beside her and began kissing her body. Neck, shoulders, ribs. His questing lips and tongue moved lower, to her belly and beyond, making her tingle with mounting tension.

She froze, her body stiffening when she felt the first feathery kisses along her inner thigh. This was definitely not something she felt comfortable doing. Eleanor jerked herself back, but the heat flashed inside her as his mouth came to rest at the thatch of hair between her legs.

Gently he parted her, pressing his lips and tongue between the folds of her body in the most intimate of kisses.

She turned her face into the pillow and moaned. It felt so incredibly good. The need inside her sharpened, yet Eleanor squirmed, trying to evade his questing tongue. She heard his wicked chuckle and felt a blush over her entire body. Never before had she felt so open, so exposed to a man.

"Joshua, I—" She tried to sit up, to shift away, but he held her in place.

"Shhh, I won't hurt you," he said coaxingly. "I promise I'll stop if you don't like it. Just try to relax. And trust me, Eleanor. Trust me."

After a slight hesitation he continued licking her, circling slowly with the tip of his tongue around the tender nub of her pleasure. Tension curled up tight inside her, hot and urgent. Her breath came in short, gasping pants. He slid his hands beneath her bottom and tilted her forward.

The need inside her spiraled out of control, and her body arched up off the bed. It broke suddenly and she cried out. Joshua held her tightly, lightly stroking her flanks as her body shuddered its release.

Completly sated, Eleanor lay relaxed and slightly dazed against the soft cushions. Joshua shifted off the small bed and she let out a cry of protest at the loss of his solid warmth.

He returned quickly, however, standing above her, his

eyes darkened with desire, gleaming down at her. She glanced over his beautiful body, hard and taut, and with a grateful blush realized he had donned a condom.

Eleanor lifted her arms to welcome him. Joshua moved between her spread legs, bending her knees back to angle her body to fit perfectly with his.

He gave her a wolfish smile before leaning over her. Gently he kissed her forehead, nose, and lips. Then with infinite tenderness he joined their bodies.

Eleanor cried out softly. She turned her head into his shoulder and nipped at the solid, warm flesh.

"Am I hurting you?" Joshua's voice was tight.

"No." Eleanor trembled. His body was shuddering with the force of his need, but she could tell he was holding himself in check.

He slid deeper and deeper inside her. Eleanor felt her body stretching to accommodate him. She exhaled slowly, forcing her muscles to relax.

He fondled her breasts, then reached down between their bodies and caressed her softly.

"Better?" he whispered hoarsely.

"Hmmm," she muttered, too involved in the glorious sensations to speak.

He moved inside her, slow and deliberate. She lifted her hips to get closer and he increased the pace, surging into her.

Her hands gripped the corded muscles of his upper arms, clenching and unclenching frantically as the tension within her started building again . . . higher . . . higher. Her heart raced and the blood pounded through her veins, the pressure so intense it almost became pain.

He froze for a second, then shuddered violently. She could feel the movement of his body deep within her, the pulsing of his release.

Her arms tightened around him. Her own pleasure was

quickly forgotten as she became caught in the wonder of experiencing Joshua's orgasm. It was incredible. She whispered his name and felt tears fill her eyes.

Spent, he collapsed on top of her. His weight crushed her, but she loved the feel of having him draped over her like a blanket. Their bodies were still joined and she reveled in the physical bond, the closeness they still shared.

I love you, she thought, realizing with sadness that it was the truth. She was in love with him. But there was no time to savor, to indulge in this miraculous feeling, for reality quickly followed truth.

An ache assaulted Eleanor, the feeling so brutal she tightened her embrace and held onto Joshua with a near-death grip.

It was unlikely they had any future together. Their lives were too different, their expectations polar opposites. She had known that before the weekend started, and everything that occurred since, from the private plane ride to the glittering party tonight, merely confirmed that fact.

She didn't belong here, could never really fit in, feel comfortable.

Yet perhaps the most difficult truth of all to acknowledge was that when this magical weekend ended, and their time together was over, she would still love him.

Joshua lay back on the pillows. It was a close fit on the small bed, but he enjoyed the cozy arrangement. Somehow it felt right, having Eleanor snuggled so close to him, warming his body pleasantly. Outside, yet inside, too.

His gaze roamed her serene face. She was sleeping soundly, had been for the past hour. Gently he smoothed the few damp strands of hair from her temples. Her complexion was flushed, almost glowing. And it had nothing to do with her slight sunburn. With a smile that was pure male ego he took credit for the glow on that skin.

They had been good together. Better than good. Still, Joshua hadn't realized he would care so much, would *feel* so much. Not just physically, but emotionally.

Her shy hesitation, her initial nerves, had brought out the protective side of his nature and added a dimension to their lovemaking he had never before experienced. In the past he had always favored tough, aggressive women. The type that just might come up and grab your crotch, in case you didn't exactly understand what they wanted.

But now he discovered he could appreciate, even admire a completely different sort of woman. A woman like Eleanor. Less aggressive, less take-charge, a bit unsure, yet smart and competent. Gentler. Kinder. It was a nice change. It was the type of change he had never even considered until now. Yet he knew it was right for him.

He picked up a tendril of her hair and rubbed it between his fingers. Eleanor stirred, moaned, and snuggled deeper into the cushions. Joshua wondered briefly what thoughts were swirling through her brain. Even in sleep she seemed pensive.

Was she thinking about their future? He certainly had been. Exactly where did they go from here? There were some large problems looming on the horizon, specifically their working relationship. Even though Eleanor didn't work directly with him, she was an employee in his firm and there were some very strict rules governing company relationships.

And that was what they had—a relationship. He hadn't known her long, but he had established a closer, more honest connection with Eleanor than he had with other women he had dated for months. In this instance he readily accepted that quality, rather than quantity, was the key.

What about Eleanor? What did she want from him?

Expect from him? He was astute enough to realize from the comments she constantly tossed out with comic delight that deep down inside she believed they were all wrong for each other.

Two days ago he would have agreed with her. Completely. But now he knew differently. He *felt* differently. That was clearly the first hurdle he needed to jump. Convincing Eleanor to take a chance on investing in a solid, meaningful, lasting commitment to him wouldn't be simple or necessarily easy, but well worth the challenge.

Eleanor opened her eyes sleepily and glanced around. He knew the exact moment she realized where she was by the startled look that came over her face. Followed briefly by a quick flash of pain. *Now what the hell was that all about?*

"What time is it?" she asked groggily.

"Nearly one A.M."

"Oh." She shifted and sat up, clutching a large pillow to her breasts. "Do you think the party is still going on?"

"Probably," he replied distractedly, his mind wandering, worrying over that look of distress. Did she have regrets? Had he hurt her in some way? Disappointed her?

The thought rankled him and he gave her a penetrating look. He knew he had brought her pleasure, but had he made her happy? It suddenly seemed very important to know that he had.

"Are you all right, Eleanor?"

She turned to him, looking mystified. "Y-yes. Of course. It was incredible. *You* were incredible." She blinked and her cheeks bloomed with color. "Are you all right, Joshua?"

"Never better." He gave a shaky laugh. She had caused him to practically lose all control, physically and emotionally. Even now he was amazed that he'd kept his head long enough to slip a condom on at the last moment to protect her.

"We should probably return to the house before anyone notices we've been gone." She frowned down at the rug. "Can you help me find my clothing?"

Her simple request wounded him. She seemed very anxious to leave. Besides, he didn't have the heart to tell her that by this time surely his father and Rosemary would have noticed their prolonged absence, along with any other guests who might have been interested in speaking to them.

"What's the rush?" He took one of her hands and brought it to his mouth. Tenderly he nibbled on the fingertips. "I was hoping we could stay here for a while. Would you mind?"

She leaned toward him. The intensity of her expression was making him hard. Again. Joshua reached out and tugged at the large pillow she had tucked under her chin to hide her nudity. Surprised, she let it go. His gaze slid over her breasts and down the length of her body. Man, she was a pretty sight. Slowly he reached out, cupping her breasts. His fingers tested their firmness, his thumb teased one sensitive nipple.

"Are you tired?" he asked.

"Aren't you?" she questioned breathlessly.

"No." He dipped his head and kissed her tender nipple.

She moaned. The long, whimpering sound brought his body to life and it tightened with need. What extraordinary power she possessed. Amazing.

It was nearly dawn when they left the summerhouse. They walked silently together through the wet grass, his arm thrown possessively around her shoulders. The party was long over. The terraced patios had already been cleared of any dirty plates and glasses.

The extra outdoor seating and tables had been removed, the citronella torches lit to keep the bugs away had been extinguished. All that remained were the strings of tiny white lights wrapped in the trees nearest the patio, twinkling like newly formed stars.

Joshua was pleased for Eleanor's sake that they encountered no one on the way. No overnight guests, no servants or, God forbid, his father or Rosemary. Explanations might have caused her embarrassment and he didn't want any negative memories to mar the perfection of their first night together.

When they arrived at her bedroom door, Joshua kissed her softly, gently on the lips and, despite the early morning hour, whispered a gentle good night.

Only then did he finally relinquish her from his possessive embrace.

Ten

Eleanor wiggled her toes on the bottom of the slippery porcelain tub, shutting her eyes as the steam rose all around her. Fifteen minutes ago she had pulled the bath curtain closed, adjusted the shower setting, and turned it up full blast. Her fingers were starting to wrinkle, along with other parts of her anatomy, yet it felt too heavenly to leave.

The water beat hot and steady against her neck, shoulders and back, soothing her joints and muscles. Turning 180 degrees, she let the spray hit her rump and upper thighs, acknowledging with a sly smile that she was aching in places she hadn't even realized existed until Joshua had shown her last night.

Memories of their incredible night and early morning together surfaced. One for the record books, absolutely. At least her record book. Deep down Eleanor had always suspected there was another facet of her personality buried inside her. That uninhibited side that longed only for the chance to show itself, without fear of retribution.

A small part of her would always be grateful to Joshua for helping her discover that part of herself and setting it free, even as the stronger, more dominant side of her practical self whispered it might have been a mistake. A huge mistake.

Still, the tension of the last few days had finally vanished when she had stretched out in her bed early this morning, with her head nestled against her pillow. Miraculously she had slept, a deep and dreamless sleep, yet awakened to a new reality. Her relationship with Joshua had taken yet another bizarre turn.

The thought filled her with a sense of melancholy along with a certain wistfulness. Maybe it would have been better to have kept it all a rich fantasy, to have dreamt of the possibility of experiencing a physical relationship with Joshua rather than actually succumbing to the passion. For now that she knew the truth—that the experience had completely eclipsed the expectation—it would be difficult to accept its loss.

She held no illusions about the future. She knew this weekend was a glitch in the reality of her life. A stolen moment, to be savored as a memory, remembered with joy and perhaps a touch of sadness.

She had quivered at his touch, had trembled at the feel of his flesh joined to hers. He had tantalized her with his kisses, had melted her with his sweet endearments and tender murmurs of encouragement. Again and again he had driven her to the brink of pleasure before finally working his magic upon her and granting her blissful release.

A wave of heat went through Eleanor that had nothing to do with the temperature of the water. Even now, hours later, she still felt bathed in some strange afterglow of satisfaction. And yet, she could not deny the feeling that it would be nice to stay in the warm, moist cocoon of the shower, instead of going downstairs to face Joshua and perhaps several strangers, who were house guests.

Morning-afters were a tricky affair. Fortunately, there hadn't been too many of those in Eleanor's life, but she had listened sympathetically to more than one girlfriend recount some horrendous experience. What made matters difficult this morning was the potential audience. Being a guest in someone's home denied her, and Joshua, the opportunity to slip graciously away if they so desired.

With a resigned sigh, Eleanor shut off the water and reached for a towel, drying herself briskly. She needed to vanquish these troubling thoughts. Self-recrimination was such an unattractive, unproductive emotion. Somehow she must find the inner strength to resist its allure.

When Eleanor finally made an appearance in the dining room, Joshua was nowhere to be found. *All that fretting for nothing!* There were a few house guests milling around the table, enjoying the delicious brunch that had been prepared, talking together with ease and familiarity.

Rosemary and Warren were also absent, taking a group of guests on a horseback-riding expedition, explained a maid. Eleanor lacked the courage to ask if Joshua was with them.

Instead, she hesitantly joined the group eating brunch. After exchanging polite greetings, she took a seat at one end of the polished mahogany table and was promptly ignored. There were very limited efforts to include her in the conversation, though Eleanor freely admitted she had little to contribute. The discussion swirled around her, sounding almost like a foreign language. It was the talk of people she had never heard of and places she had only read about.

She felt awkward and a bit shy, once again the outsider. It was an enlightening, though not altogether pleasant realization to discover that it was a far lonelier feeling to be ignored while in a crowd than when you were off by yourself.

Deciding against the rich cheese crêpes and luscious pecan waffles, Eleanor instead gratefully accepted a cup of hot tea from a pretty blond-haired maid. At least *she* was friendly and appeared genuinely eager to please. Needing something to do while she finished her toast, Eleanor started observing the various maids in the room and made another startling discovery. Exactly how many servants were employed here? It seemed as though she never saw the same workers twice.

She left the table the moment her tea was gone. Not surprisingly, no one seemed to take even a passing interest in her departure. Returning to her bedroom held no appeal, so she slipped quietly out to the back terrace.

It was close to noon, the perfect time to do some exploring. After pausing a moment to get her bearings, Eleanor deliberately chose a direction that led away from the sea, but also away from the summerhouse. She soon discovered a landscape of incredible formal gardens and eagerly followed the worn path, winding her way around the carefully tended fragrant blossoms.

After a while the trail began to slope upward, and when she came to the last row of boxwood hedges, Eleanor could not only smell, but see the ocean. She lifted her eyes toward the brilliant blue sky and spotted Joshua in the distance.

He was perched atop a high, sandy dune, his face angled out toward the water. A noisy flock of gulls seemed to have captured his attention as they swooped and soared, taking turns diving into the sea. The prevailing impression of strength and power Joshua exuded was softened slightly by the contrast of his casual pose.

Still, Eleanor staggered to a halt. She frowned, measuring him. Maybe she should turn around. Joshua looked so unapproachable and solitary. Surely she must be intruding on his privacy. And that was absolutely the last thing she wanted. To be an intrusion.

He turned his head sharply. Eleanor froze. She was too far away to read his expression, to see what his reaction was to her unexpected appearance. But he raised his arm and waved.

"Eleanor!" Her name drifted on the wind, floating down to her. She tried to tell herself it was only a call of recognition, of acknowledgement, but Joshua waved his arm again, clearly beckoning her.

She moistened her dry lips and plunged forward. Yet as she drew nearer, a sense of uneasiness persisted. Along with a strange feeling of connection. Even in the stark reality of daylight, she could still view him in a romantic haze. Goodness, she really must be in love with him.

She tucked a stray wisp of hair behind her ear and tried to prepare herself for just about anything. She knew that their lovemaking last night would forever change their relationship, but didn't have much of a clue as to how exactly it would be altered.

Joshua held out his hand. Clamping down firmly on the flutters in her stomach, she slid her fingers into his strength.

"Hello, Eleanor," he said softly after he had pulled her up to his side.

She felt a rush of warmth and desire go through her. It seemed like months rather than hours since they had been tightly locked in a passionate embrace. "Hello, Joshua." She took a deep, steadying breath. "Have you been out here long? It sure looks like it is going to be another beautiful day, doesn't it?"

"It's nearly perfect. I came out here to clear my head about an hour ago. I'm finding it hard to leave. It's the type of day that makes you want to lay around by the pool, relaxing in the sun, with a drink in one hand and a magazine in the other."

"Sounds ideal." Eleanor laughed. "Where do I sign up?"

Joshua frowned. "Regretfully we won't be able to stay

and indulge ourselves today. A minor crisis at the office needs to be dealt with quickly. I've been on the phone most of the morning, hoping to settle it long-distance. But I'm not making any headway."

She felt Joshua place his hand on her arm. "I've called a meeting for eight A.M. tomorrow and I'll need time to prepare for it. Would you mind if we left late this afternoon?"

Her throat went dry. Was it true? Or was he just looking for an excuse to get away from her? Anxiously, Eleanor studied his face for any signs of his inner emotions, but the look he cast her was indecipherable. It remained quiet and she realized he was waiting for her answer.

"I can be ready to go anytime." She gave a shaky laugh. "I just came along for the ride, remember?"

"You've done far more than that, Eleanor."

Unable to meet his eyes, she turned away, staring blindly at the ocean. How desperately she wanted to believe that statement.

Joshua let out an impatient sigh and glanced at his wristwatch. "I'd better get back up to the house. I'm expecting an important fax. It should be here by now."

A heavy somberness fell over her. She was hoping they would at least have time for a final walk on the beach together. "What time do you want to leave?"

"No later than four."

"I'll be ready." She smiled fleetingly. The air between them felt thick with unspoken words. For a moment she thought he might kiss her, but he only smiled and turned away.

Battling her disappointment, Eleanor lifted her arm to shield her eyes from the bright sun. She watched him jog across the sand, up the hill and disappear through the tall boxwood hedge, taking a small bit of comfort in the fact that she had managed to save some of her dignity.

Seconds ticked away. Eleanor remained where she was, still staring off in the direction Joshua had vanished. Already the distance between them was starting, and she admitted that it was more than just a physical separation. Up until that moment she hadn't wanted to admit that she had been entertaining a subtle fantasy of becoming an important part of Joshua's life.

She turned away and blinked her eyes. Sadly she knew there was nothing she could do to prevent the inevitable separation.

Was there?

Joshua hunched over his papers, trying unsuccessfully to concentrate on the work set in front of him. His fax had arrived, his computer was fired up and ready to go, but he was having great difficulty stringing any coherent thoughts together.

A shout, followed by a female giggle, then a splash reached his ears. These distractions were wreaking havoc with the numbers he was trying to crunch and ruining an already unhappy mood. He had deliberately chosen not to work in his bedroom, since it was directly over several terraced patios and near the pool.

He figured by barricading himself in a little-used third-floor study he would avoid most of the outside distractions. But it hadn't helped. The noise still found him, and even worse, he felt like a kid stuck inside doing his homework while everyone else got to play outside and have fun.

Was there truly no peace and quiet to be found within this sixty-five-room house? Anywhere?

Another shout, followed by the deep rumble of male laughter, had Joshua standing on his feet and pacing the room. How could anybody hear himself think with all that racket going on? For the life of him, he couldn't understand how his father put up with all this nonsense.

Sure, his dad was retired now, but Joshua remembered when he was growing up there were often guests at the house. Large groups of thirty and forty people, staying for a round of weekend parties and social events.

As a child he never realized the significance of those gatherings. Powerful, influential men in government and politics were entertained within these walls, but Joshua's only concern had been if anyone had brought a child or two along. If he was lucky, the youngsters were close enough in age to play with him.

Those events hadn't been purely social. There had been business conducted during those house parties. Important, significant deals had been struck that added to the growth and stature of the family business and to the personal fortune of the Barton family.

Joshua rubbed his tired eyes. Maybe he should call upon a few of the old family friends to lend him a hand now. Because if he didn't start working on a solution to this latest crisis immediately, there might not be much of a family business left.

A knock sounded at the door. Eleanor? The thought brought a rush of elation. Eagerly Joshua yanked open the door.

His father stood on the other side. "Another fax came for you," Warren Barton said gruffly. "None of the servants could find you, but I had a suspicion that if you were working you were probably up here."

"Thanks." Startled, Joshua accepted the document, realizing that his father was probably the only person in the world who could catch him so completely off-guard. "Do you want to come in?"

"I don't want to intrude," Warren replied, standing stiffly in the doorway.

Joshua let out a mocking laugh. "You'd only be intruding if I was getting anything accomplished. Trust me, that's not the case. Please, Dad, come in."

"Well, maybe for a few minutes. Rosemary's expecting me to help her settle some last-minute details for tonight's dinner."

Joshua's grin faded. "I don't want to disrupt your schedule."

"Rosemary can wait," Warren said in an almost gentle tone. He stepped into the room and glanced over at the desk where Joshua had spread out his papers. "So what's the problem? A deal go south?"

"You could say that," Joshua replied noncommittally. He was not in the mood to be lectured about how to run his business or second-guessed over any decisions. In Joshua's opinion, the only thing worse than trying to cope with this current mess would be to get into an argument with his father over it.

"Is the problem with a client or an associate?" Warren probed.

"Both." Joshua winced inwardly. He had not meant to reveal even that much about his difficulties. Needing a distraction, Joshua poured them each a glass of iced tea from a pitcher he had brought in earlier. As he handed his father the beverage, he closely observed the expression on the older man's face. Surprisingly, it was concern.

"Some days it feels like everyone and everything is conspiring against you, doesn't it?" Warren took a swallow of his drink. "There are a lot of things I miss about not working, but coping with employees who screw up isn't one of them. Many people used to think I was a demanding boss, and I guess I was, but the fact is that someone has to take charge, take responsibility, make the unpopular decisions. That was me. And now it's you."

His father reached over and patted him on the shoulder.

The gesture was awkward and wooden, but the emotions behind it were sincere. Joshua looked at his father and suddenly the words started tumbling out.

"It feels like the place is coming apart, Dad. Johnson has pissed off a major client and Morton blew a deal that I was counting on to raise our third-quarter profits. The competition is so tough these days I have to exert some major damage control or else these clients are going to walk. Pronto."

Joshua ran his fingers through his hair. "But those are minor concerns compared to the mess Weston might have made while putting together an initial public offering for an Internet company earlier this year. I've been reviewing some of his prospectus notes and I'm afraid he might have crossed the line with some of his decisions."

"Was the initial offering of stock priced too high?" Warren asked, citing a typical mistake.

"No. Exactly the opposite. It was too low. Much too low. The stock took off and is holding high, so the company is thrilled with our work. But I have a strong suspicion that Weston somehow purchased a major block of this stock for himself."

"Insider trading." Warren whistled softly. "This is very serious. How are you going to handle it?"

"Right now all I have are suspicions and some figures that might or might not prove anything. What I need to do is amass enough proof so that I can confront Weston directly. He's a partner in the firm, so I need to make sure I can force him to resign, before somehow convincing him to turn himself in to the authorities. That's my only hope of keeping this entire incident relatively quiet."

Warren nodded his head. "Discretion is critical at this juncture. Even if it was only one man acting on his own and the firm is cleared of all responsibility, the publicity alone could ruin our reputation. And the last thing you want is some Washington bureaucrat poking his nose in your business."

"Exactly. If this situation blows before I can resolve it, I don't want to look like I've been trying to cover it up."

"I could make a call to Washington and let one of my old buddies in the Treasury Department know you've got a situation brewing that needs a little time to get straightened out," Warren offered.

Joshua rubbed his chin. "It's a risky move. If I can't solve this on my own then I've given the government some very interesting information that will spearhead an investigation."

"That's true, but you might also be telling them something they already know." Warren regarded him skeptically. "You aren't the only one who can be looking at numbers. Red flags might have been raised over this deal back when the stock started trading in the beginning of the year."

"Good point." Joshua said. The corners of his mouth quirked in a grimace. "Any suggestions on how I should handle this?"

A slight stain of red crept up his father's neck. Joshua would have thought it signaled embarrassment, but there was no mistaking the expression of pride and delight on the older man's face.

The two men discussed various options, their voices occasionally raised to emphasize a point, but always speaking with respect. Joshua's hand flew across the paper as he scribbled notes, at times copying verbatim what his father said.

With a sigh, Joshua tossed his pen on the table, then raised his arms high, stretching his neck and shoulders. "It's afternoons like this one that make me wonder why I fought so hard to gain control of the company."

Warren chuckled. "I know just how you feel. Right now you're thinking it would be a whole lot smarter to jump on the first decent bid you receive and sell the damn company. Or ask the partnership to put together a buy-out agreement. Then all this mess could be someone else's headache for a while."

His father leaned back in his chair and crossed his arms over his flat stomach. "Problem with that idea is that you'll be looking to start up or buy another firm within two weeks. You just have to face facts, Joshua, you're too much like me. And we aren't the type of men who do well taking orders from someone else."

Perhaps it was the sympathetic tone, or the understanding look in the older man's eyes that made Joshua pause and consider, for the first time, that yes, his father really did know what it was like to deal with this sort of pressure and responsibility.

His father's empathy was not hollow or condescending. It was genuine. And more important, it was the voice of experience talking. It might have been a different era, but his father had faced and overcome many of the same challenges. There was perhaps no one else who understood more what it was like to be the managing partner of Hamilton, Barton and Jones.

In the past Joshua had always been quick to dismiss his father's business advice as implied criticism, probably due to the older man's dictatorial manner. But Joshua now conceded that he had done them both a great disservice by putting greater emphasis on the *way* his father spoke to him than *what* his father was saying.

"You've got some smart ideas on how to handle Weston. Employee problems present some of the most difficult challenges you'll ever have to face," Warren said. "It's always a fine line to walk. Just remember if you throw out an offer on the table, you've got to be prepared to live with the consequences.

"Nothing more lethal than bluffing when you offer a deal. Those are the times you can really get caught with your pants down." Warren smiled. "But why am I telling you this? You already know it. It won't be easy coping with this latest insider-trading mess, but I trust you to make the right choices, son. The tough choices."

"Thanks, Dad." *His father believed in him?* For possibly the first time in Joshua's life, words failed him.

Warren cleared his throat. "So what time are you heading out?"

Joshua raised his head with a guilty start. "Four o'clock. I should have told you earlier, but I was preoccupied with this mess. I apologize."

"No problem. Eleanor's already told us that you were leaving this afternoon. We invited her to stay on, but she said she needed to get back home." Warren nonchalantly ran his finger around the rim of his empty iced tea glass. "I like Eleanor, by the way. She's a fine woman, sincere and genuine."

His father held up his hand, forestalling any possible reaction. "Oh, I know it's immaterial if I like her. What's important is how you feel about her. But I thought I'd let you know my impressions, my opinion, just in case you were wondering." Warren lowered his head and for a moment looked almost sheepish. "Guess I do that a lot. Let you know my opinion."

Joshua laughed. "It's been known to happen." His expression lightened. "But you've been doing it for thirty-two years, and I don't think it is ever going to change, so I'd better start getting used to it."

Warren joined in the laughter. As he listened to his father's hearty mirth, a profound sense of peace enveloped Joshua. The hurt that always seemed to be hovering just below the surface was gone, along with the tension and quarrelsome attitude. For once, the gulf between them seemed neither wide nor uncrossable.

"It's my understanding you spent a good part of the evening in the summerhouse last night," Warren said casually.

With a start, Joshua realized his father, too, must have felt the positive change in their relationship, since he took the opportunity to broach another sensitive subject.

"You were standing next to me when I asked the groundskeeper to make sure the house was clean and the interior lights turned on before the party began," Joshua replied evenly. "You should have spoken up if my request made you angry."

"I wasn't angry." Warren's eyes got a misty, faraway gleam. "No one has used the place since your mother died. I have it cleaned and aired periodically. After all, I wouldn't want it to fall into disrepair. But I haven't set foot inside it in five years."

The sadness in his father's eyes deepened. "I wanted to have it torn down. Your mother had been nagging me for years to build it, but we didn't start construction until she became seriously ill. Consequently it reminds me of the end of her life. How she fought and struggled and eventually lost the battle to her disease."

"Why didn't you tear it down?"

"Because it's a piece of your mother. How could I destroy it? Besides, I always suspected you might not appreciate coming down here and finding it was gone."

Joshua battled a hot, stinging sensation behind his eyes. "You live here, Dad. I just visit. And not very often. If the summerhouse was a painful memory, you should have had it removed, taken away."

Warren cleared his throat. "No need to go to such extremes. Who knows, it might make a good playhouse for my grandchildren one day."

Joshua paused in the act of putting his laptop away. "That's the second time you've mentioned grandchildren this weekend."

"Is it?" Warren's brow knit into a frown. "I don't mean to be pressuring you, but seeing you with Eleanor must have subconsciously got me thinking about you settling down."

Guilt sliced through Joshua. Thanks to his deception, his father was definitely under the impression that he and Eleanor had a serious romantic relationship. Perhaps circumstances last night had started turning that lie into the truth, but it was far too early to start making serious plans.

"Hmmm, there's something I need to tell you about Eleanor." Emotion thickened Joshua's voice. "She isn't a librarian."

"She isn't? You could have fooled me. She certainly knows a lot about Rosemary's books."

"What I meant to say is that she isn't primarily a librarian. She's going to school to get her degree and working on Saturdays at the library. But her main job is as a financial analyst at Hamilton, Barton and Jones."

Warren's eyebrows raised suspiciously. "Are you telling me you only have a business relationship with this woman? She isn't your girlfriend?"

"She wasn't before this weekend started." Joshua slumped in his chair. "I initially asked Eleanor to join me because she knew so much about Rosemary's work, but now that I've gotten to know her better I find myself very attracted to her. Yet how can I justify continuing a relationship with her? She works for the firm, and we have a very strict rule against coworkers dating each other."

Warren slapped his palm against his knee. "I told you it was a foolish policy."

Joshua shook his head. "No, Dad, it isn't a foolish policy. It is an inconvenient policy for me, personally, right now, but even if I could change it, I wouldn't."

"You're firm on your commitments, son," Warren said with a trace of pride. "I'll have to give you that much. This policy must have some merit if it holds up to your test. I'm still not convinced, but this is one issue upon which we'll just have to agree to disagree."

"Exactly." Joshua stalked about the room. "Since I've neatly boxed myself into a corner, any ideas on what I should do next?"

Warren leaned forward, an eager grin plastered on his face. "Well, since you asked, I might have one or two opinions I'd be happy to share with you on how to handle this delicate matter."

Eleven

Seven days. Seven days had passed since she had last seen or spoken with Joshua. A full week. Eleanor shuffled the pile of papers on her desk and told herself firmly she was fine with the situation as it stood. After all, she had expected no less.

On the afternoon they had left North Carolina, he had been quiet on the plane ride home. Preoccupied, distant, absorbed in the documents he studied with an ever-widening frown. Occasionally he'd muttered something under his breath and tapped impatiently on the computer keys, but mostly there had been silence inside the aircraft cabin.

She'd thought twice of offering to help, but squashed the notion. If he'd wanted her assistance he would have asked. She told herself repeatedly that she was not disappointed nor heartsick. He had important work to do that was in far greater need of his undivided attention.

Yet the thought stung Eleanor more than she cared to admit.

A car had been waiting for them at the airport when they'd arrived back in the city. That beautiful Bentley, driven by the stiff chauffeur. Joshua had apologetically informed her that he needed to be taken to the office as quickly as possible. He'd calmly assured Eleanor the chauffeur would drive her directly home the moment that task had been completed.

Then Joshua'd picked up his cell phone and started dialing, while Eleanor huddled miserably in the corner of the luxurious car and pretended not to listen.

There had been a fleeting moment when she had caught a glimmer of the incredible man she had come to know over the weekend. The car had pulled curbside, in front of the office building, but Joshua hadn't immediately exited.

He had taken her hands in his and gazed deeply into her eyes. His handsome features had contorted in an expression of unabashed tenderness and she'd waited breathlessly for him to say something.

"I'll never forget this weekend, Eleanor," he had finally uttered. "Thank you so much. For everything."

She'd half expected, half hoped he would lean forward and kiss her. One last memorable embrace to end their time together. Yet feeling the watchful eyes of the chauffeur had made Eleanor realize that wasn't possible.

Joshua had vanished inside the building without a backward glance. Her final, morose thought as the car pulled away and merged into traffic had been at least she had been spared the humiliation of being offered a handshake.

Eleanor rubbed her forehead and glanced down at the spreadsheet on her desk. She had printed it out earlier, and even a cursory scan revealed numerous mistakes. It had been like this all week. Distractions, the inability to concentrate, to make a decision, to follow through on a project had plagued her, and her work had definitely suffered.

Admitting this afternoon would be no different, Eleanor picked up a stack of folders and headed for the copy room. She should have been sending a clerk to do the photocopying, but she needed to lose herself in a mindless task. This one seemed as good as any other.

The hallway was deserted. Yet a sudden, loud commotion at the end of the corridor penetrated her lethargic mood. It sounded like a herd of elephants was tramping her way. Curious, she lifted her head.

That was all the warning she had. And then suddenly, there he was, striding down the hallway, encircled by a group of men. They were having an animated discussion, with several people talking at once.

Joshua raised the volume of his voice slightly, and everyone shut up. They crowded closer to him, hanging on his every word, or at least pretending to. Eleanor saw one man hastily scribbling notes on a pad, while another punched the keys of a handheld electronic device.

As they moved nearer, a wave of panic assailed her. Valiantly she fought it back, nervously moistening her lips. The boisterous group bumped their way down the narrow hallway and Eleanor's heart bumped along with them.

She stood her ground as they drew even closer. Just when she thought she was in real danger of being knocked over, Joshua raised his head.

Their eyes met and held.

She noticed the immediate tension that sprang into his eyes. It cut through her heart like a knife, sharp and painful. *He's embarrassed to see me. And obviously uncomfortable with the idea that I might speak to him, might acknowledge the fact that I know him.*

She forced herself to meet his gaze directly, with as calm and carefree an expression as she could manage.

"Good afternoon, Joshua."

She realized her mistake the moment his name fell from her lips. Calling the managing partner of the firm by his first name in front of a group of curious onlookers was a definite faux pas.

Unfortunately, Eleanor's greeting rang out loud and clear, drawing the immediate attention of the rest of the group. She watched with a sinking feeling of dread as Joshua's eyes darkened . . . with anger?

The sudden silence was overwhelming. The rapt attention previously afforded Joshua by his band of faithful companions increased tenfold. They glanced at her, then at him, then back at her. Clearly, she was not the only person who was interested in his reaction.

This added pressure seemed to have no effect on him. Slowing, but not breaking stride, Joshua resumed the conversation with his companions by asking another question, nodded his head curtly in her direction, and brushed past her, his entourage in tow like a pack of faithful hounds.

The hallway fell silent as they disappeared around the corner. Eleanor felt her knees begin to tremble. She had never in her life been made to feel so small and insignificant. Even at that awkward brunch in his father's house, the guests had managed to acknowledge her existence with a polite greeting.

Now, disgusted by her own cowardice, she longed to charge after him and start shouting her anger and hurt at his betrayal. Instead she lowered her head and trudged slowly in the opposite direction.

Two hours later, back at her desk, Eleanor was still reeling from the encounter. Confusion and pain reigned in her wounded heart. Having nothing to rely on but her common sense, Eleanor questioned both her judgment and her memory.

Had they not just spent a magical weekend together, laughing, talking, making love? Didn't that time together at least earn her the right to expect a polite acknowledgment if they happened upon each other in the workplace, even if others were present?

She knew the rules, the company policy against relationships between coworkers. Like a Bible, the personnel policy had remained on the nightstand by her bed all week, and Eleanor had read and reread that particular passage so many times she could recite it from memory. Yet was it so unreasonable to expect common courtesy from Mr. Joshua Barton? Clearly they had no *relationship* that would violate the all-important firm rules.

"Hey, Eleanor, want to take a break and get a cup of coffee?" Jeanne asked as she walked over and stopped beside Eleanor's desk. "My eyes are starting to cross studying these latest financial reports. I could really go for a cappuccino, and the caffeine boost is practically a medical necessity at this time of day."

"N-no. No thanks. I've got too much to do."

"Okay." Jeanne frowned, then leaned forward, touching the back of Eleanor's hand. "Are you feeling all right? You look very pale."

"I'm fine. Just a little tired." Eleanor attempted a smile. "It's always tough getting motivated on a Monday, especially after last week's crunch."

"I've always hated Mondays, too." Jeanne quirked a smile. "Oh, I forgot to tell you. A letter came while you were away from your desk. Mrs. Jackson, the main man's personal servant, hand-delivered it herself. Guess it must be important."

"A letter?"

"Yeah. I put it right here, on your desk." Jeanne sifted messily though the neat piles on Eleanor's desk, eventually finding the missing note. "Here it is."

A letter from Joshua! Her shattered faith soared with hope. With shaky fingers Eleanor took the note. "Thanks."

Jeanne waited expectantly, but Eleanor merely smiled vaguely. Taking the hint, the other woman finally shrugged her shoulders and left.

Showing remarkable restraint, Eleanor waited until Jeanne walked out the door before savagely ripping open the envelope.

The typed words on company letterhead blurred before her eyes. Blinking rapidly, she stared again at the top of the page, then read quickly, scanning down to Joshua's bold signature at the bottom.

Hands trembling, she read the letter a second, then a third time. Eleanor sagged back against her desk with a hollow laugh. Despite the bone-jarring message, the irony of the moment did not escape her.

She had been telling herself that speculating about Joshua's feelings was a stupid, immature way to handle this situation. What she really needed was a concrete, solid indication of his opinion of her. Well, she had finally gotten her wish, in the form of this oh-so-charming letter.

There was no denying the truth now, for here it was in black and white, stated briefly, coldly, and clearly. Her services were no longer required by the financial firm of Hamilton, Barton and Jones.

She had been fired. Effective immediately.

"You did what?" Joshua clenched his teeth, fighting to keep his anger under control.

Edna Jackson, his executive assistant, stood on the opposite side of his desk and stared blankly at him. "I composed and formatted several official letters from the information notes that were on the computer disk you left on my desk yesterday afternoon. It was all fairly standard stuff, except for the letter to Eleanor Graham."

Edna's voice was calm and steady, yet for the first time in his memory, she looked rattled.

"There wasn't supposed to be a letter to Eleanor Graham," Joshua insisted.

"Obviously I know that now." Edna's brow shot up. "But there was no way to tell that from the notes you left yesterday."

Joshua's eyes locked with hers for a long, tense moment. "Didn't you think to ask me about it? Terminations always come from the personnel department. Didn't you find it odd that this one came directly from me?"

"I did think it was a little strange, but you've been under tremendous pressure since you returned from your trip," Edna replied after a slight pause. "You've been working late every night, preoccupied with far more important matters.

"I considered asking you, but you were busy with meetings all day and I thought you wanted the letter sent immediately. The file did say 'urgent' on the top," she finished defensively.

Joshua's eyes narrowed with suspicion. "You said you typed this yesterday. Tell me again how Eleanor received this letter so quickly."

Edna sighed. "It seemed ridiculous to mail the document to her house. So I brought the sealed letter to her office and left it with one of her team. Clearly she received it, since she didn't come in today."

"As I just unpleasantly discovered when I called and asked her to come up to my office," Joshua said, pressing his fingers to his brow.

The flustered expression on Edna's face deepened. "I checked with security this morning. Eleanor turned in the keys to her desk at five yesterday, along with her laptop and computer disks. I'm not certain what happened to the rest of her papers, the projects she was currently directing. I assume she left them with one of her subordinates, or maybe one of the other financial analysts. I'll make a few calls and find out."

"Don't bother," Joshua said frostily. His hand tensed with the urge to reach for something and fling it across the room in complete frustration. "You have done quite enough already, Edna."

Her spine stiffened. He could see her lower lip tremble slightly. "It was an honest mistake, Joshua, and I apologize if I've unintentionally caused any harm. If you want, I'd be more than willing to apologize to Ms. Graham, too."

"I have to find her first," Joshua muttered under his breath.

His mouth twitched with annoyance as he fought the strong urge to give full vent to his anger. What an unholy mess! Yet Joshua was forced to admit it wasn't entirely Edna's fault. Things never would have reached this point if he hadn't been such a coward, if he had taken control of the situation with Eleanor and resolved it quickly, as his father had advised.

True, this business mess with Weston had been a sensitive issue, a critical problem that needed to be addressed immediately. It had taken a considerable amount of Joshua's time and concentration, far more than he'd originally anticipated.

But now that Weston's resignation was safely in hand, and the federal authorities had been notified of the particulars, he could relax and shift his attentions away from his business problems.

To his personal problems. Namely, Eleanor. He had felt physically ill after the incident in the hallway yesterday. There had been no reasonable explanation for his behavior, for his unpardonable rudeness.

The simple truth was that he had panicked. He had

been caught by surprise by her appearance, and even more shocked by his reaction to her.

She stirred emotions in him that were so foreign, he scarcely recognized them. Both negative, as witnessed yesterday, and positive, as witnessed all last weekend.

Today he had intended to take her out to lunch and dinner and discuss their relationship. Business and personal. The two went hand in hand. Yet if all went according to plan, the problems they presented would be gone by the time they ate breakfast together the next morning, after spending the night together in each other's arms, which was also very much part of his plan.

"I need to leave," Joshua announced. He patted his pants pockets, searching for his car keys, pleased that he had decided to drive into the office on his own today instead of having his driver bring him. "I have no idea when I'll be back. Maybe not until tomorrow, if all goes well."

"Where can I reach you?" Edna asked.

"You can't," Joshua said curtly. "Any problems that turn up here will have to wait until tomorrow. Or until I can get to them. Understood?"

Edna pushed her glasses up to the bridge of her nose. "I can handle things at this end."

Joshua glowered silently at her, needing no words to convey his feelings.

He hastened down to the parking garage, but wisely took a moment to study the road map before pulling out. Eleanor hadn't answered her home phone all morning and the only other place that Joshua knew to look for her was at the library. He reasoned if he couldn't find her there, he'd find her apartment and wait out front in his car for her to get back.

Damage control. That was what was needed today. Thankfully it was an area he had expertise in, but he never thought it would be such a critically necessary skill in a personal relationship.

A horn blared angrily behind him. Joshua glanced up and saw the light had changed from red to green. He blew out his breath and made a sharp right turn, heading for the bridge.

He made the drive to New Jersey in record time, despite the traffic on the bridge and getting lost twice in the suburban neighborhood where the library was located.

Today the library lot was as crowded as it had been the Saturday morning he had first been there, but with quick reflexes and a substantially smaller car, Joshua was able to snatch the last parking space away from a woman driving an overgrown SUV.

The air-conditioned coolness of the building was a welcome relief from the sticky outside warmth. Joshua took a moment to get his bearings. For some reason he expected it to be quiet inside. After all, it was a library.

Yet the main desk was busy, humming with the conversations of the wide assortment of people checking out materials. His first thought was to inquire if Eleanor was there, but it was so crowded he decided he could locate her faster on his own.

He walked through the small archway to the left of the main desk and entered the children's department, where the volume increased considerably.

It was like walking onto an alien spaceship. There seemed to be kids everywhere—sitting in little chairs, banging on computer keyboards, crawling over piles of books. Some were laughing, a few were crying, one was screaming at the top of his lungs. How could you even think in this chaos?

Joshua shifted uncomfortably, feeling the intrusive scrutiny of a woman as she walked past. She gave him the once-over from head to toe, and two things immediately became obvious to him. He was definitely overdressed in his pin-striped suit and shiny leather shoes, and he was also the only male in the room over the age of ten.

But his height advantage gave him a clear view of the room. He scanned anxiously for any sign of Eleanor, feeling a twinge of disappointment when he didn't find her.

Joshua turned to leave, but above the din heard a twinkling female laugh. *Eleanor.* He followed the sound down a narrow row of books, rounded the corner, and found her crouched in a squatting position, pulling books off a bottom shelf.

"Okay, Carol, I've given you every single book we own on humpback whales," Eleanor said with a smile. "Now do you think you have enough material for your report?"

The young girl giggled and lifted one knee to keep the tall stack of books from sliding out of her arms. "I'll go show these to my mom. If we need more stuff, I'll find you."

"I'll be at the reference desk," Eleanor cheerfully replied. She duck-walked a few steps to the left and started rearranging the books on the bottom shelf.

"Hello, Eleanor," he said softly.

Her hands froze. Ever so slowly she turned her head and raised her gaze.

"Joshua?"

The shock made her lose her balance and topple backward. Although she was close to the ground, he could tell she landed hard on her rump by the sound she made when she hit the floor.

"Eleanor!" Joshua rushed forward.

He reached down to help her and she lifted her chin. The look in her eyes warned him to keep his distance.

Despite the cool temperature of the room, Joshua could feel himself starting to sweat.

He had expected her anger, had thought himself prepared to face and diffuse it. But he had also expected to see some of the woman he knew. Her shy blushes, nervous finger twisting, those coveted glances discreetly thrown his way that she thought he wasn't aware of.

Yet there was no sign of the former behavior he had found so charming. She regained her feet awkwardly and faced him squarely.

"Are you lost?" Eleanor folded her arms over her chest. "If you need directions to the city, they have detailed maps in the adult reference department. On the second floor."

"I'm not going anywhere." Joshua leaned against the bookshelf. "We need to talk, Eleanor."

"Oh, no." She shook her head vehemently. "I recognize that stubborn expression on your face all too well. You don't want to talk with me, you want to talk at me. No, thank you."

She turned and fled. He stood in place for a moment. *No, thank you?* He unfroze and doggedly followed her. His initial impression that she wasn't pleased to see him was confirmed when she slipped behind the long, narrow desk, with the sign on front that said, CHILDREN'S REFERENCE AND INFORMATION.

"If you have a question pertaining to children's literature, I'd be happy to answer it. If not, kindly leave." Eleanor raised her chin self-righteously. "I've already been fired from one job this week. I absolutely cannot afford to lose another position."

Ouch. That was a tough one to easily refute. Joshua cleared his throat. "That's one of the reasons I need to talk with you, Eleanor. There's been a mistake. A complete misunderstanding. I never meant for you to be fired."

"Really?" She gave a dismissive snort and turned away. "The letter I received was very emphatic about my termination. I'm certain that I didn't misunderstand the meaning. Plus, your signature was on the letter. I assume you read it. After all, it is a very unsound business practice to sign important documents without first reading them."

Joshua's jaw tightened. "Edna Jackson has been my personal assistant for six years. She can write my signature better than I can. She wrote the letter. And signed it."

Eleanor gave him a disbelieving stare. "What could I ever have possibly done to Mrs. Jackson that would cause her to fire me? I doubt she even has the authority."

"She doesn't have the authority. Edna misunderstood some notes I had made."

"Ah-ha! So the order did come from you."

"It did not," Joshua said briskly. Eleanor sounded so smug. And since her reasoning was logical and partially true, it made him feel like an idiot. "If you would just let me explain, I know you'll agree this was an innocent mistake."

"Excuse me." A young woman with a rambunctious toddler walked up to the desk. She gave Joshua a curious look. "I'm sorry to interrupt, but could you tell me who wrote *The Very Hungry Caterpillar?* I have to read a book to my son's nursery school class and he asked me to bring that one since it's his favorite story."

"Good choice. It's a perfect read-aloud for preschoolers." Eleanor smiled pleasantly at the woman. "Eric Carle wrote that story. We own several copies. I shelved one just this morning. You'll find it in the picture book section, under the first three letters of the author's last name."

"Thank you."

"If you have any trouble, just come and get me and I'll be glad to find it for you."

"Thanks." With a happy nod, the woman and little boy left.

Joshua drew in a breath. "Eleanor—"

"Why don't you have any Ramona books? My friend was here on Saturday and she got two but she said you had a lot. But there aren't any on the shelf."

Joshua glowered at the girl who had so rudely interrupted him, but she didn't even notice him.

"Beverly Cleary writes the Ramona stories," Eleanor explained. "Did you look in the fiction section under *C-l-e* for the books?"

The youngster rolled her eyes. "I know Beverly Cleary is the author. And I know how to find the books on the shelf. I looked, but you don't have any Ramona books."

Eleanor tapped her chin thoughtfully with her finger. "Which shelves were you looking on?"

"Those." The girl swung her arm and pointed to the far side of the room.

"Ahhh, I see the problem. That section is for picture books. You need to search in the fiction area. Let me show—"

"I know where it is," the girl insisted, stomping off.

"Nice kid. Excellent manners," Joshua muttered sarcastically. "If she acts like that at this age, I can only imagine how charming she'll be when she's a teenager."

Eleanor shrugged, but he could see the twinkle of amusement in her eye. Maybe she was beginning to lose some of her anger. "Eleanor, you've got to give me a chance to explain about this mix-up. Our relationship is too important, too special to be thrown away over a misunderstanding."

"We do not have a relationship, Joshua," she retorted in a bitter voice. "You just don't—"

Eleanor abruptly stopped. The rigidity left her body and she seemed to visibly soften before his eyes. Joshua grinned with delight, then realized she was focusing her attention on someone else, someone standing behind him.

He whirled around and saw a timid boy slowly creeping near the desk. His eyes were darting to and fro and it looked like a loud noise would make him take off like a shot. When he got closer to her, Eleanor bent low, meeting him at eye level.

"Can I help you find something?" she asked in a gentle tone.

The child's eyes grew big and round and for a moment Joshua thought he would turn and bolt. But he swallowed hard and asked in a whisper, "Do you have a Mexican dictionary?"

Eleanor's expression grew serious. "The people in Mexico speak Spanish," she said in that same gentle tone. "I bet you're doing that assignment for Mrs. Field's class, where you have to write the days of the week the way a schoolboy in Mexico would say them."

The boy broke into a relieved smile and nodded his head enthusiastically. "I have my homework sheet." He held up a crumpled piece of paper.

"Great. I have the perfect book for you." She reached behind the desk and pulled out a short, thick book. "If you look up the word in English, the Spanish translation is next to it. Let's try the first one together."

The boy practically sat in Eleanor's lap as they huddled over the book together. For a moment Joshua envied the child. Given Eleanor's current mood, there was no way in hell that Joshua could get that close to her.

"That's easy," the boy proclaimed with delight.

Eleanor smiled. "I knew you could do it. I don't think you'll need it, but if you want any more help, please ask me."

The boy clutched the book to his chest and replied confidently, "Thank you, Miss Graham."

As soon as the youngster left, Eleanor turned her attention back to Joshua. The pleasant expression immediately left her face. "As you can see, I'm very busy. There really isn't anything more for us to say to each other. I'd appreciate it if you would leave. Now."

Joshua frowned. He had never realized what an obstinate, hardheaded woman she could be. Of all the times for her to start exercising her independent streak! Yet this new discovery served to only raise her higher in his esteem.

He never liked women who were too meek and agreeable. During the weekend they had spent together he had needed her to be accommodating and supportive, but now he was more than willing to concede that she had a right to her anger and indignity. Even though it was proving to be a royal pain in the butt for him, Joshua was glad she had the guts to stand up to him.

"I'll leave, but just to be fair, I'm warning you." Joshua focused on Eleanor's face. "I'll be back."

Twelve

"Ready for some dinner?"

Joshua's voice cut through Eleanor's troubled thoughts. He stood in the library parking lot, arms folded casually across his chest, one hip braced against the hood of an expensive sports car. His, no doubt.

Eleanor's eyes narrowed. Part of her was surprised to find him out there, waiting for her, yet another part told her it was to be expected. She had actually said no to him, had refused to listen to his explanations. He was probably in mild shock over the event.

Besides, he had warned her that he wasn't going anywhere.

"What kind of food are you in the mood to eat?" Joshua asked, pushing himself away from the car. "Chinese, Italian? How about Mexican? If you bring that dictionary along we can translate the menu before we order our meal."

"I'm not hungry," Eleanor retorted, deliberately sidestepping him. She lifted her chin and walked briskly to her car.

Joshua's hand was on the door handle before she could get her key in the lock. "Stop running away from me, Eleanor."

Her mouth opened with a ready retort, but the words

never passed her lips. He was right. She was running away. And this whole mess apparently wouldn't be resolved until she stopped.

"Okay, we'll talk. But there's no need to bully me."

"I've hardly been doing that."

"You certainly have, but I'm sure your elevated level of testosterone has completely marred your judgment." Eleanor opened the car door, reached inside, and flipped the switch that unlocked the passenger-side door. "Get in."

He stared down at her. Something in his expression made her heart lurch. He looked like a little boy who'd just been caught raiding the cookie jar. She told herself she was glad her words had some impact on him, but a corner of her conscience cried out.

Had she gone too far? He looked almost wounded by her comments. *Stop it,* Eleanor commanded herself. Her nerves were starting to gain control of her emotions, and that could lead to real disaster. Despite the revelations she had reached about her nonexistent future prospects with Joshua, the feelings he evoked in her were strong and powerful.

It wouldn't be wise to remain in his company for very long.

Her door slammed after he got in the car. The seat was positioned forward and his knees bumped against the dashboard. His physical presence seemed overwhelming in the small space.

"As I tried to tell you before, your letter of termination was a complete mistake." Joshua turned toward her, flashing his killer, Prince-Charming smile. "If you want, you can have your old job back."

"Ha!" She cast him a sneering look. "If I hire myself a shark attorney with a track record and a taste for blood, I can have your whole damn company."

The grin disappeared. Joshua looked at her in genuine disbelief. "That was a very nasty remark."

"Not uncalled-for, however," she scoffed, her face warming. "I was treated shabbily by the firm, for no apparent reason, other than sleeping with the boss. I'm not feeling particularly charitable right now."

"I'm really sorry about this mess. It's entirely my fault." Joshua placed his hand over hers.

Eleanor gripped the steering wheel tightly. His touch still had the power to turn her insides to the consistency of warm oatmeal and her vulnerability terrified her.

"What can I do to make this right?" he asked.

"Nothing." The discussion was starting to get dangerous. His sincere regret was lessening her righteous anger, and Eleanor knew she needed it to complete the conversation.

"I was given a termination package from the human resources department yesterday. You're very generous with former employees." A thread of irony crept into her voice. "I explained my change of circumstances to the library director this morning. Fortunately there is enough money in the budget for her to add additional hours to my current schedule.

"Working part-time here will allow me to go to school full-time. Being suddenly fired forced me to make a career change a little sooner than I planned, but now I'll be a professional by the end of the year."

She felt his hesitancy. "How are you fixed financially?" he finally asked. "Do you need any money?"

Eleanor told herself that she was not going to get angry. Or insulted. He was trying to help. This was probably how wealthy individuals dealt with difficulties. They solved a problem by throwing money at it.

"Believe it or not, the county will help pay my school tuition. I have a healthy savings account that I can dip into to supplement my modest salary." Eleanor's lips tightened into a stubborn line. "My overall expenses are modest and I know how to economize. I'll manage."

A flush stained his cheeks. "I guess it would be stupid to suggest I pay your living expenses while you're attending school?"

"You guessed right." For the first time Eleanor smiled. She knew it was wrong to enjoy Joshua's discomfort, but she had suffered enough over the past week to get a lift from it.

"Well, at least one good thing came out of all of this mess." Joshua sidled as close as the center console would allow. "Since you're no longer my employee, the company rules against dating aren't an issue. We can concentrate on our relationship without any outside distractions."

Two weeks ago she would have sold her soul to hear him say those words. Up until yesterday afternoon she would have believed what he was offering was too good to pass up. But no longer.

For years, she had been completely mesmerized by the idea of Joshua. The man she had built up in her mind, the one she had formed a restless infatuation with, was a perfect, infallible male icon. Discovering Joshua's feet of clay as he ignored her completely in the hallway yesterday had not only surprised, but hurt her.

She was honest enough to admit that it wasn't entirely his fault. No human being is perfect and truly no person could have lived up to the expectations she had created in her mind. Yet it was like being suddenly awakened from an incredible dream, and she harbored a trace of resentment toward the man who had jolted her away from her fantasy.

"There is no relationship, Joshua."

There was confusion in his eyes. "I know you have feelings for me, Eleanor."

She blushed. "The feelings I had, or thought I had, were all based on a myth. An inflated, unrealistic view I had of you. It wasn't fair to me or you."

"You can't deny that we had a special time together. It meant something to me."

"Yes, it was special." Eleanor sighed and turned away, finding the intensity in his gaze unnerving. "But the reality was, we did everything that weekend exactly the way you wanted. You set the rules, from lying to your father about me being your girlfriend to the dress I wore to the party.

"As I told you more than once, I was just along for the ride. You were in control the entire time. It makes sense that you would now think it was very special, that I was special. Who wouldn't be thrilled to have a companion who catered to their every whim? Who was agreeable, quickly made concessions, did whatever was necessary to appease?"

A shadow crossed his face. "It wasn't like that," Joshua protested.

Eleanor shook her head. "Yes it was. I'm not complaining. I had an incredible time, and I'll never forget it. But it wasn't based on reality. At least not the reality of who I am."

He turned his head and forced her to meet his gaze. Their eyes locked, and something dark flashed between them. "That is pure bullshit."

"That's reality."

Eleanor's posture grew more rigid and she held her face carefully expressionless. It was the truth, though not perhaps the entire truth. He could still arouse emotions and feelings in her with a simple smile, but she wouldn't be so easily won over.

"You're afraid," he whispered in amazement. "It isn't me you doubt, but yourself."

Eleanor squirmed uncomfortably in her seat. "Spare me the psychoanalysis."

He glared over at her. "It's the truth. You're afraid, so you're running away."

"Oh, please. You sound like a badly written article in a teen magazine."

He regarded her in silence for a long moment. "If you're not afraid of a relationship between us, then prove it. Have dinner with me."

Eleanor shook her head sadly. "I don't have to prove anything, Joshua."

He got a calculating look on his face that made her shiver. Eleanor inched slowly away from him, pressing her forehead against the edge of the warm glass of her half-opened window.

"I'm not willing to walk away from this so easily," Joshua declared flatly.

"You have no choice."

"There are always choices, Eleanor."

The conversation was turning serious and obstinate. Eleanor glanced over at Joshua and felt slightly better when she saw a spark of mischief in his eyes. But she forced herself to ignore that hopeful glimmer.

Reminding herself it was for the best, she spoke the words that were swirling in her head. And yet even before they left her lips, she felt enveloped in a strange sense of loss.

"I've thought long and hard about this situation. Our backgrounds are too dissimilar, our expectations of life too opposite. The feelings and emotions we've experienced might be enticing, but they aren't enough. I've made up my mind. It would be a mistake for us to even attempt a relationship."

He opened the car door and exited without a word. Eleanor's fingers tightened on the steering wheel as confusion gripped her. This was for the best, right?

He stalked over to the driver's side of the car and leaned inside her window. "So, you've made up your mind about us?"

She nodded briskly.

"Well, sugar, it looks like I'll just have to change it."

The shrill ring of the phone echoed through Eleanor's apartment. Out of habit, she glanced over at the digital clock, but it wasn't necessary. She already knew it would read seven P.M.

She let the phone ring again, then a third time, took a deep breath, and lifted the receiver.

"It's me," a deep masculine voice said.

"I know. Hello, Joshua."

"How are you?"

"Just fine. And yourself?"

"Lonely."

Then get a dog. Or a girlfriend. Tonight she nearly said it, just to push his temper, but perversely admitted to herself that she didn't want him to follow either suggestion.

"What's new at the library?"

Eleanor sighed. He always began these nightly calls with the same questions. She hesitated, then finally blurted out what she had been thinking all week. "I can't believe you are honestly interested in what went on at the library."

His tone turned serious. "If it affects you, I'm interested. I enjoy hearing about your day." He cleared his throat and the tone changed again—to upbeat, amused.

"Tell me, what was the most difficult question you answered today?"

Eleanor twisted the cord around her index finger. "It wasn't exactly difficult, but I had a tough time convincing a third grader that I didn't have any books with a photograph of a woolly mammoth."

Joshua laughed. "No photographs! What sort of establishment are you running, Ms. Graham?"

She smiled. "Not a very good one, according to this child. I showed him at least a dozen books with drawings and sketches, but he kept insisting on a photograph. He was very disappointed. I tried to explain, but I don't think he believed me when I said there weren't any cameras several million years ago."

"Poor kid. You should have told him all the photos were destroyed when the earth froze."

Eleanor shrugged and leaned against the cushioned arm of her couch. "He still took his disappointment better than the argument I had with a woman who wanted a library card. She told me she lived in a different town, but she owned land in our community and was entitled to a card. But when I asked to see a tax bill to prove that she pays property taxes, she didn't have one. Turns out she owns a cemetery plot."

"She equated a cemetery plot with owning land?"

"Apparently." Eleanor could hear the smile in Joshua's voice, could imagine it on his handsome face. A real, open, warm grin that made his beautiful eyes dance. "I tried to explain the rules to this woman, but she wasn't listening. Finally I told her she won't be entitled to a card until she actually takes up residence in our community. She didn't think that was very amusing."

"Impressive. Are you always so tough?"

"Oh, I'm a real people person," she retorted lightly. Eleanor reached for the tall glass of lemonade she had fixed earlier and took a sip. "I saw the article in the *Times* this morning about Mr. Weston being indicted by a federal grand jury. Is everything all right?"

"I've got it all under control," Joshua replied firmly. "I was aware ahead of time that this was coming. The firm will have limited liability in the case and hopefully limited publicity."

"I'm glad," Eleanor whispered. And she was. No matter what her jumbled feelings toward Joshua were, she had never truly wished him or the company any harm.

"Okay, enough about that. What are you wearing?"

"Joshua!" Eleanor laughed into the phone, marveling at how easily he could surprise her. Still, the erotic timbre of his voice made his question seem wickedly forbidden.

"Come on, throw me a crumb, Eleanor. What are you wearing?"

She glanced down at the oversized T-shirt and baggy shorts she had on. "Support hose, sensible black shoes, a gray dress with a high ruff collar and a hem that hangs below my knees."

"Is your hair tied up in a bun?"

"Naturally." Eleanor giggled. The man was impossible!

"Mmmmmm. Sexy. I like your hair piled up tight on your head. It looks so prim and proper. Makes it all the more fun to try and muss you up. Let's see, first I'd take down that hair, pulling the pins out slowly, one by one. When they were finally gone, I'd massage your neck and make you shake the curls loose. Doesn't that feel better, sugar?"

The hint of Southern twang in his voice had her sliding down on the couch. What should she do? Just one icy comment would completely kill the mood. The words hovered on her lips, but she hesitated. Should she be daring and play along?

"I-it does feel better. My hair. Hanging loose."

Eleanor covered her mouth and groaned. She sounded like a moron.

"Good. Now we need to get rid of those shoes. I must confess, I've never liked the boxy, square-toe style on you. I like to see you wearing thin, spike heels. In red. Shows off those great calf muscles."

"I'd fall off heels that high and thin and break my ankle," Eleanor replied dryly, then winced, thinking she had unintentionally killed the mood.

"Perfect. I'd catch you as you fell. At this point, I'll take any excuse to hold you in my arms."

Eleanor slowly let out her breath. Nice save. Yet the silence on the other end of the line told her Joshua was waiting for her to say something. "W-what next?"

The deep growl he made was pure male excitement. "The support hose have got to go. But I'd peel them off slow and easy, letting my fingers glide over those smooth legs of yours, massaging your tired muscles until you were sighing with pleasure. Then I'd move higher, searching until I found that sweet, soft spot at the top of your inner thigh."

"Oh my," Eleanor whispered, as she felt the heat spread across her face. And other parts of her anatomy.

"Would you like that, darlin'? I know you would, so I'd keep at it, circling the same spot, lazily. Then your eyes would drift close. I'd start moving my fingers higher and higher, until I heard that catch in your breath, the little cry of excitement that lets me know how much you need me, how much you want me."

Eleanor's nipples sprang to erect attention. Sensations she thought she'd never experience again with Joshua started coursing through her. She knew if she protested he would stop at once, yet she felt helpless to resist the deep, sensual timbre of his voice.

"Could I have a kiss?" she whispered in a small voice.

He groaned. "A dozen. To start. First your sweet lips. I love the taste of your soft breath, the warmth of your tongue, that rumbling noise you make deep in the back of your throat. Then I'd let my lips travel, kissing you all over, sinking my mouth into your pale flesh until your skin starts to burn, until your body starts to soften.

"My hands would wander, too, and I'd stroke you gently, lightly where you are sweet and scented and made just for me. And I'd wait, anticipating that joyous moment when you'd start to make that purring, pleasured sound that tells me you are near the peak of your climax."

Eleanor could hear herself panting. Her knuckles brushed against her neck and she could feel the heat on her skin, could almost imagine that it was Joshua's firm lips caressing her fevered flesh.

"You're just playing with me," she croaked out.

"Ahh, sugar, you are my favorite toy. Unique, precious, irreplaceable. The only one I refuse to share with anyone."

His toy? The whimper of need that was shuddering in her throat stilled. She waited for the anger and outrage to take hold, but his voice drifted over her indignation.

"I'd swing you on top of me, sprawled naked across my chest, so I could give myself the sheer pleasure of watching you move, so I could see as well as feel your body clamp down around me. Rising up a little faster and thrusting down a little harder."

She bit her lip, tensing with expectation. He seemed to possess the power to so easily tap below the surface of her proper self and transform her into the passionate woman lurking inside. She had never tried the position he was suggesting, even though it had always intrigued her. How had he known?

Her mind formed a picture of them together. Joshua on his back, with her astride him. Their bodies joined tightly together, the heat surrounding them. Eleanor could almost feel the passion mounting, as she imagined his hands on her breasts, teasing her nipples to hard peaks, her thighs quivering tightly each time he surged up to fill her.

"If I'm on top, I'm in control," Eleanor gulped.

"Sure you are," he whispered seductively. "Completely in control. Of me, of us. And that's where you'll stay, as I fill your swollen flesh fully and deeply. Your back arched, your lovely face etched with passion, the climax building harder and faster until you sob my name in pure satisfaction."

Eleanor barely managed to refrain from grinding her teeth. Her body felt alive with excitement, throbbing with need. She was drowning in a sensual onslaught brought on by his suggestive words, the mesmerizing way he spoke them, and the incredible images they produced.

She remembered reading in a woman's magazine once that satisfying lovemaking was just as much a mental fulfillment as a physical release. She believed that now.

There was nothing on the other end of the line except the sound of harsh, deep, masculine breaths, telling Eleanor that Joshua was still on the phone.

"Wow. I think I need a cigarette," she said weakly. "And I don't even smoke."

"Hell, Eleanor, I can be at your apartment in forty-five minutes." His voice was harsh, raspy. "Thirty-five if I disregard the speed limit."

"I don't think that would be wise." Eleanor blinked rapidly. What had she done? "It's getting late and I . . . ah . . . have to go."

He made a noise that sounded like steam escaping a radiator. Eleanor's heart started thudding. "Good night, Joshua."

Without waiting for a reply, she promptly hung up the phone.

Joshua heard the definitive click. It wasn't a surprise, more of a disappointment. He had pushed her as far as he dared for tonight. Gently he punched the Off button on his portable phone and placed it on his desk.

He inhaled a ragged breath. His body was singing with sexual tension, so hard and aroused it was almost painful. She was killing him!

It was no contest. There had never been another woman in his life who excited him as much, who made him feel so alive and eager. She had something totally unique to offer him and no matter what it took, he was determined to get it.

He never had to try very hard to get women, never worked very hard at keeping them once he had them. Since his teenage years, women had always seemed to be easily and conveniently in his path.

Maybe this was what had been missing from his other relationships. The courting rituals. Joshua had actually started to enjoy the novelty of it, had been enticed and intrigued by the chase. Especially since Eleanor presented such a challenge. She wouldn't be impressed by the obvious gestures, was in fact consciously resisting his advances.

And resisting, he was convinced, her own feelings. Joshua was slightly miffed that after a week of nightly phone conversations she was still refusing to see him. But he was very determined to change that—and soon.

He needed a new plan of pursuit. One that would bring him in physical contact with her. He needed the added advantage of being able to attract her attention as well as being able to witness her reactions. She wasn't very adept at hiding her true feelings, and he was counting on that honesty to guide him in his quest to win her over.

After a discrete knock, the door to his study opened.

"Dinner is ready, Mr. Barton. Would you like it served in here instead of the dining room? I can bring a tray in for you."

Joshua glanced up in confusion at his middle-aged housekeeper. She had probably been placating his temperamental cook for the past half hour. Yet the last thing on Joshua's mind right now was food.

"I'm not very hungry this evening. Please extend my apologies to Cook. I'm sure she has gone to a great deal of trouble, as always, but I couldn't do justice to a meal. Have a plate made up that can be reheated in an hour or so. I'll ring when I want it."

He waited until his housekeeper had left before slowly rising to his feet. He was still excited by the thought of Eleanor, as evidenced by his physical arousal. With a grim smile he headed toward his private bath, intent on doing something he hadn't done in years.

Take a long, ice-cold shower.

Thirteen

The tables were covered with books and puzzle pieces, scraps of paper and small pencils, piles of videotapes and stuffed animals. Two small chairs were tipped over and one of the computer screens was obviously malfunctioning, blinking a nearly blinding pattern over and over.

"It looks like a cyclone blew through here," Rosalind commented wryly.

"The Peterson triplets." Eleanor grinned at Rosalind, a fellow library assistant, as they surveyed the damage wrought to the children's section. "Even with their mother, an aunt, and a grandmother along those three boys managed to destroy the place in ten minutes flat. A new record."

"Did they at least check out any books?"

"No." Eleanor laughed. "Mrs. Peterson couldn't find her library card, and the triplets had reached their breaking point. I selected a few titles I thought the boys would enjoy and left a stack of books at the circulation desk for her. She said she'd try to come back later to check them out. Without the kids."

"Poor woman." Rosalind shook her head. "I only have one toddler at home and she runs me ragged."

Eleanor smiled in sympathy, remembering the chaos that occurred the time Rosalind had brought her energetic daughter to the library. "I agree that Mrs. Peterson usually looks exhausted, but she told me once that she and her husband had tried for six years to have a family. Thanks to a successful fertility procedure the boys were born. She may be bone-tired much of the time, but she seems so thrilled to finally have children, I don't think she minds."

"All I can say is, better her than me," Rosalind quipped with a small shudder.

Eleanor's gut reaction was agreement, yet as she tossed a few toys into the toy box, her thoughts drifted to families and babies and the lengths some people were forced to go to in order to achieve their dreams. The Petersons' situation was all too common these days. Would she be willing to do that much to have a baby if she found herself unable to conceive?

She honestly didn't know. Yet when she tried to imagine a dream family, Joshua's handsome face popped into the role of proud papa.

Eleanor groaned softly. Those nightly calls were starting to have an effect. Try as she might, she could not keep him from invading her thoughts at odd, unexpected moments.

Eleanor lifted a stack of picture books and headed for the shelves. She glanced at the title on the top of the pile and shivered. *All Different Kinds of Daddies*.

The fantasy swirling in her head took flight. What sort of parent would Joshua be? Would he be involved in his children's lives or would he be too busy with business to spend much time with them?

And what of her? Would she take to motherhood with the patience of Mrs. Peterson, or would she be flustered, nervous, unsure? Eleanor liked children, that was one reason she had decided to work with them, but she had little experience with or knowledge of newborns. They were mysterious and rather terrifying entities.

But there would be extended family to help. Her own mother would be joyous over the prospect of becoming first a mother-in-law and then a grandmother. And what child wouldn't adore having as a grandparent the talented author Rosemary Phillips, whose wonderful stories celebrated the joys and trials of childhood?

Even the gruff Warren Barton seemed enthusiastic over the idea of having a grandchild or two to spoil. Eleanor remembered he had made several references to the lack of them during her visit.

She could envision the children playing on the beautiful grounds of the Barton estate, swimming in the pool, the ocean, riding horses, building sandcastles on the beach. Surrounded by love and laughter.

But the fantasy turned dark as Eleanor tried to imagine herself raising a child in an environment of great wealth and privilege, where she felt uncomfortable and out of place, self-conscious and insecure. What sort of mother would she be then?

"What's next?"

Rosalind's cheerful voice brought reality crashing back. Eleanor almost felt relieved to escape those disturbing daydreams.

"The community day camp is bringing over three groups of campers for a video program," Eleanor replied, consulting her watch. "They should be here in an hour. I've already brought the projector and films into the program room. Would you check and make sure the electronic equipment is connected correctly? This is the first time I've done it on my own and I want to make sure it works properly."

"No problem." Rosalind picked up the remaining puzzle pieces and fitted them neatly into place. "The

Play button on the video machine has a tendency to stick, so I'll be sure it's not jamming. There's nothing more horrifying than being trapped in a roomful of kids all psyched up to see movies and having the projector break."

"Sounds dangerous."

"It can be."

With a laugh and a wave, Rosalind left. Eleanor retreated to the office she now shared with two other librarians, who were currently at lunch. She was just starting to make a dent in the stack of professional journals on her desk when she heard a familiar voice.

Eleanor peeked around the corner of the opened office door and saw the library director headed toward her.

Good, Eleanor thought. The director had mentioned earlier in the morning that a new volunteer would be starting today. It looked like she would now be able to get that person started on a few basic projects before the campers arrived.

"I was hoping I'd find you here," a no-nonsense female voice declared. "I've brought someone down for you to meet."

Eleanor turned away from the material she had been sorting with a ready smile on her lips for the woman who had been so kind and supportive when she'd needed it most.

"This is our newest volunteer, who specifically requested work in the children's department," the director continued. "Joshua Barton, meet Eleanor Graham."

The director stepped aside and the smile on Eleanor's face instantly disappeared. *It couldn't be!* But of course it was. Looking tall, commanding, and impossibly handsome. For a brief instant she fought the impulse to break into nervous giggles.

When it became obvious Eleanor wasn't going to be

speaking anytime soon, Joshua broke the awkward silence.

"How are you, Eleanor?"

"I've been better, Joshua."

The director's eyebrows rose. "Do you two already know each other?"

Eleanor could feel her face burning. "Did Mr. Barton fail to mention that I used to work for his company? For nearly six years. Then one day I was rather unexpectedly fired."

"No, he did not mention it," the director replied. She glanced suspiciously at Joshua. "Is that going to present a problem for you, Eleanor?"

"Not at all." She straightened her spine and cinched the belt on her dress a little tighter. "It will be a refreshing role reversal, having Mr. Barton under my supervision. Unless he has a problem with the arrangement?"

She looked him directly in the eyes. He was smiling, but she could see a small muscle dancing in the corner of his mouth. Good. It was about time someone let him know he couldn't command everything in his path like some demented dictator.

The library director regarded them thoughtfully. "If you're sure this is acceptable, then I'll leave you to get started. Call me if you need anything, Eleanor. Anything at all."

Eleanor managed to hold onto her pleasant facial expression until the director left. Then she turned to Joshua.

"What kind of joke are you playing now?" Eleanor asked, leveling an accusing finger at his broad chest.

"Please, give me a minute," Joshua replied, with a lazy, half-formed grin that was so sexy and intimate it made Eleanor's knees weaken. "I'm still trying to shake off the mental image of being under you."

"My God, is that all you ever think about?" Eleanor asked tersely.

"Not at all. Other positions intrigue me, too."

Thankfully he didn't elaborate, but his smoldering grin filled with sexual promise had Eleanor squirming with embarrassment.

"I want to see you, Eleanor. You keep refusing my invitations to dinner. To lunch. For coffee." Joshua crinkled his nose. "And as much as I look forward to and enjoy our nightly phone conversations, they just aren't enough."

Eleanor flushed scarlet, remembering the sexual nature of their phone call last night. She tried to hold herself rigid, but the memories made that impossible. With just the power of his words and the timbre of his voice he had created visual images that made her feel passion and excitement.

She had spent a sleepless night, restless, unsettled, her mind and heart filled with an unbearable sense of longing.

"Becoming a volunteer for the library is hardly a viable solution," she insisted.

He folded his arms across his chest, regarding her with a look that she swore was amusement. "You aren't giving me many options. Volunteering at the library for a few hours a week will at least give me an opportunity to see you. It sure beats the heck out of becoming a stalker, which was my second choice."

Eleanor stared at him. "It's hard to be inconspicuous stalking someone while you're being squired around in a chauffeur-driven Bentley," she said dryly.

"Give me some credit." He gave her such a long, exaggerated look of despair, she knew he was teasing. "I would never involve my staff in an illegal activity. I drove myself to the library today."

A NIGHT TO REMEMBER

Eleanor bit her lip to keep the smile from forming on her lips. She would not be amused, nor charmed by him. With determination she walked toward the windows that faced the parking lot and looked out, scanning the neat rows of cars. "Red Ferrari, right? I stand corrected. You'd make an excellent stalker, completely inconspicuous in that sports car."

"You're not listening. Stalking was my second choice. I haven't done it yet." His expression turned hopeful. "If you want, I can give it a try."

She almost gasped as another slow, sexy smile of delight crossed his face. The rat. There was nothing worse than a handsome, virile man who knew how potent his sex appeal could be.

"No thanks." She returned to her desk and started busying herself with a stack of papers. He was right on her heels, like an annoying car salesman.

"What do you want me to do?"

"Go home," Eleanor answered automatically.

"I can't do that. I've agreed to work and I intend to honor my commitment."

"Stop being ridiculous," Eleanor said scornfully. "Our volunteers are usually teenagers who need to do community service for their church or school, or retired seniors who want something useful to occupy some of their free time."

Joshua bristled. "I can have just as much civic pride as anyone else."

"Oh, please." Eleanor rolled her eyes. "You don't live in this community. You don't even live in this state. How much civic pride can you possibly have? Why don't you write out a big fat check instead? I'm sure the library could put the funds to good use."

"I'd be pleased to make a donation," Joshua replied

smoothly. "But that won't change my mind about the volunteer work. I'm staying."

Eleanor nearly screamed and stomped her foot, all the while itching to hurl something big and heavy directly at his head. She felt completely frustrated. Flattered more than she would ever admit by this attention, this persistence, yet totally confused by it, too. But worst of all, she was feeling utterly powerless.

"You're breaking the rules," she hissed at him.

A frown creased his brow. "I didn't know there were any."

She gave him her best cut-out-the-crap stare, then started shifting from foot to foot when he didn't even flinch. It took her aback for a moment. There was something vaguely disturbing about his even-tempered manner in the face of her anger. It made her want to push and prod him until he reacted as she expected. But nothing she said or did seemed to set him off.

"There is no relationship between us," Eleanor said firmly. Joshua's calm persistence was fraying her already taut nerves. "I've already explained my feelings and reasons. They haven't changed."

His chiseled features clouded. "Your reasons are a bunch of bull and I'm not buying it. I plan on using any means necessary to change your mind. Haven't you ever heard the expression, 'All's fair in love and war'?"

"This is neither," she huffed, crossing her arms defensively.

"It sure feels like a war from this side." Joshua stiffened, his set expression emphasizing his determination. "You refuse to go out with me, and if this is the only way I can spend time with you, then this is what I'll do."

Eleanor threw up her hands in disgust. There would be no changing his mind. Fine. If he wanted to work there, then so be it. Her eyes seethed with the frustration of all the emotions she couldn't put into words, but she commanded herself to let them go.

Compressing her lips, she glanced at his clothes. He wasn't wearing a suit or a tie, but the neatly pressed slacks and cotton shirt were equally inappropriate for this environment.

So he thinks he wants to work here? She smiled grimly, wondering how enthusiastic he would be when some child accidentally dropped glue on those expensive leather shoes.

"If you won't listen to reason, there's nothing else I can say or do," Eleanor retorted ungraciously, barely managing to stop short of glowering.

She normally wasn't such a surly loser, but she was getting sick and tired of Joshua always getting his way. This was precisely the sort of problem, she contended, that made a relationship between them impossible.

"Maybe my motivation for volunteering is different from the norm, but I'm both able and willing to work." Joshua glanced around nervously. "I won't . . . umm, have to do anything directly with the children, will I? Like read stories?"

For a moment she was thrown by the glimmer of vulnerability in his eyes. There was a rush to her heart that felt strangely like tenderness, but she squelched it. Finally, she had discovered something that seemed to crack that ultracompetent veneer.

"Don't you like kids?"

"I don't dislike children," he clarified slowly. "But I know very little about them. I'm an only child, remember? No nieces or nephews to practice my child-friendly skills on."

"Then you shouldn't be working in the children's department," Eleanor declared, determined to exploit this marginal weakness. "I can send you up to the adult reference department or, better still, the technical services division. They work behind the scenes. You won't come in contact with any library patrons, only staff members. I noticed several cartons of books were delivered today, and an extra pair of hands is always welcome."

"That rather defeats the whole purpose of my being here," Joshua responded firmly.

Eleanor sighed. The discussion had come full circle and she was in exactly the same position she had been when it started, stuck with Joshua as a volunteer. The irony of that was not lost on her.

"How are your cutting skills?" Eleanor asked, giving into the inevitable yet hoping once he realized the type of simple jobs he would be asked to do, he'd change his mind. "The volunteers pre-cut the crafts for our programs. I'm sure you'll find that job riveting and intellectually stimulating."

His gaze rambled over her body. "As long as I'm near you while I'm working, I'll be stimulated enough."

She let out a sigh that was part frustration, part excitement. How would she ever be able to concentrate on anything with him around, when one sultry glance had her heart kicking nervously against her ribs? She probably would have found that flicker of admiration in his eyes demeaning coming from any other man, but not from him.

Beyond Joshua's head she could see the story room door move the barest fraction. "Okay, Mr. Volunteer, here's your first task. Seems like I've got some curious kids fooling around in the story room."

He turned, then nodded his head, apparently understanding where she was indicating.

"I'd like you to go and chase whoever is in there out, and make sure they stay out of the room. If they've messed up the books and puppets, which I'm sure they have, put the materials back in their designated locations. All the cupboards are clearly marked, so you shouldn't have any difficulty figuring out where everything belongs."

She pushed past him out of the office and headed in the opposite direction.

"Where are you going?"

The slight edge of panic she detected in his voice brought the first real smile to her lips. "I've got to check on the video equipment for my program. But don't worry. As you are so fond of saying, I'll be back." She turned her head, smiled sweetly, and without breaking stride added, "Eventually."

Joshua hefted the heavy stack of books onto the top shelf and lined them neatly along the edge, precisely as Eleanor had shown him. He flexed his shoulder muscles and reached for a second pile, surprised at how heavy they were. If he kept this up for a few weeks, he could cut his workout time in his home gym in half.

Once the books were all correctly aligned, he glanced over at the story room, verifying that the door remained closed. When he had gone in the room earlier, as ordered by Eleanor, he had discovered two energetic youngsters busily rifling through the books and puppets stacked on the shelves. They had shrieked with terror at his arrival, before he had even had a chance to ask them to stop.

Hearing the children's screams had brought their mother charging through the door, glaring at him like he was some sort of monster intent on brutal harm. Only his bright red volunteer badge had saved him. After seeing that he was in fact a member of the staff, the mother had left in a huff, shepherding her dear wee ones away from the *nasty man,* oblivious to the fact that if she had been keeping an eye on her kids in the first place, the incident never would have occurred.

Years of dealing with employees, clients, and competitors might have given him some keen insight and excellent instincts toward people, but they were useless in this environment of children and their mothers.

Joshua took another glance at the story room door and started on the next section of shelving. A tingle of awareness crept up his spine and he experienced the distinct feeling of being closely watched.

Preparing a sultry smile, he lifted his head, but instead of encountering Eleanor's lovely face, he found himself returning the stare of a little boy, possibly four, maybe five or even six years old. Having no frame of reference made it difficult for Joshua to judge.

"What are you doin'?" the child asked, coming closer.

"Moving the books."

"Can I help?"

The eager, hopeful look on the boy's face canceled the immediate urge to refuse. "Maybe when I reach the lower shelf you can place a few of the books on the bottom," Joshua replied, hoping the child would lose interest by then.

No such luck. Ten minutes later, the kid was still hanging around, chattering up a storm. About his dog, his little sister, his friend Mike, his mother, his new sneakers, and the toys he wanted Santa to bring him at Christmas, which was months and months away, but he was already making a list.

Joshua listened distractedly, trying to nod or offer an *uh-huh* in the appropriate spot. The high-pitched voice droned on, and Joshua managed to shift an entire section of books before noticing it had grown quiet. He glanced down, realizing the child's rambling flow of words had finally stopped, and the boy was now staring at Joshua with an expectant, hopeful expression. Problem was, Joshua had no idea what had been said.

"That's great," he answered ambiguously.

The flashing sunny smile of delight was the only warning Joshua got. The child stretched up on his toes and reached for a book on the top shelf. He yanked it hard, knocking over several others. Like a stack of dominos they tumbled, then pitched forward, off the shelf. Joshua saw the books falling, but he couldn't move fast enough, and several hit him directly on the foot.

"Goddamn it!"

"Uh-oh, you said a bad word."

"No, I didn't." Joshua gritted his teeth against the stinging pain in his foot.

The boy shot him a conspiratorial look of admiration. "That's okay, I won't tell."

"Thanks a lot," Joshua muttered under his breath, gingerly lifting his injured foot, trying to shake off the throbbing pain.

Apparently unperturbed by the incident, the child of disaster bent over the mess on the floor and sorted through the pile. "I'm ready," he declared.

"For what?"

"I asked you to read me a story. I like this one best." He proudly held up the book he had selected.

Joshua opened his mouth to refuse, but stopped when he saw the title. *General Explorer Meets Miss Audry's Class*. It was one of Rosemary's books! And one of the few children's titles he was familiar with.

Following the trick he had observed Eleanor using the other day, Joshua knelt down until he and the child were at eye level. "Have you ever heard that story?" Joshua asked.

"Sure, lots of times. Will you read it?"

"I guess I'm about due for a break," Joshua decided.

He followed the child to a table and with difficulty folded himself into one of the pint-sized chairs.

Joshua read the book in a quiet tone, not wanting to disturb anyone else in the room or incite the tempers of any angry mothers. He had no notion of either the attention span or patience of a child at this age, but his new little friend appeared engrossed by the story.

The boy listened raptly, his forehead wrinkled as he concentrated on the drawings, occasionally running the tip of his finger over a section of the page. He smiled with pure enjoyment when the story ended and whispered a sincere thank-you. It gave Joshua a jolt of real pleasure to hear those words and see that smile. For the first time he felt a true understanding of what drew Eleanor to this type of work.

Joshua's legs were starting to cramp, but he felt reluctant to leave his young friend. "I bet you didn't know that I know the lady who wrote this book."

"Really?"

"Her name is Rosemary Phillips. She's married to my dad."

"My dad is married to my mom," the boy replied philosophically, reaching across the table for the book. He fiddled with the plastic cover. "I like General Explorer a whole lot. Do you think maybe, sometime, you could get Rosemary's autograph for me?"

"Sure." The suggestion lit a light bulb in Joshua's head. "If I can work things out, you might even get to meet her. Would you like that?"

"Yeah!"

"Great. I've got to talk it over with Ms. Graham first." Joshua glanced over at the pile of books still scattered on the floor. "When I'm finished, maybe you can help me put those books back on the shelf."

"I'm a good helper," the child declared proudly. "My name is Henry. What's your name?"

"Nice to meet you, Henry. I'm Joshua." He tried shaking hands with the youngster, but Henry just laughed. "Don't start picking up those books until I get back, okay?"

"Okay!"

Joshua pulled himself out of the small chair, but midway to his feet realized the pocket of his slacks was caught on the edge of the table. He hesitated, stuck in a half sitting, half standing position. While contemplating his next move he felt the chair starting to tip. Instinctively he reached back, righting it before it crashed to the floor.

The sudden movement saved the chair, but the distinct sound of material tearing told Joshua he hadn't saved his pants.

Henry must have heard it, too, for he announced in an authoritative voice, "Your mom's going to be really mad at you when she sees that."

Joshua just shook his head. With an aching foot and a sizable rip at the side of his pants, he hobbled toward Eleanor's office.

"My goodness, what happened to you?"

"Volunteering," Joshua responded with a flat smile. Her stricken expression made him feel like an inept fool. Slowly he eased into a chair, more relieved than he would admit that it was adult-sized. "Now I understand why you have volunteers to do these jobs. Regular staff would demand combat pay."

"Joshua—"

"A few books fell, that's all. No big deal."

"But your pants are ripped. I can see your underwear, for goodness sakes."

"Is it turning you on?"

"Oh, please."

He squeezed his eyes shut. "I take it that wasn't a cry of unbridled passion."

"I think there's a sewing kit around here somewhere."

His eyes remained closed as he listened to her opening desk drawers, searching for the sewing implements. A small cry of success let him know when she found it.

"Scoot closer to the edge of the chair so I can sew that rip closed. The thread color doesn't match your slacks very well, but this temporary repair will prevent you from getting arrested."

Joshua opened his eyes and gazed with interest at her. "Maybe I should take my pants off?"

She arched one eyebrow.

"Got it. Pants stay on."

He did as she instructed and moved to the edge of the chair. Without further comment, she knelt by his side and started stitching. They were alone in the office. Eleanor's face was a mask of concentration and she nibbled on her bottom lip as she pushed the needle carefully through the fabric.

Joshua took advantage of her relaxed proximity and nearness to observe her. The top buttons of her blouse were unfastened at the throat, affording him a perfect view of her tanned skin and lovely, full breasts that were straining against the cups of her bra. It was a heavenly sight.

"Stop looking down my blouse."

She hadn't paused in her sewing or lifted her head. How had she known? Joshua cleared his throat. "I had an idea I wanted to run by you."

The needle sailed in and out of the fabric. "I'm listening."

Joshua launched into his pitch. "One of the many books that fell on my foot just now was one of Rosemary's, and I thought it might be nice if she came here to visit with the kids. She mentioned making appearances at bookstores, so she shouldn't object to coming to a library. If you want, I can call her and try to set something up."

Finally the needle stopped. "Would you really ask her?"

Eleanor's hopeful eagerness reminded him of young Henry. "I can't guarantee she'll agree to come, but I'd be glad to ask."

"That would be wonderful. We were really hoping to have an author visit this year, but there wasn't enough money in the budget." The excitement left Eleanor's face. "Do you think Rosemary will expect an honorarium? Most authors do."

Joshua shook his head. "She hardly needs the cash. I'll make all the transportation arrangements and she and my dad can stay with me while they are in town."

"I'll get the program schedule so you can give Rosemary a wide selection of dates." With a flourish Eleanor finished her stitches, knotted the end of the thread, and cut it off with small scissors. "I can't believe you thought of this! I almost asked Rosemary if she would visit the library when we were down at your father's, but I thought it would be too presumptuous. Especially since she believed I was your girlfriend. That would have definitely pressured her into saying yes."

His girlfriend. Joshua stroked his chin thoughtfully. He had nearly forgotten about that little white lie.

"That gleam of mischief in your eyes is making me very nervous, Joshua." Eleanor slowly lowered the large calendar she was clutching. "You aren't going to put any conditions on this favor, are you? Like having me pretend again that we're dating?"

He hadn't thought anything of the kind. His father already knew the truth about them, but Joshua realized he had never told Eleanor about the conversation he'd had with his dad before they'd left North Carolina. He could very easily tell her that now.

But the words remained unsaid. Maybe, just maybe, if he could get Eleanor to let her guard down for a few hours, he'd have a chance at penetrating that wall she had erected between them.

"You don't have to pretend about anything, Eleanor," Joshua said. "I'll simply tell my father and Rosemary the truth about us. I can't, however, vouch for how they'll react. Especially my father. You've witnessed firsthand that stubborn temperament of his."

Joshua's answer couldn't have been any more ambiguous. Frankly, he felt twice as shocked by the words he had spoken as she looked. But he didn't refute them. He picked up the stapler on her desk and idly toyed with it, letting her take her time, hoping desperately she would draw the wrong conclusions and thus make the decision he intended.

He knew he had her firmly on the ropes by the conflicted expression on her face and the way she kept tapping her chin with the tip of her finger. Feeling only a twinge of remorse, he moved in for the score.

"It's your call, Eleanor. Do you want me to tell them the truth about us?"

"N-no." The tapping ceased. "I don't want you to lie to your father or Rosemary, but then again there's no need to reveal all of the ugly truth."

It was hard not to gloat, but Joshua somehow managed. "Fine. When they come north, we'll be a couple again. I'm sure I'm just stating the obvious, but you do realize you'll probably have to spend some time with me entertaining them? They'll expect it. I promise to try and keep the activities to a minimum. I certainly don't want to impose on your time."

She glanced suspiciously at him and he realized he was probably laying it on a bit thick. Eleanor might be gullible, but she wasn't stupid. "Do you have those dates handy?"

Distracted, she returned her attention to the calendar, but her expression remained mildly suspicious. The minute he had the list safely secured in his pocket, he jumped to his feet. "Better get back to work. There's a pile of books and an eager helper waiting for me."

He hurried over to the bookshelf, feeling oddly guilty that he was being so deceptive and not experiencing much remorse. He smiled ironically, remembering that he had made an offhand comment to Eleanor about all being fair in love and war. With surprise, Joshua realized he had absolutely meant every word of it.

Fourteen

"What exciting things have you two been doing lately?" Rosemary asked Eleanor, once they were all seated at a quiet table in the restaurant.

Eleanor gave her a vague smile and deliberately turned toward Joshua. As much as she feared his outrageous answers, she was very uncomfortable with the notion of lying or even exaggerating the truth to either Rosemary or Warren.

"It's been a rather hectic time at work for both of us, so we haven't had the usual free time available to indulge ourselves," Joshua replied, draping his hand possessively over the back of Eleanor's chair. "We manage daily phone conversations and weekend dates, but that's starting to frustrate us both. Isn't that right, sweetheart?"

"Mmmm," Eleanor mumbled, deliberately pushing a large portion of the warm bread that had been placed on the table into her mouth, reasoning that it was better if Rosemary and Warren thought she was very hungry or had appalling table manners. Anything to avoid furthering the lie that she and Joshua were involved in a romantic relationship.

Eleanor had been greeted like a long-lost family member by the older couple, with hugs and kisses and genuine smiles. It made her feel awful. Even though she had agreed to attend this dinner, she vowed right then not to do anything that would encourage the lie that she and Joshua had a serious future together.

Although there *had* been moments over the past three weeks when Eleanor had questioned her feelings toward him. After returning from North Carolina she might have realized that she had fallen in love with a mere image of the man she believed him to be, but recently discovering aspects of the man he truly was now forced her to revise her opinion once again.

He was still dictatorial and demanding and could on occasion be downright rude. But he also had a wicked sense of humor and possessed the rare ability to laugh at himself. He also had an abundance of charm, intelligence, and incredible wealth.

After being fired from the firm, she had felt so strongly that a relationship between her and Joshua was an impossibility. Yet that certainty had been tested more than once over the past few weeks.

She never believed he would return to do additional volunteer work after his disastrous first afternoon. But he did, every Saturday morning, coaxing her into a lunch date before he left. Those days had been punctuated with flirting, teasing, sometimes arguing, but they were never dull afternoons.

Often he would make comments that bordered on the improper, letting her know in no uncertain terms that he found her desirable. That always gave her a secret thrill, yet left her feeling the most confused, the most unsure.

He had followed up immediately on his promise to ask Rosemary to come to the library. Her writing schedule could only accommodate an immediate visit and Joshua had performed nothing short of a miracle to get everything ready. He had even arranged for some local press coverage, which would be beneficial to both the library and Rosemary.

"Work is important, but don't forget to take some time out to play," Warren said. "If you two ever need a place for a quick getaway, don't hesitate to come visit us. We're only a short plane ride away. Since it's summer, the weather is still hot, but it starts cooling down nicely in autumn. Nothing more romantic than a stroll on the beach in cool weather. Perfect excuse to cuddle."

"Warren, stop it." Rosemary patted her husband's hand. "You're embarrassing Eleanor."

"Thanks for the invitation, Dad." Joshua smiled at his father. "We might just take you up on that offer when things settle down."

Eleanor shifted uncomfortably in her chair, saying nothing. In the face of their generous hospitality she felt like even more of a fraud. She fiddled with the stem of her water glass, hovering on the brink of confessing the truth, when the waiter arrived with their menus, followed by the wine steward with the wine selections.

Warren and Rosemary began a detailed discussion with the steward. It was clear they were connoisseurs and the steward was obviously pleased by their knowledge and eager to share his own expertise.

Normally Eleanor would have been fascinated by the discussion and pleased at the opportunity to gain some firsthand knowledge on a subject that she knew very little about, but had always been interested in. Yet she found she had trouble concentrating on the details.

Halfheartedly, she took a sip of each of the three wines that had been suggested and decided they all tasted the same. Expensive and bitter.

"Have you decided on your dinner entree?" Joshua asked, leaning close.

She risked a frown at him, since Rosemary and Warren

were occupied with the wine steward. "How about liar's delight?"

Joshua looked as if he was about to say something, but he must have changed his mind. "Try the salmon. Or the lobster. All the seafood is excellent here."

With a petulant expression, Eleanor scanned the menu. Maybe she should order something spicy. If anyone noticed her lack of conversation she could always say her mouth was on fire from the food.

She turned the page on the large menu and hit upon the perfect choice. Pepper-crusted beef fillet, pan-seared in garlic butter. When the waiter asked, she devilishly ordered the dish to be prepared with extra garlic, deciding that the first time Joshua stepped out of line she was going to breathe on him. Heavily.

The moment their hands were free of the large menus, Eleanor felt Joshua fumbling under the linen tablecloth. There was a bump against her leg and then his palm came to rest possessively on her upper thigh. She fidgeted in her chair, trying to scoot away. It was a spacious table, but there wasn't much room to maneuver.

The hand moved fractionally. A delicious quiver worked through her and she almost forgot to be annoyed with him. She glanced over at him, but his head and attention were centered on his father and the conversation they were having. Deciding to be magnanimous, Eleanor concluded that Joshua's touch was accidental.

Yet his hand stayed on her leg, putting her nerve endings on full alert. Eleanor grew increasingly uncomfortable, dismayed at how easily he could get her flustered. It took enormous self-control not to respond in a big way, but she was very aware of Rosemary and Warren. Had they noticed the gesture? Mortified at the thought, Eleanor sat up straighter and pulled back, as far away from Joshua as she could, trying not to seem too obvious.

Finally, he glanced in her direction. She immediately narrowed her eyes and glared. Joshua grinned down at her, shrugged his shoulders, and noisily moved his chair closer to hers. His hand remained where it had been, inappropriately perched upon her thigh.

". . . so I told the guy there was no way—" Warren abruptly ceased talking and glanced at them suspiciously. "Is something wrong, Joshua?"

"No, Dad. Finish your story." The moment Warren resumed speaking, Joshua's hand glided further up Eleanor's leg and started a journey toward her inner thigh. Her skin broke out in goose bumps. She gritted her teeth and clamped her knees together tightly, trapping his fingers.

She heard his startled curse and smiled. Feeling triumphant at finally thwarting him, Eleanor smugly glanced his way, disappointed to discover only a hint of strain about his lips.

"How's the golf game, Dad? Is Rosemary still beating you?"

Rosemary grinned with delight. "Two out of three times. He starts out strong, but usually runs into trouble on the back nine. And he grumbles about it all the time."

"I grumble because you make me walk the course," Warren insisted. "Zaps my strength and takes us twice as long to play a round."

"There is nothing wrong with your stamina." Rosemary winked slyly at her husband. "Do you play golf, Eleanor?"

"No." Eleanor squeaked out her answer. Joshua's hand was now firmly wedged in between her thighs and she couldn't figure out how to get him to remove it without causing a major commotion. "Golf looks like a fun sport. I've always wanted to learn how to play."

"I didn't realize you were interested in golf. I'd be

happy to teach you," Joshua offered with a charming smile. He shot her an assessing look and wiggled his fingers.

Eleanor nearly groaned out loud. The heat from his hand was starting to send shivers of sensation throughout her body. Her eyebrows rose in alarm. Was he actually going to try and carry on a polite conversation with his hand wedged between her legs?

The thought alone was enough to make her break out in a cold sweat. Thankfully, the arrival of the salad course saved Eleanor from having to make any further conversation. As the waiter expertly wielded a large pepper mill, she began wickedly imagining what she would do if she held a golf club in her hand right now. Perhaps bash Joshua over the head with it?

Eleanor shifted in her seat. To her great consternation, the movement gave Joshua better access to her sensitive flesh. He wiggled his fingers again and the light, fluttery movement nearly made her jump out of her chair. She speared a piece of lettuce forcefully, took a small bite of her salad and tried desperately to ignore the warm, glittering sensations his touch evoked.

It wasn't easy. With each slow, circular stroke it felt like her insides were melting. Joshua next slid his hand downward, confining his caresses to the soft, vulnerable spot on her inner thigh just above her knee. It drove her nuts.

Eleanor seized the opportunity the moment the waiter appeared and started clearing away the salad course to tilt her head near his and hiss in his ear. "What in the world do you think you are doing?"

"Being friendly?" He actually had the nerve to sound affronted by her question. There was still a hint of strain about his lips, but no other sign of distress.

She flinched away from him. "I ordered steak for dinner and I'm sure it will be served with an extra sharp knife. You'd better behave, or else it might end up in a most indiscreet part of your anatomy."

"Your occasional nastiness I can learn to live with, but a violent streak really intrigues me." He lowered his voice to that sexy, sultry pitch she found so irresistible. "Have you ever fantasized about being tied up on a bed and ravished?"

Eleanor nearly sprayed her mouthful of wine all over the table. A coughing fit ensued and by the time it was over her face was the same color as the lovely burgundy wine—deep red. But Joshua's hand was also gone.

Eleanor stifled a smile. He might be shameless, but he was incredibly inventive, too. Dinner arrived and the conversation between the four adults resumed. Eleanor deliberately took her time eating, cutting the delicious steak into tiny pieces so that every time she was asked a direct question by Rosemary or Warren, she could give a very brief reply and then fork in a bite of food. That left Joshua to carry the bulk of their side of the discussion.

She was pleased to note that he seemed far more comfortable around his father and Rosemary than he had been in North Carolina. As Joshua launched into another story, she realized that she was the center of several of his anecdotes, always emerging in a positive light.

When he finished one particularly outrageous tale about her and some of the children at the library, he grabbed her hand and lifted it to his lips. She snatched it back before he had a chance to kiss it and gave a small cough, letting him know she wasn't going to put up with any more of his manipulation. She generally was slow to anger, but something about the way Joshua was acting tonight seemed to get her blood boiling in record time.

They placed their orders for dessert. When fifteen minutes had elapsed without any additional antics, Eleanor finally began to relax. Apparently Joshua had declared a moratorium on his juvenile behavior. Yet just when she thought she had herself—and Joshua—under control, she felt a light caress against her leg. Her head swung immediately toward Joshua, but his hands were in plain view. She had almost convinced herself she had imagined it, when it happened again.

Thinking fast, Eleanor pushed the linen napkin off her lap.

"Oh, I've lost my napkin," she announced softly, to no one in particular, ducking her head under the table. Even in the darkness it took only a second to see that it had been the tip of Joshua's shoe intimately caressing her calf.

Eleanor's patience snapped. Without another thought, she sat upright in her chair, pulled her knee up, and kicked him in the shin as hard as she could.

Joshua's barely muffled curse let her know she'd scored a direct hit. It was a small, petty, infantile act and it made her feel ten feet tall.

"Was that your leg, Joshua?" Eleanor asked in sweet innocence, bestowing her best facsimile of deep concern and worry upon him for Rosemary and Warren's sake.

"That's okay," Joshua gritted out. "I have another one."

"How clumsy of me. I'm so sorry." Eleanor kept her gaze directly on Joshua, certain there were wicked lights of devilment flashing in her eyes as she gazed at him.

He raised his snifter of brandy toward her in mock salute. She drew her knuckles to her mouth to prevent a full-blown laugh from escaping. She didn't think either Rosemary or Warren had realized she'd kicked him. Eleanor almost wished they had, deciding it might be amusing to watch him try and explain why his *girlfriend* was acting so oddly.

Eleanor took a sip of her coffee, deciding to hold onto

A NIGHT TO REMEMBER

her cup with both hands, lest it leap out, dumping its contents into Joshua's lap. If the situation weren't so completely ludicrous she might succumb to the absurdity and burst into laughter.

Miraculously they finished the meal without further incident. Eleanor was relieved when the waiter finally presented the bill. The strain of the evening was really starting to wear her down, so much so that she barely tasted her beautiful chocolate soufflé.

After a bit of scuffling over the check, Warren reluctantly agreed to let Joshua pay for the meal, vowing he would pay for the next. As they adjourned to the cloakroom to retrieve the lightweight coat Rosemary had worn, Joshua's pocket started ringing. With an apologetic shrug he retrieved the cell phone from his suit jacket.

He spoke for a moment, then turned to them. "Sorry, I need to take this call."

He moved to a small alcove off the coat room for privacy. Eleanor saw him reach into his pocket again, this time extracting an electronic notepad. He tucked the phone into the crook of his neck and began punching the buttons of the device.

"Looks like Joshua will be tied up for a few minutes with that phone call," Rosemary commented. "I think I'll take a quick trip to the ladies' room. Eleanor?"

"I'm fine."

Eleanor realized her mistake the minute Rosemary left. She hadn't wanted to spend any time alone with either Warren or Rosemary, but given the choice she belatedly decided it might have been better to be with Rosemary.

"Did you enjoy dinner?" Warren inquired.

"It was lovely," Eleanor replied, working hard at keeping her features free of the pained expression that would reveal her true feelings. "Both the food and service were excellent."

The tension heightened as they stood together in the opulent foyer, listening to the sedate classical music that was piped into the restaurant at a discreet level.

"I'm glad that you and Joshua are dating each other," Warren said. Leaning close to Eleanor he whispered, "For real."

For real? "We aren't exactly dating." Eleanor's hands started shaking. She knitted her fingers together for strength. "All that much."

To her great relief Warren nodded his head. "I understand. You want to keep the relationship under wraps for a while."

What in the world has Joshua told his father about us? Something completely outrageous, judging by the look Warren was giving her. Perfect. All this pretending and confusion was starting to make her feel like the drama queen in a soap opera. The only truth she could honestly acknowledge was the pure absurdity of the situation.

It was past time for it to all end and somehow set the record straight with Warren. But where to begin?

Eleanor swung around and faced Warren squarely. "I sincerely hope you haven't gotten the wrong impression about my relationship with Joshua," she said. "We really are just friends."

The words sounded lame even to her own ears.

However, Warren was apparently a man who heard only what he wanted. "That's fine." He patted her on the shoulder sympathetically. "I know you must be harboring some resentment toward Joshua over getting fired. It's only natural. I'll bet he never explained that the whole idea was mine."

"Yours?" A flush rose in her cheeks. But how did Warren even know she had worked for the firm? It had been deliberately kept a secret so she could pretend to be Joshua's girlfriend while they were staying with Warren and Rosemary. "I hadn't realized you knew that I worked for Joshua. So, you told him he should fire me?"

"Yes." Warren smiled, seeming genuinely pleased with himself. "I could tell that idiotic rule about employees not dating was making him miserable. The best solution was for you to leave, especially since you had already found another career that suited you."

Warren folded his hands together with a heavy sigh. "Naturally, I didn't mean for him to go about it quite the way he did. Even as a boy he had trouble controlling his intensity sometimes. I wanted him to discuss the notion of you leaving the firm first and if you agreed, then you could resign. I never suspected you would be blind-sided with a letter of termination. That must have made you pretty angry."

"You could say that." Eleanor slid her fingers up to her temples and tried massaging her brain. It didn't help. "When exactly did you discover I worked for Joshua?"

"The afternoon you left North Carolina," Warren answered promptly. "I think the lie was making him feel guilty. Joshua really opened up to me, probably for the first time in years. It staggered us both to realize, and admit, how much alike we are. I know you've had a lot to do with my son's change in attitude toward Rosemary and my marriage. Heck, even toward me. I'm grateful to you, Eleanor."

"Grateful?" she echoed in astonishment.

"Certainly. You're good for Joshua. Rosemary thinks so, too. That's why I was so pleased when he called and invited her to speak at the library. I knew you had forgiven him for his earlier misjudgment."

Eleanor's head was spinning. She had a dozen more questions, but wasn't sure if she was prepared to hear the answers. Suspiciously, she glanced over at Joshua. He was still engrossed with his phone call. Realizing she'd probably never get a better chance, she plunged ahead.

"I'm afraid Joshua might have given you a slightly skewed picture of our relationship."

Warren would never win any prizes for hiding his emotions. His jaw clenched and his eyes grew stormy in an instant.

"Unintentionally," Eleanor quickly added. "The point is, I'm not sure what sort of a future exists for us. Our backgrounds are so dissimilar. I had a very modest upbringing. As you have no doubt realized, I'm not from one of those upper-class, cosmopolitan-type families where everybody seems to instinctively know how to handle any situation with ease. I'm afraid I don't fit in all that well with the way he lives."

"You're referring to Joshua's house, right?" Warren's expression changed from anger to understanding. He sighed. "I told him not to buy that old mausoleum, but he wouldn't listen to me. It took him two years and I don't know how many dollars to restore that place. Then he hired a team of New York decorators and they completely ruined the house. Looks like a museum.

"It doesn't have that same comfortable, homey feel that my place does. Too many rooms and too much staff. I suppose he needs the help because of all the business entertaining he does out there, but it could be better managed and made to be more of a home. By a smart wife."

Fortunately Eleanor was in too much shock to be blushing over Warren's none-too-subtle hint about marriage. His father thought that Joshua's home was even grander than the North Carolina estate? Where exactly did Joshua live, Buckingham Palace?

With effort, she cleared her throat. "I'm glad that you understand how Joshua's lifestyle might overwhelm a simple girl like myself."

Warren arched one eyebrow. "I'm not sure where you got the idea that we're such snobs."

Great. Now she'd insulted him. "Oh no, you've always been so gracious, Warren. Both you and Rosemary. But I won't lie about my feelings. Joshua's position and especially all his money definitely spook me."

For a second, Warren looked almost sentimental. "Lord, you remind me of Joshua's mother."

"His mother?"

"Before she became my wife, she was my secretary," Warren said in an affectionate tone. "She was always harping about the differences in our social standings. As if I cared about such malarkey. I think I fell in love with her the second day she worked for me, but it took me nearly a year to convince her to marry me. I'm proud to say she never regretted it."

Eleanor had never heard of any such story. "Joshua's mother worked at the firm? As your secretary? Are you kidding?"

Warren stubbornly crossed his arms over his chest. "Why would I joke about something like that? She was a smart woman, and a damn fine secretary, back in the days when women didn't resent being called secretaries. Now they have to have fancy titles like administrative assistant or personal manager or some such nonsense, but they do the same type of work.

"You may not believe this, but I had a difficult time finding the right girl to work for me. It was a real tough spot to fill. I went through half a dozen secretaries until Joshua's mother took the job. She was the only one who could put up with my brisk business attitude and not get emotional every time I had to raise my voice."

Eleanor couldn't help but laugh, imagining Warren in action. "You must have been a tyrant."

He lowered his gaze, looking almost bashful. "I might

have gone overboard once or twice, but only when I had just cause. I was thrilled when my beautiful wife became pregnant, and at the same time frustrated as all get-out because she left her position at the firm. It wasn't easy finding a replacement."

Warren eyed Eleanor with an expression that was strangely hopeful. "I want my son to experience that kind of love and joy in a relationship. I want him to be happy. And I believe he can be. With you."

Eleanor flinched. Warren's hearty and sincere endorsement of her character should have pleased her, but it only made her feel greater guilt for not being completely honest with him about her relationship with his son. Yet how could she possibly explain what she didn't even understand herself?

"It's getting late." Eleanor fumbled in her purse for her car keys, then realized the car had been valet-parked when she'd arrived at the restaurant. Fortunately she was able to find the stub quickly. She gratefully handed it over to an eager young employee waiting in the lobby. "I'd better get home."

"You're leaving?" Joshua asked.

Eleanor closed her eyes and sighed. He joined them just as she was voicing her plans to Warren. It would have been inexcusably rude to leave without saying goodbye to him, but she had seriously considered it. "I need to get home."

"So soon?"

"Yes." The possessiveness in his tone made her immediately feel defensive. "Tomorrow's Rosemary's big day at the library and I still have a million things to do."

Joshua frowned. "But it's early. I was hoping you would join us back at my house for the remainder of the evening. If you're feeling too tired later, you can leave your car and I'll drive you home."

Eleanor shuddered. Visit Joshua's fabled restored, decorated, and overstaffed museum? The place that his father felt was too stiff and formal? Wouldn't that just be the perfect ending to the evening?

I'd rather eat glass. With a concentrated effort, Eleanor managed to keep her initial reaction to Joshua's suggestion to herself. Luckily Rosemary also reappeared, making an escape possible.

"Good night, Rosemary, Warren. It was a lovely evening." Eleanor impulsively hugged them. "I look forward to seeing you both at the library tomorrow."

She heard Joshua mutter something under his breath, but she kept the smile plastered on her face as she bid him a polite good night. Her heart was pounding so violently she could feel the pressure in her eardrums, but she turned away and starting walking.

Eleanor wasn't certain how she managed to get home without driving her car accidentally off a bridge. Her mind was totally consumed by confusion and doubt. She entered her apartment like a creature seeking refuge, a safe harbor from a cruel, uncertain world.

The message light on her answering machine was blinking furiously, but she deliberately ignored it, already knowing whose voice would fill the room if she played the tape.

Joshua Barton, the princely god who had haunted her dreams, the infallible, all-too-human man who stalked her days.

Maybe she had been lying to herself. Maybe Joshua had been right when he told her that she was really more afraid of herself than she was of him. She had used his money and his position as a shield, proof that there was no reason to try and establish a relationship that was doomed to failure.

But his mother had done it. Most successfully. And during a time when social rules were stricter, more rigid.

Dry-eyed, Eleanor picked up a sofa pillow and hugged it to her chest. She did not want to pursue this avenue of thought and feelings. Question was, how much longer could she avoid it?

Fifteen

Rosemary's presentation was very entertaining. She had definitely captured the attention of the crowd in attendance, which was equal parts children and adults. They laughed and applauded, jockeying in their seats to see the delightful drawings she was showing.

Unfortunately, Joshua was unable to keep his mind focused on the slides projected on the screen because his eyes kept wandering about the room, searching for one particular female shape. Eleanor's.

It had certainly been an interesting few weeks. What began as a challenge to his wounded male pride had turned into the realization that she was even more special, unique, and irreplaceable than he had first thought.

She brought out feelings and behavior within him he didn't even know he possessed. Protectiveness, humor, gentleness. He had learned patience and cooperation, had experienced joy and excitement, had shared thoughts and feelings more easily and naturally with Eleanor than with any other person in his life. Quite simply, she made him happy.

Okay, there may have been a few times over the past three weeks when he would have preferred the gentle, amenable woman he had taken to North Carolina, the one who had blindly followed his commands, had deferred to his decisions in most things. But apparently that woman didn't precisely exist.

Instead Joshua had discovered a confident, self-assured woman who wasn't afraid to speak her mind, who didn't shy away from the sparks of disagreement between them. She almost seemed to relish them at times. Despite their occasional feuds, they got along well, better than many other couples he knew, and he greatly enjoyed spending time in her company.

Yet the tension and suppressed passion that lingered between them was escalating. He felt it more and more each time he was near her. Without warning, that unexpected rush of desire would suddenly ignite, spreading through him like wildfire.

He missed the intimacy between them, and there were nights when his body actually ached with frustrated desire. He had taken so many cold showers they were almost ineffective now, since his body was starting to become accustomed to them. But it wasn't only the physical intimacy he missed. Eleanor was doing her best to keep him at an emotional distance as well.

If not for the small, occasional cracks in that impressive wall she had erected around herself, he might have lost hope. Yet somehow, some way, something had changed between them last night. After dinner, Eleanor had literally bolted from his company. She wouldn't speak with him on the phone, had refused to even argue or express her anger.

Joshua was finally forced to admit to himself that this impossible situation could no longer continue. Clearly, it was time for him to move on.

He had thought seriously about giving up on her, especially when she wouldn't answer his phone calls last night. There were plenty of women out there to date, to fall in love with, to build a life and future with. The problem was, none of them were Eleanor.

He was in love with her. He was certain of that, if nothing else. And he wasn't leaving today until he had heard from her own lips exactly how she felt about him.

"Thank you, Rosemary Phillips, for giving us such wonderful insight into how you create your lovely stories." Eleanor stood before the crowded room and looked out at the sea of delighted faces. Adults and children alike had been enthralled by Rosemary's presentation. It made Eleanor feel like a small part of the success of the afternoon, though in truth it had been Joshua who had arranged for everything.

"Let's all give Rosemary a round of applause to show our appreciation," Eleanor instructed. The room broke out in enthusiastic clapping. Rosemary blushed and almost looked shy. Eleanor consulted her watch. "We have a few more minutes until Rosemary has to leave. Does anyone have any questions they would like to ask her?"

There was total silence for a brief instant, then several hands shot up in the air. Eleanor looked down at the eager young faces and pointed to a chubby boy in the second row.

"I took one of your books home from the library one time and I left it on the couch in my family room and my dog ripped the pages and chewed on them and then my mom brought the book back to the library and she had to pay for it and she was mad."

"Oh dear, that is quite a story," Rosemary remarked. "Maybe it would make a good book one day. I'll have to remember all those details."

The child's face lit up. "You can use it if you want. I don't care."

"Yes, that's a very interesting tale," Eleanor interrupted. There were several hands now waving madly in the air, all eager she suspected to relate stories for Rosemary to turn into future masterpieces. "I want to know if someone has something they want to ask Rosemary. Not tell her. Does anyone have a question, something they want to ask?"

Half the hands immediately lowered. A few arms wavered, then dropped, but one girl kept hers firmly raised in the air. Apprehensively, Eleanor called on her.

"Hi, I'm Jennifer. I really like your books too, especially the ones with Allyson and Alex, because they're rabbits and I have a pet rabbit. He's white and has brown eyes, a wiggly nose, and a black spot on his back. His name is Thumper." Eleanor waited impatiently while the child took a deep breath, hoping young Jennifer would eventually get around to actually asking something. "My question is, what kind of car do you drive?"

The room seemed remarkably quiet as Eleanor started removing the decorations from the wall. She was alone in the program room. There had been a long line of children and adults waiting to have books autographed, and Rosemary had graciously spent nearly an hour signing every one.

Afterward, she and Warren had left, promising to call soon. Joshua, too, had disappeared, presumably to visit with them until it was time to leave for the airport. Eleanor was glad he had gone. Her thoughts and feelings were still so jumbled she wasn't certain how to act or react around him. Maybe distance was the answer. At least for a while.

Although she had only had a brief conversation with Warren last evening, it had seemed that overnight her perceptions of Joshua had once again changed dramatically, leaving her feeling far more vulnerable than she wanted to be.

Without the barrier of impossibility between them she was forced to confront her true, inner feelings toward Joshua. She was in love with him. And it frightened her more than anything she had ever before encountered.

She still wasn't exactly sure she was right for him, that she had the type of personality needed to thrive in the wealthy, upscale lifestyle he seemed to relish. There were even doubts that she wanted to.

But if it meant having him in her life, wouldn't it be worth it?

Sure, they had gotten along famously when she had been under his thumb, amenable to his every wish. Yet when she had defied him, their relationship seemed to rise to a new level. It had sparkled with awareness and laughter despite the occasional tension. Being on an equal footing had added greater dimension and depth, even as Eleanor tried to deny it.

He had pursued her. And she had liked it. Yet she had pretended to him and herself that she didn't.

Stop it! Eleanor clenched her hands into fists, angry with her self-indulgent attitude. There was nothing more pathetic than a weak, weepy female who had no just cause to be acting that way.

What she needed to do now was keep herself occupied. She ran her gaze about the room. The rows of chairs would be broken down and put away by the custodians on Monday morning, but there were still plenty of other things to do to set the room to rights.

With a determined attitude, Eleanor retrieved a step stool from the utility closet and began taking down the many pictures tacked up on the wall. There was a colorful welcome banner that everyone had worked on together, along with scores of drawings the children had made of their favorite characters or scenes from Rosemary's books.

Some were rather good, but many were an indistinguishable mass of colored scribbles. Eleanor noticed that an adult had written on the bottom of most of them, identifying the scene, presumably so the viewer would know what was supposed to be depicted.

One entire section on the wall was covered with drawings devoted to safety tips, taken straight from Rosemary's General Explorer books. *Never play with matches. Look both ways before crossing the street. Always wear a helmet when riding a bicycle.*

"Would you mind saving those safety tip pictures in a separate pile?" a male voice inquired. "I promised the kids I'd give them back after the program."

Eleanor didn't have to turn around to identify the speaker. She knew that voice all too well. As usual, her heart began to pound incredibly hard. "Sorry, I didn't know you wanted to keep the pictures. No one mentioned it."

Eleanor carefully climbed off the step stool and started rummaging around in the trash bin. She stacked the crumpled drawings on the table where Rosemary had done her book signing. "A few got rumpled, but they should be fine."

Joshua joined her at the table and they started smoothing out the wrinkled pictures. "I thought Rosemary's presentation went very well," Joshua commented. "Were you pleased?"

"I was thrilled. Rosemary was remarkable. Funny, informative, totally entertaining. She's a marvelous public speaker. I don't know who had a better time, the adults or the children." Eleanor took her time pressing the final drawing flat. "Thank you, Joshua, for arranging everything. It was very kind and generous and I really appreciate it."

"I was happy to be given the opportunity to help out." He settled his back against the wall and lifted his intense gaze to hers. "However, I will confess to an ulterior motive. I was hoping that you would finally realize the truth about me."

Eleanor stilled, staring at him warily. "The truth?"

He nodded his head. "I'd do just about anything for you, sugar."

Taken off guard, she stiffened noticeably. That Southern drawl of his slid through her senses like melted butter. She had never been very good with diversionary tactics, but decided one was needed now. Desperately, she clutched at the drawing on the top of the pile. "These pictures the children drew are so sweet. Have you seen them?"

He shifted his broad shoulders. "Sure. I wrote most of the text so everyone would know what they were supposed to be. After I saw them, I thought that would be the most diplomatic way to handle the situation. Some children can be really sensitive about that sort of thing."

Eleanor found herself staring at him. He had written the text? To save a child from feeling less than confident in his or her self. Blindly, Eleanor stared down at the drawing she held. Then her mouth started twitching.

"I thought these were supposed to be safety tips," she said with a shaky laugh. *"Never step on hot lava?"* I wonder where in the world this child lives. It must be a very exciting household."

Joshua glanced down at the drawing, then joined her smile with a tight chuckle of his own. "Hey, I'm not responsible for editorial content. I only wrote what I was told."

"Right." She gathered the pile together, intending to

hand them over to him, but his hands were already full. "Did Rosemary forget something?" Eleanor asked, pointing to the large book Joshua held.

"Ah, no." He cleared his throat. "I asked her to sign a copy of her latest release for a friend. He couldn't be here today."

"A friend?" Eleanor curiously reached for the book and read the inscription. "Henry? Is that someone from the firm?"

"No. Henry is a little kid, one of the library regulars. I'm sure you would recognize him if you saw him." Joshua tucked the book under his arm. "I met Henry the first day I was volunteering. He actually gave me the idea to ask Rosemary to do a program for the children. Henry was really disappointed that he wouldn't have a chance to see her this afternoon, but his family was going out of town to visit his grandparents this weekend."

"Sounds like you and Henry are good buddies," Eleanor said softly.

"We're pals. Sometimes he helps me put the books on the shelves. When he's not dropping them on my foot."

Eleanor couldn't hold back her smile. Yet as she looked at Joshua she felt an aching deep in her heart. It was as if she were seeing him for the first time. Without the trappings of wealth and position, beyond the physical perfection of his masculine good looks, just as a man. A man who was surprisingly good with children, tolerant of most adults and incredibly patient with the foolish woman who was so very much in love with him.

"Why did you fire me from the firm?" Eleanor asked, realizing that she was finally ready—no eager—to hear his answer.

"I told you that was a mistake." He stood there for a moment, searching her gaze. "Yes, I wanted you to leave the firm, but I never meant for you to be fired. I hardly slept the night after I discovered the error. I was so worried about you, about how you would manage financially. I suppose I shouldn't have doubted that you would land on your feet."

"I left that job a year ago, in my heart at least." Eleanor touched a fingertip to the corner of her mouth. "We both know you did me a favor by letting me go, even if it wasn't done in the most diplomatic fashion. But why exactly did you want me gone from the firm?"

"We couldn't be together if you were my employee, Eleanor. After our weekend in North Carolina, I knew that was what I wanted. And I was prepared to do whatever it took to achieve my goal."

His expression was so serious, but the tenderness in his eyes warmed her heart. "I never meant for you to be hurt in the process. I'm sorry." He dipped his chin. "I'm sorry also for the shabby way I treated you when we met in the hallway at the office. I know my coldness hurt you. There's no excuse for such rudeness, but I hadn't settled on a way to cope with our relationship, so I panicked and resorted to being the high and mighty boss."

Eleanor blinked. He was being so open with her, so willing to share his emotions. How could she do anything less than bare her own soul, reveal her own feelings now that she finally understood and trusted them?

"I'm a real idiot," she whispered. "Did you know that?"

"Ahh, sugar." He took a step forward.

"No, stop. Don't come any closer." Her throat constricted with unshed tears. She had to get it out before she broke down and starting crying like a three-year-old. "I'm in love with you," she said softly. "I think I've known it for quite a while, but I haven't had the courage to admit it. To myself, mostly."

She shifted her weight from one foot to the other. "I

keep waiting for you to disappear, Joshua. To stop making those nightly phone calls I so look forward to, to stop coming to the library and doing this silly volunteer work that is so far beneath your talents and intelligence. To realize that who I am is not the type of woman you want or need to have in your life."

"And?" he prompted gently.

"And!" Eleanor's shoulders dropped in frustration. "You keep coming back. Just to spite me, I think."

"I keep coming back because I love you," he said quietly.

Her head shot up. "Say that again," she whispered.

Joshua reached out and took hold of her, lifting her in the air. He lowered her slowly to her feet, sliding her body down the length of his. She trembled but kept her eyes locked on his.

"I love you, Eleanor."

Her heart soared. Was it possible? One glance at the honesty in his eyes told her it was indeed the truth.

She cupped his face in her hands, then trailed her fingers down over his neck and shoulders and arms, slipping her smaller hand into his. Joshua smiled tenderly, linking their fingers. She moistened her bottom lip, lifted her chin, pressed herself forward, and kissed him.

The warm, sweet pressure of his mouth soon gave way to deeper contact, and his passion poured into her, filling her with a sense of love and comfort that was as undeniable as it was miraculous.

She reached up and moved her hand through his hair, deepening the kiss, still dazed at the notion that he was really hers. Finally. And forever.

Eleanor quickly felt herself becoming lost in his heat and strength. She arched herself closer as the yearning, urgent feeling began building inside her. Oh, how she had missed this! The closeness, the intimacy, the wondrous sense of connection.

Just as the coiled, inner tension began to grow out of control, Joshua broke off the kiss.

"Does the door to this room have a lock?" he asked urgently.

Eleanor laughed, then groaned. "No."

"Damn!"

She bit back another laugh. Then, suddenly overcome with emotions, Eleanor felt the tears starting to gather in her eyes. Concerned that Joshua might misinterpret them, she buried her face against his broad chest. He slowly stroked her hair, then reached down to catch a tear from beneath her eye with his thumb.

"Do you have something you want to ask me?" he inquired with amusement in his voice.

She rubbed her head back and forth against his chest and sniffled.

"Oh, you have something you want to tell me."

"Yes." She lifted her chin and almost burst into fresh tears. His expression was filled with such love and tenderness it nearly stole her composure. "I'm finished with pretending to myself that I don't want us to be together. I really do want to be someone in your life, Joshua. Someone important. Special. Although I am mature enough to admit there are some things about you that bother me."

"Such as?"

"Well, did it ever occur to you that I might feel a bit insecure because you're prettier than me?"

Joshua moved his hand from her waist to push the stray wisp of hair from her cheek. He bent low and tenderly kissed the spot he had just cleared. "Thanks for the character assassination. Naturally I'm too shallow a man to love you for your inner beauty. I happen to think your outer beauty is damn hot, too, but I don't suppose you want to hear that right now."

"Mmm, you suppose wrong, Mr. Barton." Eleanor ran her hands over the solid muscles of his upper arms, still trying to comprehend that this beautiful, physically perfect man was hers. All hers. "I think honesty is essential in a relationship."

"Absolutely," Joshua mumbled, nibbling on the sensitive lobe of her ear. "I expect you to be honest with me. As I will be with you."

"Right." Eleanor paused for a moment in confusion. The touch of his lips was spreading that lush, fiery feeling way down to the pit of her stomach. For a moment, she completely lost her train of thought and forgot what she wanted to say. "Oh, and by the way, all your money makes me a little nervous."

"Get used to it." Joshua didn't even lift his head, but continued kissing and nibbling her neck. His mouth felt warm and rough against her skin. "I'm not giving it away."

Eleanor pulled back sharply, breathing heavy. "Did I say that I wanted you to? You jump to conclusions much too quickly."

With a sigh of frustration, he grabbed her by the shoulders. "Okay, I'm too rich and I jump to conclusions. Anything else wrong?"

Eleanor did some fast considering. She cocked her head coyly to one side, then laughed from sheer happiness. "One last thing," she said, molding herself softly against his hard body. "You talk too much."

And then she kissed him again, with all the love and intensity that was no longer trapped within her soul.

Epilogue

Six months later

Buried contentedly amid a tumble of silken sheets, Eleanor Graham Barton sighed languidly and drew closer to the muscular male body stretched beside her on the large bed. She felt like she was floating somewhere up in the clouds, awash on a sea of love and intimacy.

The distant sound of lapping ocean waves invaded her mind and she felt the soft kiss of a warm sea breeze against her uncovered back. They had left the windows wide open last night. Or was that yesterday afternoon? Eleanor took a deep breath and tried to clear the fog from her brain.

Time had ceased to have any real meaning. The mornings, afternoons, evenings, and nights had all run together in her mind, creating one giant sensual memory.

She inched closer to her handsome husband, entwining their fingers. Joshua, sprawled on his stomach and snoring softly, instinctively squeezed her hand despite his deep slumber.

She pulled her hand away, but the movement didn't interrupt Joshua's even breathing. She nuzzled his forearm, rubbing the tip of her nose back and forth over the solid muscle. But he continued sleeping. And snoring.

Eleanor smiled. Clearly, she had worn him out. Correction, they had worn each other out. This fabulous wedding trip was turning out to be a test of endurance for both of them. No winner had yet emerged, but she entertained grand hopes of victory.

She giggled out loud and rolled onto her back, hugging herself tightly about the waist. *Just think, I have an entire lifetime of this to look forward to.*

Propping herself up on her elbow, Eleanor studied her husband's sleeping form. He was as beautiful as ever. His face was turned toward the opposite wall, so she admired the shape of his head and his gorgeous dark, thick hair. She traced a sensual line down the middle of Joshua's back, then curled her arms around his shoulder blades and kissed the nape of his neck. He stirred and opened one eyelid, but promptly closed it again. Eleanor gave him a playful slap on the butt.

"Time to get up, mister. They have a rule at this swanky hotel. If they don't see their guests at least once every forty-eight hours, they send up a security team to check on them to make sure they're breathing."

Joshua turned his head toward her, but his eyes remained closed and burrowed in the soft pillow. "I, or rather we, own the controlling interest in this place. Any security personnel that cross our threshold will be instantly dismissed."

Eleanor knew he was joking about firing anyone, yet a jolt of surprise raced through her. She had no idea he, or rather they, owned part of this very exclusive, very expensive resort. That usual moment of panic hit, but thankfully faded quickly. Realizing how far their wealth extended still had the power to quicken her pulse with fear, yet the reactions were getting milder and were vanishing sooner.

She was gradually starting to get used to the money

and all its trappings. She was also honest enough with herself and Joshua to know that it wouldn't be an easy adjustment, but at least it wasn't a major difficulty any longer.

"Joshua, please." She glanced over at the ultramodern clock on the wall, then pressed her face close to his, their noses touching. "I'm starting to feel like a vampire. We never venture beyond these doors in the daylight. We've been here for five days already and the only time that we even left the room was for dinner in the lovely restaurant on our second night. Or was that our third night?"

"Third." His voice was gruff with amusement. "We came here to rest, Eleanor. And that's just what I'm doing. Resting."

She pulled back and gave him a disapproving stare. Resting. Hardly. More like passing out from exhaustion between bouts of mind-bending lovemaking. This was the ideal honeymoon spot, private, secluded, and tropical. Everything they needed to afford them the chance to reconnect after the frantic weeks leading up to their wedding.

And what a glorious wedding it had been! Exactly the type of wedding that Eleanor had always dreamed of—small, intimate, and wildly romantic. Yet despite the much-appreciated assistance of her mother and Rosemary, it had left Eleanor and Joshua physically and emotionally drained.

This time together following the beautiful marriage ceremony was wonderful, precious really, but they couldn't spend the entire fourteen days in bed. Could they?

A large, warm hand snaked through the covers, came up, and possessively covered her breast. Eleanor sighed with resigned pleasure. Apparently Joshua believed they could.

Her eyes drifted down to his waist. The sheet barely covered his arousal. Gracious, the man was insatiable. Yet it gave her female ego a huge boost, knowing it took so little to make him instantly ready for her.

He started stroking her breasts, then reached between her legs. She slid closer, bent her head, and plunged her tongue into his mouth. A deep, sexy growl rumbled in his chest. She could feel his hardness pressing insistently against her hip.

"I want you," he murmured against her mouth.

His words brought joy to her heart. To be wanted by this man was all she had ever desired and now, now they had a lifetime together to savor that passion. To nurture and grow with it.

Eleanor gave him a fierce squeeze, then rolled out of his reach.

"Hey, get back here."

"No." Eleanor scrambled quickly across the bed. Joshua was tangled in the silk sheets, unable to move fast enough to catch her. She reached for the first garment she could find, a lush terry cloth robe with the hotel's insignia embroidered on the breast pocket. After shrugging into it, she wrapped the belt twice around her waist and tied it securely. "If I climb back in that bed, then we'll never get out of it. Or out of this room."

Joshua looked mildly affronted. "Complaints already, Mrs. Barton?"

She pursed her lips and tried to look serious. "We have been on this glorious island for five full days and haven't once gotten to the beach. Or the pool. I am going to be thoroughly embarrassed returning to the library after my two-week honeymoon in the Caribbean without a tan. At this rate I'll return paler than before I left."

Joshua cocked a lazy eyebrow. "You could tell everyone it was raining."

"Joshua."

"How about a sunlamp? I'll have one installed on the jet. You can relax in a comfortable chair and bake in front of it on the flight home."

Eleanor cleared her throat. Wild memories of their energetic lovemaking on the private plane ride down to the island made her blush. They had practically attacked each other the moment the pilot had signaled it was safe to move about the cabin.

"I . . . ummm . . . want natural sunlight," she mumbled.

A frown creased his forehead, but his grin was so sexy she knew he was remembering that airplane ride, too. "You're right. We might not want to make any definite plans for our return flight that would interfere with our pleasure."

"Joshua!" she blushed hotly.

"I love you, Eleanor."

Her throat closed up and tears filled her eyes. No matter how often Joshua said it—and he had been saying it quite often these past six months—she never got tired of hearing it.

Smiling through her tears, she returned to the bed. "I love you, too," she whispered, touching his cheek.

He pulled back the covers and patted the mattress. "Come back to bed." He reached out and grabbed her waist, then slid both palms over her curves until one rested on each hip. "I'm lonely without you."

"Oh, Joshua." Eleanor felt her resolve melting, yet she knew the moment she lay upon those silken sheets she wouldn't be leaving the room. Again. "Why don't we take a nice stroll on the beach? Or how about a swim?" She lowered her voice to an alluring whisper as inspiration struck. "I can see the ocean from our window. The waves look great. We could try body surfing. Who knows where that might lead."

"Body surfing?" His hand stilled, then his head lifted. "Will you take off your bathing suit?"

Eleanor bit her lip. Oh dear, now what had she started? "If there's a private beach," she finally conceded.

Joshua jackknifed out of bed with admirable athleticism. "I know just the spot. The perfect spot."

Naked, he padded over to the closet. "I know I packed a bathing suit." He rambled about the room, opening drawers, rifling through neat piles of clothing.

Eleanor quickly grabbed her suit and matching cover-up and headed toward the bathroom.

"I'm ready," she called out gaily a few minutes later.

"Wait a second." Joshua narrowed his eyes. He was still naked, but his swimming trunks dangled from the closed fist that rested against his hip. "The last time we went body surfing in North Carolina you teased me mercilessly with that sexy body of yours. And the water was too darn cold for me to do a thing about it."

"Oh, darling." She moved forward and embraced him possessively, luxuriating in the feel of his warm chest. "The ocean temperature down here is warm. Nearly eighty degrees. Why else do you think I insisted we come to the Caribbean for our honeymoon?"

COMING IN DECEMBER FROM
ZEBRA BOUQUET ROMANCES

#73 TAMING BEN, by Colleen Faulkner
____0-8217-6733-X $4.99US/$6.99CAN

Ben Gordon is dead set against long-term relationships. But when he meets Mackenzie Sayer, he can't forget her. And it feels like they've met before.... Mackenzie can't believe Ben doesn't remember her from high school.... *She* remembers *him!* And when their volatile professional interaction turns into a very sensual personal reaction, she can't stay away. Maybe this time ...

#74 SOLITARY MAN, by Karen Drogin
____0-8217-6734-8 $4.99US/$6.99CAN

Rugged cop Kevin Manning had promised to care for his murdered partner's sister. But when comforting her leads to a night of passion, he leaves, sure he has nothing to offer. Months later he returns, to find her carrying his child. She can't forgive him for abandoning her. Still, something in his gaze tells her he needs her as much as she needs him....

#75 HEARTS AT RISK, by Suzanne Barrett
____0-8217-6735-6 $4.99US/$6.99CAN

Forced out of his lucrative start-up company, Tom McKittrick retires to his family estate and cancels the long-term lease on his caretaker's cottage. But the charming, reclusive woman who lives there is not about to let him order her out of her cozy retreat. She just has to teach this hunky guy to relax ... sow the seeds of romance ... and let nature take its course....

#76 THE LITTLEST MATCHMAKER, by Laura Phillips
____0-8217-6736-4 $4.99US/$6.99CAN

Lindsey Latimer wants Justine Shaw to marry her daddy, tycoon Kane Latimer. Justine soon learns Kane can easily destroy her hard-won career, yet he *still* makes her forget he's the last man she'd ever wed! Kane is well aware of Justine's charms. But he's decided a new mother for Lindsay will be *everything* Justine *isn't*. Meanwhile, he'll resist everything she is—beautiful, talented, perfect for him.

Call toll free **1-888-345-BOOK** to order by phone or use this coupon to order by mail. *ALL BOOKS AVAILABLE 12/05/00.*

Name _____
Address _____
City _____ State _____ Zip_____
Please send me the books I have checked above.
I am enclosing $_____
Plus postage and handling* $_____
Sales tax (in NY and TN) $_____
Total amount enclosed $_____
*Add $2.50 for the first book and $.50 for each additional book.
Send check or money order (no cash or CODs) to:
Kensington Publishing Corp. Dept. C.O., 850 Third Avenue, NY, NY 10022
Prices and numbers subject to change without notice. Valid only in the U.S.
All orders subject to availability.
Visit our website at **www.kensingtonbooks.com**.

BOOK YOUR PLACE ON OUR WEBSITE AND MAKE THE READING CONNECTION!

We've created a customized website just for our very special readers, where you can get the inside scoop on everything that's going on with Zebra, Pinnacle and Kensington books.

When you come online, you'll have the exciting opportunity to:

- View covers of upcoming books
- Read sample chapters
- Learn about our future publishing schedule (listed by publication month *and author*)
- Find out when your favorite authors will be visiting a city near you
- Search for and order backlist books from our online catalog
- Check out author bios and background information
- Send e-mail to your favorite authors
- Meet the Kensington staff online
- Join us in weekly chats with authors, readers and other guests
- Get writing guidelines
- AND MUCH MORE!

Visit our website at
http://www.zebrabooks.com